# My Mother's Daughter

# My Mother's Daughter

## NICKY SINGER

ORION

First published in Great Britain in 1998 by
Orion
An imprint of Orion Books Ltd
Orion House, 5 Upper St Martin's Lane, London WC2H 9EA

A CIP catalogue record for this book is available
from the British Library

ISBN 0 75280 478 2 (cased)
ISBN 0 75282 158 X (trade paperback)

Typeset at The Spartan Press Ltd,
Lymington, Hants
Printed and bound by Clays Ltd, St Ives plc.

For A.
Whose song, God willing, is strong

# ACKNOWLEDGEMENTS

I acknowledge a huge debt to all the parents who spoke to me with such extraordinary courage and honesty about their decision to give or receive a child: most especially L and Roy, Steve and Res, Tina and Jeff. God bless the children of their unions, now and always.

I am grateful to Clarissa Pinkola Estes whose book *Women who Run with the Wolves* first got me excited about the nature of myth and sea and song. I thank Arnold Rose, Angela Stannard and the inimitable Dale for the wisdom of pots; Jan Sullivan-Chalmers and Diane Pattee for insights into the life of the Ombudsperson; Doctors Jane Pateman and Joe O'Dwyer for their patient explanations of the history of anaesthesia (any errors are mine); Anya Saunders and Lizzie Forte for their lively interpretation of the teenage mind; Joy Westphal for her passionate understanding of motherhood; and Judy Marling for her brave and poignant telling on how it is to be given away.

I honour my agents, Sarah Lutyens and Felicity Rubinstein, who both became mothers during the gestation of this novel and who have shown themselves so impressively even-handed between their glorious sons and their needy book-children. I also thank my editor Jane Wood whose many good suggestions are incorporated in this book. .

And last but not least I pay tribute to Philip Franks, that

valiant friend who read the book in manuscript and was unstinting with his cool, intelligent eye. The book is better for his care as I am better for his friendship.

# DUSK

# I

You can't see my father's studio from the house. Not its entrances and exits anyway. The door from the garden is obscured by my mother's mock orange and the double doors on to the road are the other side of the building. It's here that the lorries come to deliver brick clay and collect burnished pots. We moved to this place when I was five. 'Your father needs the road access,' Grandma Bridie said. 'That's why you had to move.' I'm not supposed to be able to remember anything that happened before I was five.

Very bright light is painful to the eyes, the pain increasing in direct relation to the brilliance. Whereas darkness, no matter how intense, does not hurt at all. I was thinking this as I climbed the stairs to bed last night touching, as I always do, the glazed hollows of the five bowls I pass on my way from drawing-room to bathroom. I just tap them, very lightly and precisely in the centre, with the nail of my right forefinger. The bowl in the drawing-room is not one of my father's, though he would have been proud to make it in the days when he made bowls. Which isn't now. The glaze is deep brown with bubbles of colour bursting its surface, like a very young star system exploding into being. My staccato tap here finds a tiny crater, always the same one, of course, which feels to my nail like two minuscule ridges just a pinprick apart.

3

Out in the hall there is the ocean blue bowl with the pot-pourri. The pot-pourri offends me because it puts dead petals where there should just be the shining swirl of cobalt. Sometimes I think it's the shine that makes my fingers itch, but it can't be that because I still pause here, where there is only dust, to scrape my blue gap. On the half-landing is the pair of Gaia bowls. At least, this is what I call them, because they are the sustaining greens of Earth herself. The left-hand one is the waxy evergreen of magnolia and laurel, inter-leaved with the forest dark of firs. It's here that my mother keeps the six wooden apples she bought in New York. I push my finger between the painted russet and the bleached ash. If I tremble either fruit I have to do it again. The bowl on the right of the window-ledge is a paler green, the undulating colour of the English countryside, pierced through with the fresh green of new shoots. This bowl is normally empty, though it sometimes attracts a pin, a coin, a key. An offering bowl, I think, a hopeful bowl. Sometimes I give it two taps.

The last bowl is in the bathroom itself, broad and shallow, as yellow as a child's sun and crazed in grey. The crazing is smooth to my fingertip, when I get to it through my mother's international soaps, the small boxed sort you get from smart hotels. Nobody remarks on my tapping. Partly they are as used to it as I am. Also, mentioning it makes me worse. Yesterday I saw my mother looking. When I got to the bathroom I had to take a toothbrush and tap the bottom of my water-glass. This glass is too tall for a finger. You'd have to smash it to get your fist in.

'What do you want, darling?' my mother asked three weeks ago, smiling, zipping up the skirt of her navy suit.

She meant my birthday, of course. But oh, Mama, I am not

the stupid child I once was. I am seventeen now. Seventeen today. I ask for bland things, I mention soap, a CD. A little money, perhaps, for clothes to wear to the Rockette. Or just to wear 'out', since the Rockette implies Adele, and it is wiser not to include Adele where she may be safely excluded. More than anything I'd like books. But books are problematic, they are what Bridie used to give me. No harm in that. Dry, academic grandmother Bridie and magical, fairy-tale books with passages marked in ink.

'She's too old for those,' my mother told her mother, when I was ten, twelve. 'Why do you give them to her? What do you mean by it?'

'Mean?' says my grandmother.

The book I want most – still want – is the one with the seal story in it. But Bridie won't let me have this one. In fact, she denies it exists. I never saw it at her house, she says. Not lying on the window-seat where I picked it up and read it with my back pressed against the glass.

'I don't know what you're talking about,' she says.

Then there's my father coming in late from the studio, crumpled and thoughtful, clay in his hair. He sees me standing there on the eve of my seventeenth birthday and he says, slightly startled, as though it's only just occurred to him, 'What do you want, Grace?'

Grace. Such a still, poised name. And me – churning. But, then, names are part of it too.

'That's what I want,' I said in reply to the same question when I was seven. 'I'd like a name.'

'You have a name,' said my mother, arranging delphiniums in the drawing-room, snipping, tweaking. 'A beautiful name, Grace, Grace Thomas.'

'Charlotte Amy Richards,' I say, 'Zoë Scarlet Cowall. They

5

all have them. All my friends. Middle names. Why don't I have a middle name?'

And then she stops, a blue delphinium stem held in mid-air. 'Darling,' she says. She lays down her scissors and her stem. 'Darling.' She takes me on to her knee where I sit, too large on her bird lap. Her dark face is terribly beautiful, I think, as I sit there looking into her eyes, which are the blue of blackbirds' eggs. 'You are so grown-up now,' she says. 'Almost eight. I think you're old enough, clever enough, to choose a name for yourself, don't you?' Then she murmurs at me, just as she did when I was a baby, supposing I can remember those times. Which I can. She tells me not to hurry. Her hair is on my cheek, soft as a raven's wing. 'Take your time,' she says. 'It's not just a birthday present, but a present for a life, for a lifetime. What could be more special?'

It's a spell and I don't want to break it. But, as always, I do.

'Miranda,' I say. It's not, of course, as if I have only just begun to think about this.

'Miranda,' she repeats, and she swallows. I feel the swallow because I am so very close to her. 'Miranda. Who told you that name?'

And I don't want to tell her that Miranda is the name of the most popular girl in the class, because surely she knows that. Nor do I want to get off her lap or hear again that swallow, which I know is dangerous, because I've heard it, or think I've heard it before, so I say, 'Rumpelstiltskin.' Which is a stupid answer because it's about the stories she knows I read under the cover of dark, about the book of Grimms' fairy tales Grandma Bridie gave me the previous Christmas, about the things we don't speak about because they cause that swallow. So why do I say it, 'Rumpelstiltskin,' as I sit, where I crave to sit, on her knee?

'I see,' she says, and she kisses me. 'I love you so much,' she says into my neck. 'It's a wonderful name. Good for you. Happy birthday, Grace Miranda. Oh, happy, happy birthday.' Then she cries.

After that I'm not sure whether Miranda is my name or not. In any case I don't dare write it out. Not in full. I call myself Grace M. Thomas. That is as much as I am able to risk. Does either of us inform my father? I don't think so. It's just a difficult little thing we share, my mother and me. Something, like the marked texts, which I see at the blurred edge of my vision. A peripheral haze, which I know I should be able to pull into focus, identify, understand. But I can't. All I know is, when my next set of name-tapes arrives, they say Grace M. Thomas in green stitching. As if my mother and I have had a detailed conversation about it. Which, of course, we haven't.

So am I Miranda now? I don't think so. If I ever was. There is a tribe of Aboriginal Australians who constantly rename themselves as they change and develop through life. 'Now,' a tribesman will announce after many years of fashioning makeshift desert instruments and composing around the evening fire, 'I have become Great Singer of Songs.' Or Sturdy Hut-builder. Or Wise Woman of Wounds. Do the others of the tribe demur? No. They accept and embrace the wise woman and the hut-builder and the great singer of songs. I would like to name myself anew. But I have found this out: you cannot name yourself unless you know who you are.

'You're a Leo,' says Ruth, my mother. 'July the twenty-ninth. If you'd come when the first pains came, you might have been a Cancer. But you hung on. Trust you. You wanted to be a lion.'

'Leo.' Adele peals laughter. 'Virgo more like!'

7

But I think in this they are both wrong. I should have been a crab. It would have suited me to scuttle across the silent floors of oceans. In the dark. Perhaps that's what I feared, clinging to the inside of my mother's womb, that violent expulsion into light. I must have known that it would be July, be high noon when I finally screamed into existence. Seventeen years ago today. For just as Grace knows and does not know, and Miranda knew everything and nothing, so the infant who drew the first breath for us must have known.

It is dawn now. In a couple of hours I will get up and face the day. If I'm lucky nothing will be said and then we can all go on pretending a little longer.

# 2

It is eighty degrees and for the last three hours Alan has been dipping wall pots. He has yet to make a mistake working, as he is, at a pace designed for maximum efficiency not maximum speed. He takes each pot in his large hands, up-ends it and lowers it precisely three inches into the grey glaze. Then he blocks the three drainage holes with his index finger, middle finger and a blob of clay. The trapped air pushes against him as he submerges the vessel almost, but not quite, to the base. This is how a man would fight, he thinks, if you were pushing his head underwater. He releases the pot but not his fingers so that the interior, below the three-inch line, remains bone dry. The head he'd like to be dipping is Lee's. The thought surprises him because he likes

Lee and Lee is merely sick. And employees, as he has discovered, do get sick.

He takes another pot, begins the rhythmic process once again. The John Lewis lorry will arrive on Monday at eleven a.m. So he will fire the kiln on Saturday and let it cool on Sunday. On Sunday he will also fire the second kiln, otherwise Jerry's longtoms will not make the Tuesday shipment. When he came for interview, Jerry said that he could throw seven longtoms an hour and that he'd been doing the job ten years or more. But, on average, he throws between five and six. Which are why there are not enough of the tall, wide-necked vases stacked on the drying shelves. Without taking his eye from the grey glaze, Alan sees Jerry erase his fingermarks and cut off the longtom tail with a bamboo rib. Although he is not close he is aware that the pot is not quite right. It will be a second. Jerry has worked in the pottery for just over a year now.

'For God's sake,' says Ruth. 'Sack him.'

But there are orders to fulfil and Lee is off. Besides, Alan has other things on his mind. Slow, bubbling things. He was mulling as he mixed the glaze, as he stirred the three white powders in the bucket, china clay, chalk, feldspar, as he added fritted lead and water and copper oxide. It's a soft grey glaze that fires into the hard Victorian green so favoured by his customers, the John Lewis buyer says. He quite enjoyed mixing the glaze although, by rights, this is Lee's job. Just as dipping the pots is Lee's job. At fifty-four, Alan thinks, he is too old to be dipping garden pots. But if Lee had been working Alan would probably have been in the office. Or, more likely, sitting alongside Jerry trebling longtom production. He raises his head just a little, observes Jerry and behind him the office. Office. Still just a barely screened corner of the workspace. A

9

thin half-glass partition, a phone, papers without cabinets, an address book at the bottom of the in-tray or on the floor, or in the pocket of his jacket in the house, or . . . There seems to be so much administration, these days, and there just isn't time. Not any more. Not the 'ring-fenced' time Ruth talks about. The clean, clear-headed time to think things through. And now the phone is going and he has to put down his wall-pot and wipe his hands and answer it.

'Yes. Yes, I got it.' Shuffling the envelopes, the invoices, the newspaper, trying to locate the order. 'No, I'm sorry. I don't normally confirm in writing. I speak with Mr . . . Mr . . . Lomax.' The paper under the clay-spattered paper-weight after all. 'He knows me.'

Ruth has made suggestions about office systems. She's mentioned efficiency and profit ratios and time management and filing and computers and even secretarial assistance.

'I can't afford it.'

'Put your prices up.'

'There's only so much people will pay for garden pots.'

And that is it. Garden pots. It has silenced her. It has almost silenced him. He puts down the phone and pulls open the shallow desk drawer. There are the crumpled pictures, the designs for the light-shedders. Vases, each one a fluid hollow inside a skin of a different shape. Bland exteriors concealing secret spaces. An incurious viewer would see only the outward form. A curious one would lift and turn, trying to twist light into the shadowed interior. Knowing that there was something covert, something to be discovered. But the light, being forever sun-straight, would not bend to the viewer's will and he would be forced to guess, to push his mind into the darkness. To predict, from the way the light fell on the throat he could see, the dimensions of the core he could not. Finally he would put the vase down. He had it mapped, could draw each contour in his imagination, describe, specify, itemise. Know. And he would be right. Perhaps. But not be sure. Because you could never be sure. Unless you broke the pot. Alan shuts the drawer. The drawings have begun to curl at the edges.

She will go to the Rockette, of course. With Adele. He wants her to. He wants her to enjoy her seventeenth birthday. Friday night. They will have a family party on Sunday, perhaps, as one kiln cools and another fires. She is not the baby who lay at his feet in a Moses basket. Can it really be seventeen years? His rented studio was tiny then, above a garage in someone else's mews. It smelt of clay and the peppermint tea he kept because there was no fridge for milk. She lay by the Calor-gas fire and gurgled. Ruth was always afraid of the fire, though the flames were behind bars and he never left her by it, even when she was asleep, but carried her with him, wherever he went. Always. She was so beautiful. So utterly beguiling. Sometimes he would stop whatever he was doing, preparing a salt-firing, Vaselining his hands to stop them drying out, and just stare at her. His daughter. Her first year of life was a culmination and a beginning. And he'd never worked so well. Fruit bowls. The giving and receiving of gifts. It was his theme. She was his theme. The intake of his own breath. The rhythm of the clay itself.

He didn't have a pug-mill then, didn't mince his clay in a machine but laid it in beds to winter. Even though they lived in London at that time. He found an allotment, bedded his clay where other people grew vegetables, where the buddleias pushed through concrete. Let the air come to it, the frost break it down and the fungus grow in it to increase its plasticity. He placed damp sacks upon it so that it would not desiccate and crack like a piece of earth. In the spring, with eight-month Grace beside him, he mixed his clay in a blunger. She laughed at the wild, rotating drum, with its sixty gallons of water. He let her feel the metal vibrate, told her about the giant rotating blades, held her tiny body safe. But then he let her plunge her hands into the thick slip, the consistency of double cream. She sat in her coat, bought new in America by Ruth but soon old, stiff with clay, and watched him pour the liquid earth into a brick-lined pit. It dried slowly and yet they played the Hawk's game with it. Ever watchful, daily, twice daily when the weather warmed. It wasn't to dry on the surface. They mustn't let it dry unevenly. In early summer he jumped in the pit and turned the clay over with a spade. She was crawling by then and took herself to the edge, turned her part of the pit with her hand. When he finally dug out the clay, she was walking. He hired a van to take the clay to the mews. Stacked it in a dark corner, sacked it up. She held the hosepipe as they watered it to keep it moist. You can't make clay that way any more. It's not economic. It wasn't economic then. But that wasn't the point. The point was to move in time with nature. To celebrate the seasons of his child and the seasons of clay. To be part of growth and change and endeavour and the turning of the world. To be in love.

And he was in love, with his child and with his wife. By day he took clay in his hands, by night his wife. Clay, he thinks, is a very feminine thing, skin-like. You have to get it to show itself. When you work at the wheel you can close your eyes and feel the form of it, the sensual run of your fingers against voluptuousness. That's why he will not buy red clay even now. Not because it is twice as expensive as brick clay, though it is, but because it doesn't live, it doesn't breathe. Red clay cannot be kneaded into being, it sends the hands to sleep. 'Boil-in-the-bag' clay, that's what he calls it. Brick clay has to be worked. You have to cut it, lift it, take the whole weight of it from the bottom, with both hands. Pit yourself against it, muscle by muscle, and yet remain gentle, responsive. It is hard, absorbing work, which requires total attention. Besides, brick clay contains ground glass. Tiny translucent shards that can cut a man's hands to ribbons. A run of blood, red as the clay itself, kneaded in, becoming part of the clay and the things the man makes with the clay. Fired hard. Scarred. He didn't mind that then. With Grace beside him, in her basket, on her bottom, on her hands and knees, on her tiny summer feet. With Ruth in America, in the house, in the office, in his eyes, part of him, of the life they'd made together. No he didn't mind it then. Now, sometimes, he gets Jerry to take the yeddle and knead the clay. If he ribbons his own hands he cuts a finger from a yellow plastic glove and places it over his finger. He secures it with plaster. It keeps out the constant wet. But it dulls his finger. It takes away his touch. He never used to cover his fingers, even when they were injured.

Of course they should have told Grace. He always said it. Though it was never quite his place so he said it softly. But now it is too late. There is no point in pain for the sake of pain. He dips a garden pot. That is what he has learned after all these years.

# 3

Ruth and the enquirer sit on opposite sides of the round white table. The word 'enquirer' no longer jolts Ruth. The office of the ombudsperson exists to break down the old barriers between employer and employee. The term 'enquirer' is simply part of the new language. Ruth is as used to it as she is to the glass in the ombuds-suite windows – glass that allows those in the office to look out but not those in the street to look in. Ruth is composed, her gaze steady, sympathetic, corporate. She is wearing a discreetly expensive navy suit with a flare of pink silk about the neck. Her hands are still and her pencil, notebook and small plastic cup of water are untouched. She is listening intently.

The woman in the enquirer's chair speaks in sudden low bursts. In the pauses between Ruth hears white noise. But she is used to that too. The room is sound-proofed. 'Slab to slab,' they told her, when they built the place four years ago. People, apparently, try to crawl through walls. There are two doors in the room and both had to be checked for decibel leakage, even the one that is never opened. Both doors failed. Four times. The engineers brought a piece of equipment that sounded like a jet engine and set it going in the adjacent room. 'Shouldn't be able to hear a thing. Not a pip,' said the chief technician, working on the padding, the wadding, the fibres, the sealant.

'There now,' he said eventually. 'Perfect,' he was delighted. 'Now nobody can hear you scream.'

That's why she has her own fire alarm in the room. And also why there is a panic button under the table across which she leans towards the enquirer.

'I understand how you must feel,' she says softly.

She is not going to push the button. There is a wire that runs from here to security. The lightest of pressure on the red button will bring a man. Running. He will be with her in under two minutes. But she's not going to push the button. She hasn't pushed it for four years and she's not going to push it today. July 29. Grace's seventeenth birthday. They say women forget the pain of childbirth. Ruth has not forgotten, though mainly she remembers the clock. She was always panicked when other mothers, at playgroups, in the park, began to share birth experiences. 'The episiotomy? Like the noise when you slice the rind off a thick piece of bacon. A heavy crunching sound.' Or 'He was the wrong way round. I never even felt the contractions, it was the backache that nearly killed me.' Then they'd laugh and turn to her. 'How was it for you?' And all she could remember was the clock and how, for the five days of the stop-start labour, time seemed to stand still. It was a home birth – though not the home she has now – and every time she looked at the clock, day or night, it was a quarter to four. The insistent, green hands of the alarm clock, luminous in her mind: your baby is refusing to be born, she is holding her breath, if it's a quarter to four when you look again, she will be born dead. Of course the midwife said, 'If there is a problem we will go to hospital, but there is not a problem.' And yet, when she thinks back, this is what Ruth remembers.

'It was a near-death experience,' she tells the other

mothers. 'It was as though I was standing outside my body. I was just a prick of light looking over the shoulder of the pregnant self. The swollen belly seemed a mountain I had to climb. As the contractions hardened I felt them not in my womb but in my head, my heart. Each one tighter, tighter. I breathed and I screamed but I couldn't hear myself. My ears were blocked and the time was a quarter to four. I hadn't eaten or slept for three days and nights and I was at the limit of my strength. I kept thinking, If this goes on another hour, another minute, another second, I will die. And then she was born. Finally, finally, finally she arrived. Her perfect crown of hair and the slither of her tiny body. And they gave her to me while the cord was still attached, only I was shaking so much I could hardly hold her. Perhaps that's why she cried so suddenly, so fiercely. And in that moment my soul returned to my body. With her first breath she gave me back myself, made me whole. My daughter. And I knew as I held her naked in my arms that I could never let her go. I would kill for her. Die for her.' Sometimes it seems a little excessive to tell all this to the other mothers. So she just says, 'I remember the clock.'

'Clearly,' Ruth murmurs at the enquirer, 'it upsets you very much.'

On the round table in front of them is a vase of flowers. In the spring it is always tulips. As summer comes it is sometimes anemones, or dahlias, or stocks. Today, for some reason, it is pink roses. They are dead on the stem. Ruth has noticed this, over the years, how no flowers seem to be able to open out in this room. How the buds remain tight, and then how they seem to moisten and sag, leaking colour, becoming wet and translucent before withering properly, when they can be decently thrown away. Perhaps, she thinks, trying to remember her school science, it's because of the lack of oxygen. Plants take in carbon dioxide and exhale oxygen, that is the way, she thinks. And she is using up the oxygen. And the enquirer (who is crying now) is using up the oxygen. With the leak-proof doors shut and the slabs butted so close, it must be only a matter of time before there is too little air in this room to sustain life. Tick tock, tick tock.

'No,' replies Ruth, 'I am a designated neutral. My job is not to be an advocate either for the management or the employee. But to be the advocate of fair process.'

In the adjacent office is a safe and a shredder. While a case is being surfaced all relevant documents are locked each night in the safe. Only Ruth and her assistant know the combination. Management doesn't know. Security doesn't know. When a case has been dealt with, or gone cold, the documents are shredded. This is part of the Pharmakon promise: fear not, there are no records, there can be no retribution. The clean, fawn machine cuts and hums and little curls of paper land in the blue bin-liner. The brain's shredder, thinks Ruth, is memory. It's supposed to order things, file things, let things go. But her brain has all the blue bin-liners, has all the curls of paper, which look like nesting material, and something has begun to nest there.

'There is another option,' says Ruth. The enquirer has stopped crying but the tears have streaked ugly channels in her makeup. She looks, Ruth thinks, not unlike Grace's friend Adele. Not that she can imagine Adele crying. Ruth concentrates. The enquirer has Adele's bottle-blonde hair, cheapish clothes and sharp features. But it's not this. It's the eyes. Eyes at once provocative and defiant. Eyes that dare. Is that what has spurred on the senior manager, if needed he has been spurred on? Simon Trevor, fifty-four years old. Finance director. Ruth has known him ten years. Ruth tries to imagine Simon Trevor's hand placed where the enquirer says it has been placed, on the enquirer's breast. The comfortable, padded hand on the bony breast. Purple liver spots pressed to white flesh. Or perhaps just to white polyester. Tears have got in the way of facts. Adele's face has got in the way. Adele would have seduced Simon Trevor.

Tonight Adele will take Grace to the Rockette. And she, Ruth, will leave the air-conditioned, white-noise room, place in the safe the notes she has taken today and spin the combination dial, lock the bunker room (the term 'bunker room' is only a joke), lock the outer door of the Office of the Ombudsperson, Pharmakon International. She will push her way out into an evening as airless as this room, only hotter, more dense, petrol-fumed. In the haze of her own exhaust she will drive from seething July Brighton to the muggy heights of nearby Lewes.

Over the weekend, Grace's birthday weekend, she will not speak to Alan about any of the cases she is surfacing. She will not speak to Grace about any of the cases, not that Grace would be interested. On Saturday night she will take two calls at home from enquirers who, for various reasons, can neither phone during normal working hours or visit her in the office. On Monday morning she will re-enter the bunker suite and listen to other members of the company raise issues about leadership, control, policy, discrimination, harassment, discipline, benefits and the work environment. They will be enquirers not complainants. But they will not be happy. They will not be full of praise. She must be careful to guard against believing that Pharmakon is falling apart. She must remember that her job allows issues to be raised and, sometimes, resolved. She provides an invaluable function. She is a sick-bowl, she is toilet paper, she is absolutely indispensable. The chairman says so. Her boss, in New York, will remind her not to have sandwiches at her desk, but to force herself downstairs to the cafeteria where she may meet someone with whom she is allowed to interact. Some companies forbid any interaction by ombudspersons. Pharmakon is enlightened in this respect. Pharmakon has given Ruth Thomas awards for service. They appreciate her. She is supremely good at her job. Her job is moving forward other people's issues.

The thing nesting in the curls of shredded paper has wings and an angry, open mouth. Its shrieks are sudden and violent. Soon, Ruth thinks, she will get up and burst out of the soundproofed room. She will not go through the door marked Ruth Thomas, Regional Ombudsperson, Pharmakon Europe, but through the door opposite, the one that's never been opened and only has a handle on the inside. This door leads, so she is assured, though she's never been there to prove it, to Marketing. The men and women in Pharmakon marketing have ceased to see the door, for a door that is never opened begins, after time, to look like a wall. So when she bursts out of her office into theirs, they will naturally be astounded. But how will they react? What will they do? There will be a moment, she imagines, of pure silence, a paralysed pause that will elongate while they try to remember who she is, while they wait for the appearance of whatever terrible thing has finally driven her from her lair. They will see monsters, machetes and rivers of blood. But there will be only her in her immaculate navy suit and high-heeled shoes. And then what will they do?

Ruth takes a small sip of water. It is only the heat getting on her nerves. She looks at her watch. Nearly one o'clock. The enquirer has been in the office for two and a half hours. Time moves swiftly now. Grace is seventeen. In a moment she will be eighteen. She will be an adult. She will have rights. She will be due what is fair. Perhaps, Ruth thinks, there are market gardeners who return to their own slug-infested back-yards, accountants who fail to complete their tax returns on time.

She stands up. She shakes the enquirer warmly by the hand. She opens the door marked Ruth Thomas, Regional Ombudsperson, Pharmakon Europe. It makes a smooth whooshing sound as air escapes.

'Of course,' she says, ushering the woman out, 'I will do everything in my power to progress your issue.'

# 4

If I feel lonely late at night, I sometimes go to my bedroom window and look out towards the river Ouse hoping to see a light on in Adele's house. It's a futile gesture because you cannot, in fact, see a single one of the two thousand houses on Adele's estate from here. But I've never stopped believing that you ought to be able to. Partly because Adele and I live less than ten minutes' walk from each other and my house is on the rise of the hill, and partly because I know that if I look for Adele she will always be there.

Adele's mother, Julie, thinks the planners deliberately

chose to build the estate in the dell between Offham Road and the river, precisely because it is so effectively, and apparently naturally, screened from the posher suburbs. Her theory is supported by the fact that there is only one road into, and therefore only one road out of, the estate.

'Beats me why they don't put a sentry up there,' says Julie. 'Impose a curfew. Note our comings and goings in a pocket book.'

Of course, Adele and Julie haven't always lived in Caldicott Road. They moved here when Adele was nine, the year after Julie and Dave split up. In the eight years since then Adele has not seen her father.

'Good riddance to bad rubbish,' says Julie.

On a map the estate follows the perfect hexagonal grid-lines of a honeycomb. The reality is starker but also more charming.

'You don't live here,' says Julie.

Adele's small two-up, two-down is in a sixties terrace, painted the lime green of chocolate fondants. The brightness of the sun today has the effect of toning it down, and the street would look gay and a little Mediterranean, if it wasn't for the shut doors, the mismatched net curtains, and the hospital-style white metal railings that flank the steps to the flats opposite.

'Were they aiming for the blind market?' asks Julie.

Yet still my heart lifts as I open the wooden gate to walk the scant few concrete feet to Adele's front door.

'Got some money!' A small fat girl wearing a too short and too tight pink skirt, comes hurtling out of the house next door. 'Mr Softee! Mr Softee! Stop! I've got some money!'

Mr Softee continues to slalom down the street with the girl in flailing pursuit. The road is narrow here and the only space

21

where he might park with any safety is currently occupied by a rusting Cortina jacked so high at the back where its wheel is missing that it looks like a huge metal dog pissing up a lamp-post.

'Mr Softeeee!'

I pause to watch ice-cream van and girl plunge round the corner where they both come to a jerking halt. It's really not so very long since the girl in the pink skirt was me. Puppy-fat Grace with her new bone-thin friend Adele. We didn't run, of course, had the dignity of thirteen-year-olds. We just swung nonchalantly on the gate, waiting. I used to give my Flake to Adele to make her fatter and me thinner. But Adele has one of those bodies that will never be fat.

I have a key to Adele's house but today I ring the bell. It chimes with what my mother considers a lower-class tone. I feel happy. Maybe because Carl's motorbike is not parked outside. This means, I hope, that Carl can't come. That Adele and I will go to the Rockette alone. That we'll take the train together and walk along the seafront to the club. That it will be at least two drinks, possibly three, before some slavering young man plucks up the courage to ask Adele to dance and she says yes. It's not that there's anything particular I want to discuss with Adele. It's just that Carl's presence, and he's very present at the moment, blocks some of the light.

'Come in, come in.' It's Julie who answers the door. 'It's the birthday girl,' she yells, although Adele is less than ten feet away, standing at the mirror. As soon as you step into the room you're aware of that mirror, glaring from the right-hand wall. It captures you, splits your body in two around the S-shaped crack that divides its oval glass. Julie claims to have found the mirror complete with crack and rusted frame in a skip.

'Someone else's bad luck,' she said, buying Hammerite. 'Eat your heart out, Snow White,' she said, painting the frame a thick gold.

'Hi, babe.' Adele finishes the sweep of her blue eye-liner, releases her eyelid and comes to embrace me. 'Happy birthday. Let's see, then.' She pushes open the light jacket I'm wearing over my clothes for the Rockette, studies my pale yellow shift for a minute. 'You look great. Absolutely great. Doesn't she look great, Mum?'

Julie is in front of the mirror now, sugar coating her mouth candy pink. She smacks her lips, pouts. 'Great.'

'Only you'd colour-co-ordinate better if you dyed your hair.' Adele's grin is quick and affectionate. It's a long-running argument. I like my mouse-brown hair. It gives me anonymity, privacy. I think Adele actually likes it too, it makes her blonde all the more distinct, obvious, glossy. This theme carries over into our clothes, I favour soft, neat, inconspicuous colours and fits. Adele prefers lamé and psychedelic satin, fake fur, big boots, seersucker crop-tops and diamanté shades. This evening she's in her burnt-orange satin micro-mini and a see-through silver lace top, which must be new. Her sandals are big, strappy and purple, the huge Cuban heels emphasizing the length of her slim, summer-bare legs. I love to look at her, to watch the men coming to her vivid flame.

The concept of being a moth to someone else's butterfly does not impress Julie. 'You should wear electrics,' she tells me. 'Shocking pink. That'd suit you.'

Julie wears shocking pink and burnt orange and acid green. Unlike my Jaeger mother, who's fifty-one, Julie's a defiant thirty-six. She likes clothes, makeup and men, despite how she harangues them in their absence. People on the estate say she and Adele look more like sisters than mother and daughter. Adele allows the comparison, it flatters her mother, makes her feel good about herself, more likely to go out, give Adele a free rein. Though she's always had a pretty free rein. I don't envy this any more than I envy Adele's attractiveness. It's a bright sunshade under which I can sit in the cool.

'Hey, babe. This is for you.' Adele thrusts a small spangly package into my hands. 'Just what you always wanted. Happy birthday. Go on, open it.' She hovers impatiently as I slide my finger under the shiny wrapping.

Inside are two discs of yellow plastic connected by a metal hinge. 'Look.' Adele snatches the object from my hand. 'First, it perfectly matches your outfit. Lucky or what? Second, it's a mirror.' Dextrously she flips it open and engages the catch. 'This side's just ordinary. Just your lovely face. And this side,' she twirls the little yellow sun, 'magnified.' She pushes the glaring circle into my face making me blink. 'All your pimples in glorious technicolour.' She laughs. 'Great, isn't it?'

'Thanks,' I say. 'Thanks very much.' And I squeeze it shut, clip it tight. The first time she came to my house Adele couldn't believe that I didn't have a mirror in my bedroom. Just four empty screw-holes at the back of my dressing-table where the mirror should have been.

'How do you do your makeup?' she asked, aghast.

'I go to the bathroom,' I said quickly. 'Better light.'

'Oh, right,' she said. And left it there. Didn't question whether, aged thirteen, I really wore makeup. Didn't remark on the screw-holes from which it looked as if a mirror might have been ripped. Perhaps it was gratitude that first made me fall in love with her.

She smiles, takes the yellow contraption from me and drops it into my handbag. I won't use it, but she won't notice that, will just lean across and borrow it when she needs to.

'Right.' Julie, at the gold mirror, sprays herself with something compellingly sweet. She sniffs, turns her head this way and that, puffs her hair a little with spread fingers and then snaps shut her makeup purse. 'That's me done. See you later, girls.' She swings her red heart-shaped leather bag over her shoulder and sashays like a teenager out of the door. There isn't much more flesh on her than on Adele. She doesn't tell us where she's going or ask about our evening's events. She doesn't mention times to be home or taxis from stations. My mother thinks she's irresponsible.

' 'Bye,' says Adele to her back. 'Right. Let's be having you.' She pulls me across the room to the mantelpiece, where the gas fire is, where the cracked gold mirror is. There are no theatrical light-bulbs around the mirror, but there might as well be. The mantelpiece, which is really just a wide, white shelf, looks like it carries the cosmetic freight of an actor's lifetime. Makeup seems to have been born and to have died here. There are scraped out pots of Leichner creams, lidless eye-tints and plastic spikes, which were once sponge-tipped brushes. There are frosted spills of Silver Dazzle, Blueberry Ice and Translucent Rose, daubs of cranberry lip gloss and Brick Red No 7, glue tubes, lash curlers, nail extensions, polish and perfect sable brushes. There are palettes for blue days, pink days, gold days, silver days, shadows and silk. There are mascaras and cleansing gels, pencil shavings, matt finishes, hardeners, softeners, concealers and balms. At Julie and Adele's altar you can become anyone.

Adele stands me to the left of the crack so my face will be whole. Then she lifts her hand to my cheek and strokes me.

Automatically I focus on the foreground, on her white lacquered nail, on the soft pad of her forefinger. Behind her hand my face is a safe blur.

'I'm going to make you shimmer,' she says.

Normally she leaves me alone. Allows me my thin thread of kohl, my colourless lip-gloss. But today is my birthday. I turn my gaze to the mirror's edge, consider the stickers, which say 'Hello Petal', 'No Plastic Pecs', and 'Confess!', the postcards from Spain and the photo of Carl, on which Julie has drawn devil's horns.

'But first,' Adele says, 'I'm going to do your hair. Big hair. That's the biz. Big mouse hair.' She laughs her suddenly soft, cascading laugh. And she pushes my head down, down below my waist.

'Adele . . .' I say, but I don't resist because there is pleasure in darkness, in being behind my hang of hair. Something is making me nervous. Perhaps nothing more than being confronted by mirrors I didn't expect. I'm so much, it seems, a creature of habit.

'Perfect for you,' she says. ' "Makes fine hair thick," ' she quotes and there's a spurt of something cold and airborne into my mouse roots. 'Now shake your head,' she commands. 'Shake. Shake! You'll never get megahold unless you shake.'

I shake slightly. Then she grabs handfuls of hair and scrunches it in her fists. 'This is great,' she says. 'You wait.' There's another squirt and bubbles of tangerine burst, acidic and sticky, in my nose. 'Great,' she says. 'Great. Head up.'

I put my head up. She lightly combs the strands from my forehead, pays attention to wisps, tucks them up, touching me with expertise and sweetness.

'There. What do you think?'

My glance is sidelong. But Big Hair is big enough to be seen at any angle.

'I look like a mouse in a wind tunnel.' I take my comb from her and try to flatten the effect. My effort to reclaim myself disappoints me probably more than Adele. If Big Hair isn't me, she will think of something else.

'OK, OK.' She's already browsing among the paler palettes of her art. 'But you must let me do a little shimmer. Just a tinsy one. Bit of glitter on the cheekbone. How about that?'

She takes me by the chin and holds me still as she scrutinizes the contours of my face. She is quick and thorough, and her stare so intense I begin to feel the shape of my own skull. I want to reach up to see if I still have flesh over the bone. But I must have because she's talking about creme blusher and cinnamon-tinted glaze.

'Hop up.' She pats the red plush seat of the aluminium swivel stool Julie was given by some grateful barman. If you ask her what for, she just laughs. I climb up as instructed and Adele swings me round to face her, braking my pirouette with a clump of her heel on the foot-rest. She holds me in place as she works on hollows and highlights. Brushes and fingertips flutter on my face. I close my eyes and hope it will go on for ever.

'Wake up,' says Adele. She is wielding the Antique Gold Eye Definer. 'Now keep still.' She pulls down my eyelid and draws a faultless line. 'Good.' She progresses to the second eye. 'There.' She gazes at her handiwork. 'You know,' she says suddenly, 'you really have beautiful eyes.' And she swings me round to face the mirror. 'Look!' she cries.

And I look. I just can't help it. Not because Adele's taken me unawares, she hasn't. I know I must not look directly into a mirror. But I do. Because I so much want to see what she has seen. A Grace who can be beautiful. My Grace is not distinct enough to be beautiful. She's brown and shaded, soft at the edges, a sketch of a person not coloured in properly. The drawing of a three-year-old, incomplete, with a few lurid, exaggerated features; large, flat feet, bright red embarrassed cheeks, and breasts that swell against her clothes, push at them. So it's vanity, hopeless and wilful, that finally impels me to take a risk. To look through the glass. To stare straight into the pit of my own eyes.

But, of course, they're not my eyes. Though, in the split second of my decision to look, I hope that they might be. But, as always, they're the child's. And I want to scream, 'Stop it! Go away! Leave me alone! You're spoiling this too!' But I don't because the minute I look at her, I feel the same furious welling of compassion that I always feel.

'Brown,' coos Adele, over the stamping of my heart. 'Brown-hazel. Did anyone ever tell you?'

I only have to kick at the floor and I'd spin away on Julie's stool. But I don't kick at the floor. I'm pininoed by the gaze of the child and the memory which, once triggered, comes in remorselessly. She's four and a half years old. The same age I was when my mother sat me on her knee in front of the kidney-shaped dressing table that was hers but now is mine. But where I have grown the child has refused to grow. And now she's here. In Adele's house.

Behind me Adele's mouth moves. She's saying something to me but I can't hear it because her voice has begun to stretch away, to fade just as everyone and everything fades when the child comes. It is the week before Easter and I know my mother wants to whisper something incredible to me. I am bathed and ready for bed, warm and curled into her, secure in a happiness I am unable to name. Her head is so close to mine that her mouth is in my hair. She is kissing me, murmuring to me. And at first I'm not really listening, just snuggling, replete with love, watching, in the mirror, the perfect circle that is us. Then she says it. Doesn't make a speech, just tells it like a story, softly, punctuated by kisses. For a moment I don't think I react at all. Perhaps I pretend. Perhaps I hope. Then I look in the mirror and, quite suddenly, the girl is there, staring out at me with stunned pain in her eyes. She is utterly still, tearless, her hands folded meekly in her lap yet I know, as certainly as if I'd crawled in her heart, that she is destroyed.

Then I forget about me, about whatever it is that my mother has whispered, and I pour out all my grief for this child. And I want to reach through the glass and take her, hold her, crush the suffering out of her, but I can't. So she just sits and waits, seeming to need my pity, feeding on it. Then my mother blows her nose and the girl disappears. But she comes back, of course, returns to me, time and again, in dreams, in mirrors, haunting me with her helpless, hopeless look. Wanting something that I am increasingly unable to give. And that's when I begin to turn my head, avert my eyes. When I grow older and she does not. Then the time between her visits lengthens and, once or twice, I let myself believe, perhaps, at last, it is all over. She will not come again. That finally, she is gone for ever. But then a day comes like today and there she is. Just behind the glass. Sitting. Waiting. Blowing me the kisses of the unloved.

'That's enough ogling,' says Adele. 'Ogling gives you pimples.' And she wheels me around to face her.

'Jesus,' she says, 'are your eyes watering? I don't think this stuff is run-proof.'

'Oh, Adele, Adele,' I cry because I can hear her. 'Can we go? Please, Adele. Let's go.'

'Hey,' she says. 'I haven't done your lips yet.'

And I let her brush a colour because to do it she needs to hold me still. To hold me. And I want her to take all of me in her arms and I know she can't and won't, so I make that touch enough. Allow myself to come quietly back into the room, creep once again into my own body and inhabit, for a blessedly solid moment, the dependable here-and-now of Adele.

'There, that's you done,' she says.

'Thank you,' I say. 'Thank you, Adele.' She hears the gratitude tremor my voice.

'Don't be soft,' she says. Then she opens her purse and counts the notes inside. 'Great,' she says. 'This is going to be a great night. I'm going to get smashed, slaughtered, absolutely out of it. Off the planet.'

And then, with a miserable flurry of shock, I realise I do envy her.

# 5

I have made a mistake, thinks Bridie, as she watches her friend of forty years wheel about the drawing-room, exclaiming, touching things.

'It all looks the same,' cries Irene Potts delightedly. 'Just as though I'd never left. Home from home. After all these years. Just imagine.'

Bridie is imagining, trying to remember the time when the girls were small, when Mungo was still her husband, when Irene Potts was an important, comforting part of her life. She looks at the tray set with her mother's silver tea-pot, pierced silver strainer and Crown Derby cups. In a minute, she thinks, the tea will be brewed and then, surely, Irene will have to sit down.

'Except the chest,' says Irene. 'That was on the landing, I think.'

It is fourteen years since Bridie moved the chest. On the landing the chest seemed to invite attention. It had a hinged lid. It was obviously a storage place, had a spacious cavity beneath the dark wood exterior where one might reasonably look for pillows or extra blankets. In the drawing-room, set with the green majolica plant pot with its little orange tree, the chest seems no more than a table. People remark on the orange tree, its tiny, bitter globes of fruit. No one mentions the chest. No one sees it or stops to wonder what it might contain. Even a hideous scar, thinks Bridie, passes unnoticed if you see it every day. She recomposes herself in the chair. As she has got older she occasionally feels her heart-rate increase for no obvious reason. Now is one of those occasions.

'A little cake?' she says to Irene, who is standing by the piano reaching for the bevelled glass photo frame.

'Yes. Yes. Thank you.' And then, as she studies the photo in her hands, 'Let me guess, one of Laura's daughters.'

'No,' says Bridie. 'That's Grace. Ruth's daughter.'

'Gosh, a real chip off the Laura-Mungo block.'

Mungo. They do not speak of him now. He is never mentioned in this drawing-room, which used to be his, both of theirs, thirty years ago. She pictures the blond mass of him leaning on the mantelpiece flicking cigarette ash into the glass ashtray which, she realises with disquiet, is still within arm's reach of the hearth, in its old place on top of the bookcase. No one smokes now and yet the ashtray remains. Why hasn't she thrown it away? Mungo would have thrown it away if it had belonged to her. 'You have to move on,' says Mungo. 'There's no point living in the past,' says Mungo. When I'm dead, thinks Bridie suddenly, he will stand there again. The old dog will outlive me. He'll come here and flick ash at my funeral. Excuse himself. Say none of it was his fault. It was all to do with Alice Watling.

'Do you see him at all?' asks Irene.

'No,' says Bridie.

'So he doesn't see the grandchildren?'

'No.' Bridie makes her voice sharp. Irene is presuming too much. She is a foreigner now. She lives in New Zealand. She must understand that her relationship is purely postcard, Christmas card. Besides, Bridie is not used to this and her heart won't take it.

'Do sit.' Bridie pours Lapsang Souchong from the elegant silver spout. The smoky aroma of the tea calms her, as does the sight of the twigged tea-leaves gathering in the silver strainer. No wonder the Japanese have made an art of this. She does not offer Irene milk but places a perfect half-moon of lemon on the woman's saucer.

Irene sits. 'Could I have sugar?' she asks.

Bridie begins to lift herself from the wing chair.

'Oh, sorry, let me get it. Top cupboard near the kitchen window. Am I right?'

'You must think my life very dull.' Bridie is upright. She is not going to have Irene Potts in her kitchen.

'I'm so sorry.' Suddenly Irene looks flustered, mortified. 'I didn't mean . . .'

Then Bridie remembers how it was Irene Potts who came and made tea on the days that Alice Watling's parents parked at the end of her drive and sat for hours in their car. Irene Potts who said, 'You shouldn't take it personally. I mean, I don't think they're accusing you of anything. I mean, wouldn't you, if your daughter had died?' And it was that 'had died' not 'had been killed' that comforted her through the interminably long weeks of the enquiry.

Bridie softens. 'Of course,' she says. 'Still in the second cupboard. Thank you so much.' She sits stiffly, to make it clear to Irene that her seventy-five years weigh more heavily on her than Irene's sprightly seventy-one. In Irene's absence she looks out of the french windows and down the drive. They came so often. First Mr and Mrs Watling together and then, later, just Mrs Watling. Sitting alone in her car, behind her dark glasses, staring up the drive. Not just during the enquiry but afterwards. At first she came once or twice a week, then fortnightly, monthly, then every two months. Later on, much, much later on, she just came on the anniversary itself. August 2.

She must have known that the leylandii were planted against her. 'Oh, yes,' the man at the garden centre had assured Bridie. 'By far the fastest growing of the firs. If you're looking for a screen, you couldn't do better.' Now the trees are thirty foot high, though Bridie has had them pruned. Their roots are so thick they are prising apart the concrete driveway to the garage. There are eruptions and cracks. Ruth has said she ought to have the trees dug out now, plant something else, something lighter, more in scale. Fruit trees, perhaps, plums or greengages. But who knows if Mrs Watling still comes? With the leylandii still in place, this is not a question to which Bridie needs to know the answer. She is not forced to think about it as Irene Potts is forcing her to do today. Making her imagine that behind those trees (after all, it is very close to the anniversary) sits old Mrs Watling in her cracked dark glasses. Mr Watling is dead now. Bridie read that in the newspapers. And Alice, who was six when she died (the same age as Bridie's daughter Laura) has been gone forty-three years. Perhaps Mrs Watling has finally laid the ghost of her daughter to rest. But, then again, maybe she has nothing better to do now than sit at the bottom of Bridie's drive and brood. She could be there right now. Just the other side of the trees. Waiting. Mungo is right. It does no good to brood.

'I know what I meant to tell you.' Irene, a voice in the hall, appears through the door with the sugar. 'Dr Gilliebrand has retired to Auckland. Bought a plot just three down from ours. Can you believe it?'

'Gilliebrand,' says Bridie vaguely.

'Yes, yes, you must remember him. The handsomest man in medicine. Well, after your Mungo. The houseman who arrived in the hospital the year before – you must remember. Dr Gilliebrand. Those long fingers and incredible eyes. Well, they started building on the plot and I saw this old man standing there. Well, young by your and my standards. Sixty-nine. And I just knew it was him from the way he stood. And do you know what? When I went up and tapped him on the arm, he turned round and said, "Sister Potts, as I live and breathe." Sent shivers down my spine and no mistake. All the widows in Auckland will be after him. His wife died, you know. He offered me tea right then and there. Out of a Thermos. And we sat on the grass like a couple of twenty-year-olds and watched them mixing concrete, pouring the foundations. Talked about the hospital. Talked for hours. He remembered you, of course. "Our first woman anaesthetist," he said. "How could I forget?"'

And Irene begins to walk Bridie down the long corridors of the General, towards the gowning room and the surgical masks, the Boyles machine, the halothane gas and the double doors of operating theatre number one.

'No,' says Bridie, 'I don't remember.'

'Oh, but you must –'

'I remember how your daughter was set on the medical life,' interrupts Bridie. 'Meggie. Dermatology, wasn't it? What happened to all that?'

'Oh, Meggie. Just like your Laura. Two of a kind, that pair. Gave up everything when she married. I wrote you, didn't I? All suddenly nothing beside the children. Work, qualifications, aspiration.' Even Irene pauses. 'They were supposed to be the new generation.'

'Yes,' says Bridie, grateful for this firmer ground. 'But we were much more the pioneers.'

'Where are they?' says Irene suddenly, wheeling again, searching the photos on the piano, the mantelpiece, the two occasional tables. 'The children. Laura's children. The boys must be quite grown-up.'

'Michael's . . .' The pain is there again. Bridie's breathing is shallow. If she takes deep breaths it hurts more. 'Twenty-six now, I think. That would make Toby twenty-four and the girls about twenty-two and fifteen.'

'I have to see pictures. I promised Meggie a full report.'

'Of course,' says Bridie, lifting the lid of the silver tea-pot and, despite everything, pouring in boiling water with a nerveless hand. 'But I'm sure you have pictures. Meggie's boys. Priscilla's. I think I should see those first. Fair's fair.' Irene has not hired a car. She has a train to catch. A taxi booked. The end of the afternoon must come. If Bridie smiles and pours tea, if she eats cake and controls her breathing then Irene Potts will leave, she'll go away. There will be no damage done.

And so they talk. Or, rather, Bridie lets Irene talk, encourages her. A few small questions are all Irene needs and Bridie does not, necessarily, have to listen to the answers. Certainly there was a time when the girls were close, Meggie and Priscilla, Ruth and Laura, girls of an age, sharing secrets together as they shared the door Mungo cut in the fence between their gardens. 'No point having them go round on the road,' Mungo said, returning from Venezuela, crashing into their lives with his lickety-split ideas and his hired chain-saw. The door was cut in an afternoon and used almost every day. She can remember exactly where that door was, though it is now behind a flower-bed, the lock rusted shut, the hinges a green tangle of climbing hydrangea. Irene is still talking. Priscilla's husband has not been well, but he's better now. Bridie expresses sympathy, surprise, repeats, 'Really,' with different intonations. This seems to be enough now. It was only that she wasn't prepared. That was all. And, of course, time does pass. The taxi arrives.

'Not already, surely,' says Irene. 'We don't seem to have covered half the ground.'

'No,' says Bridie.

'And I won't be back for a decade,' says Irene, and laughs. 'If ever.'

'I'll write,' says Bridie, knowing she won't.

'Oh, and so will I,' says Irene. 'And thank you so much.'

'A pleasure,' says Bridie. 'My pleasure.'

Irene, tired now, walks to the car slowly enough for the driver to jump out and open the passenger door. Bridie waves as her friend disappears down the drive, behind the leylandii, out into some future that need not concern her.

It is a quarter to six. Bridie goes inside and bolts the door behind her. She feels as if she needs tea. But she has had tea and it hasn't helped. It is not yet supper-time and far too early to go to bed. She rarely watches television these days, with its noisy, false companionship, and the radio would be only background to her thoughts tonight.

She clears the tea-things as slowly as she can. She hand-washes the cups, the saucers, the cake-plate, the spoons and knives. She takes the opportunity to empty the sugar bowl and scour its ceramic insides with a rough metallic sponge, though there is no stickiness there, no crust of sugar. She dries the bowl with a clean tea-towel (she has to go to the airing cupboard for this) and carefully pours in new sugar, pure, clear crystals. The silver service is next. She soaps and wipes and rinses. The tea-pot is dried inside as well as out, though this stains the white linen cloth. Then all the pieces, milk-jug, tea-pot, strainer and saucer, are buffed with the special silver cloth. When they shine like mirrors she places them in their separate drawstring bags of lined green baize and puts them away in the sideboard. Finally she wraps the remaining seed cake in tin-foil and empties the bin of general rubbish and Lapsang Souchong leaves. The time is now six twenty-five.

Bridie goes to the oak bureau and pulls out the runners. She lays down the lid and hopes to pay a bill or consider her savings account. As she sits she watches her right hand reach for the small centre drawer. She gives the brass handle a little tug and the drawer slides out noiselessly. She removes it completely and peers into it as though she just wants to see exactly what's inside, to count the different coloured envelopes, to know how many air-mails she has left. But already her hand is moving again, feeling into the dark cavity that the absent drawer has revealed. There is no spring to be sprung, no wooden panel waiting to be slid aside. There is just a small rectangular space with Bridie's fingers already inside. She brings out the photos but doesn't look at them immediately. Holding them in her hands she rises to shut the drawing-room curtains, though it is still quite light. Then she returns to the bureau and switches on the desk lamp. Michael. Toby. Manda. Sadie. Laura's children. Her grand-children. Lanky Michael, thirteen, up a tree, his face too big, blond like Mungo. On a branch beneath him Toby, eleven, smaller, wirier and more tense, reaching a hand upwards. On the ground, dark Manda, nine, sitting on the rug with baby Sadie, two. Manda playing peek-a-boo and Sadie in chubby raptures. Bridie remembers taking the picture, when she was allowed, when she was still the children's grandmother, Laura's mother. The summer before the ultimatum. This photo and the one of Michael as a baby, of Manda as the Angel Gabriel and Toby, blurred, riding a bike, these are the only photos to have survived. The ones Ruth missed.

Bridie puts the photos back. It is stupid to have looked. It is not as if she can't conjure the faces exactly, the lie of the children's limbs, their dated summer clothes, the way the light falls in the tree, on the rug, all of it she knows so intimately. It is printed behind her eyelids, branded on her heart. But how the children look now, over a decade later, that she doesn't know. Hasn't seen. She pushes the drawer back in and closes the bureau lid. The runners bang in their slots. It's because they're loose, Bridie thinks.

Her mind is made up now. It is not Irene Potts's fault. It is not Alice Watling's fault. And it is not her own fault. She switches off the desk light and opens the curtains. Sunlight pours in. She is seventy-five years old. She will not live for ever. There will never be a right time, so why not now? Mungo is right. '*Carpe diem*,' said Mungo, as he strode out of her life.

She goes into the kitchen and lifts the phone. Then she realises she does not know the number off pat. She replaces the receiver while she searches the kitchen-table drawer for her telephone book. Irene Potts will be in London now, gently tearing the roof off someone else's life.

Bridie presses the buttons and listens to the phone connect and ring. She has thirty seconds, maybe, to change her mind. But she will not change her mind. Not this time.

'Hello?'

'Manda,' says Bridie, 'is that you, Manda?'

'It's Sadie. Who's that?'

'Bridie. Your grandmother Bridie.'

'Oh.' There is a pause but the phone is not put down.

Sadie. Fifteen-year-old Sadie. What can she say to this granddaughter of hers? 'How are you, Sadie? Is everything OK?'

'I think you'd better speak to Mum.' Now the receiver does go down. But only as far as the table. 'Mum . . . Mum, it's for you.' Bless Sadie. Precious Sadie. She does not say who's calling, so Laura comes, footstepping to the phone. 'Yes?'

Bridie waits. It is her daughter's voice. 'Yes?' says her daughter, not angry, not distant, just neutral. Bridie lingers, collects the shining word, stores it.

'Who is this?' A slight tension now.

'It's your mother,' says Bridie.

A tight, clenched silence. 'So you've passed it on?'

'I . . .' says Bridie. 'Laura . . .' She has not planned a speech. What, after all, is there to say? I saw Irene Potts. I remembered you as a child, happy, making daisy-chains with Meggie. I saw you skip through the fence-gate when there was nothing more to darken your life than the thought that Meggie might be out. And then, even if she was out, there was still nothing lost, I could make it better with kisses, promises, ice-cream. This small summer memory and inside it my own death. For it cannot be long now, Laura. And I don't want you to have to get to my age before you feel the pointlessness of it all. Laura, my child.

'So you haven't passed it on.' Laura's voice low and deadly. 'Then you've got me the address, perhaps? Sent a photo?'

'Laura . . . Laura . . .'

'Mother, we have an agreement.' There's an electronic click and the line disconnects.

But not before Bridie hears the keening. This frantic noise cracks along the phone wires, it howls through the branches of the leylandii, finally coming to lodge, with other hardened griefs, between the bones of Bridie's skull.

# 6

Ruth and Alan are sitting on the patio. Alan, who has fair skin, has turned his chair against the sun and is reading the newspaper in the shade of his hat. Ruth has her recliner positioned so that her olive limbs stretch towards the sun and her dark-glassed gaze falls naturally on the girls, who are lying, so close together, on the rug thirty yards away. They giggle, Grace and Adele, knowing they are seen but not heard. Ruth moves in her chair, leans forward, listens intently. She hears birdsong, lawn-mowers, the rumble of passing cars, the fury of a child in an adjacent garden. At Pharmakon International, she thinks, people make appointments to tell her their secrets.

'What do you think the joke is?' Ruth asks Alan, who turns a breezy page, flattens it with his hand and continues to read about Algeria. Sometimes she thinks the joke is her. Ruth Thomas. Her need to know. Her constant expectation of exclusion.

When Grace was ten, eleven, she still came every morning to Ruth and Alan's bed. Lay between them with as much ease as she had when she was five, occasionally reaching out a hand to tickle the backs of their necks, just as they always had with her. The distance began at twelve, thirteen. She began to stand at the edge of the bed, leaning only to give – but not receive – a quick, dry kiss. At fourteen she remained in the doorway, hand on hip. At fifteen she ceased to come at all. Now, at seventeen, she lies full-stretch. With Adele. Their bodies so close you cannot see a thread of rug between them. They also lie together in Grace's room. On Grace's bed. In her bed. They pull the sheets high around their necks and whisper. When Ruth knocks, the whispering stops. Ruth walks in to silence, just as she did when she was a child herself and the silence was Bridie and Mungo's. Though her parents' silence was downstairs. Every time Ruth stands outside her daughter's room and the talking stops she remembers how, aged nine, she would return from school, dropped off by another mother, and walk into a kitchen that hushed at her approach.

'Hello,' her own mother, Bridie, would say, smiling around the pinched rage in her cheeks.

Her father would simply leave the room, banging the door behind him.

Of course she learned to creep, tiptoed into the house, flattened herself against walls, asked God each night to make her invisible, make her good, make her parents love her. Well, now she is the parent and Grace is the child, but her heart still drums in her throat when the whispering stops.

'What colour is my hair?' she asks Alan now, in the sun.

'Grey,' he says, without having to check.

Of course, she's aware that her hair has lightened, silvered, in the year since she was fifty. Just as Bridie's did. A genetic quirk. Nothing more. She's paid it scant attention, except perhaps gradually to tone down the colour of her lipstick. Besides, under Bridie's instruction, she has learned to pride herself not on her physical self but on her intellect. It was always her sister Laura who was beautiful.

'When did it change? How long ago?'

'A year. Two years.' Sports page now. 'I really don't remember.'

'And before it was grey?'

'What sort of question is that?' Alan asks, lifting his head at last.

'It's a question Adele asked. When she arrived this afternoon.' As if she hadn't been here, day after day, when Ruth's hair was jet black.

'Don't,' says Alan. 'It's not important.'

But it is important to Ruth. Just as the photograph album Alan has told her to 'leave be' is important. It's appropriate, Alan says, for pictures of one's parents to give way to pictures of one's friends. But that is not Ruth's point. There are no pictures whatsoever of Grace's mother now. It is as if Ruth is a ghost. A disappeared. In Grace's snapshots of family life, Bridie's still there, Alan too, occasionally. But Ruth has ceased to exist. It is as though God, forty years too late, has finally granted her wish of invisibility.

'I think you're making too much of this,' says Alan.

And maybe she is.

The girls have stopped talking now and are lying in sun-drenched quiet.

Alan lays down his paper. 'Would you like tea?' he asks.

Of course, it's only natural for him to walk across the lawn, towards his daughter, towards Adele, and ask them the same question. Ruth watches her husband move with his customary slow, casual grace. He is a large but agile man, not unlike her father Mungo. She remembers thinking this the first time she ever met him. Alan was one of the exhibitors in a group show being sponsored by Pharmakon International. It was a canapé-and-warm-white-wine private view. She noticed him immediately; unironed, sensual, magnitudinous.

'This is the chair of the sponsorship committee,' a grateful administrator simpered, introducing her. Some of the artists hadn't been able to see beneath her suit, others had stared at her handbag, pricing the leather, wondering how free she was with her chequebook. Alan looked her in the eye and talked about pots. 'Jug amphorae with the curves of women,' he said. The hot, burnt colour of terracotta, each with a small swell of clay breast, a tiny golden nipple. In the throat of the pots words, inscriptions, runes, love chants. On the pots, on each breast, the imprint of his thumb. 'You cannot,' he said, 'divide the maker from the made.' She knew she'd marry him even then. A man like Mungo but one who'd stay. A man of toil and soil, earthy, earthed.

43

The girls are lying on their backs and they lift themselves towards Alan as he nears them, leaning up on their elbows, shading their eyes to focus. Adele is white and bony, all elbows and knees and jutting hip-bones. But Grace, Ruth thinks, is a flawless beauty. A fluid piece of mythology, some young man's dream made peachy flesh. Small and gamine but with the flush of womanhood upon her. Her skin firm and golden, with a down of fine hair. Her neck white for stroking, her lips the pulse of a kiss. But she does not yet seek a god for her goddess, will not, in fact, look directly at any man but her father. Turns her head away, casts her eyes down, remains hidden. The scent of her maddening them. Is this what Mungo saw in Laura, why he looked at her with those panting eyes? Why Bridie consoled her, 'Ruth, you are the intellectual one.'

Ruth observes her own arid limbs. She is fifty-one. She has grey hair. But it is not this. For she never had luxurious flesh. Never felt the gaze of lust upon her. Never moved inside her own body as if she belonged there, like Mungo, like Laura, like Alan. Like Grace. All of them peas of one swelling pod. And her a husk. Parched like Bridie. The rind of a woman only.

Of course, Alan would not say so. Of course.

Adele is gesticulating. She wants something. Alan laughs and nods. Then he turns to his daughter. She shrugs. It's all the same to her. She will have whatever Adele is having. This is what Ruth interprets, sitting thirty yards away on the patio. Ruth wishes that Grace did not yield so easily. There are penalties to be paid for being too considerate, too accommodating. Kind. That's what Ruth's sister Laura says.

Alan passes her on his way to the kitchen. Ruth doesn't ask what he is going to prepare for the girls. She doesn't want to know. Alan also yields too easily. She watches Adele settle herself again, laying her face on her hands. Beside her Grace picks up the orange tube of Ambre Solaire and squeezes a spiral of the fragrant cream into the palm of her left hand. Then with small circular movements of her fingertips, she massages the lotion into Adele's shoulders, her back, her neck. Adele squirms under her touch, rolls a shoulder-blade, then relaxes, seems to sleep. Grace then does her own shoulders and back as best she can, twisting around herself, stretching, leaving gaps where she cannot reach.

Ruth toys with a book. 'I will teach my children,' Laura's voice says, 'not to give. To say no.'

The garden drowses. Ruth waits. Alan comes out of the house, precariously balancing a large tea-tray. At one end there is a tea-pot with cosy, a milk-jug and one small floral cup and saucer. At the other end are three huge, brimming drinks. He has used the tall, curvaceous Guinness glasses she bought from a pub sale many years ago. Pint glasses, with gold lettering and gold harps, used in a drinks promotion. He has made iced coffee, filling the glasses to the rim. He has mounded in vanilla ice-cream, cracked ice, dropped cube after cube of it into the creamy mass. Yellow froth has bubbled over, it flows down the outside of the glasses. He has crushed real coffee grains, swirled on chocolate powder. She can smell it melting, aromatically, in the sun. There's a scarlet straw in each drink and beside each glass a long-handled spoon.

'I didn't think you'd fancy this,' he says, indicating the froth and passing her the small cup of tea. Then he sets down a quenching coffee for himself and crosses the lawn to the girls. They both sit up and gesticulate wildly. They giggle. They are in raptures. Adele rises. She's going to kiss Alan.

45

Ruth closes her eyes. Mungo would return to such a welcome. From Peru, Argentina, Venezuela. From the west coast of Africa. From wherever the oil company had sent him their airborne doctor, their tropical disease specialist. At first it was just troubleshooting, a week here, two weeks there, checking the local facilities. Then he began to get involved, needed to be on site. The weeks turned into months, two months, three, six. It was no longer possible for Bridie to accompany her husband. The children were at school now and her own job too demanding. The girls began to see him less. In his absence the house was calm. Bridie prevailed. She kept a neat, an exact house. Despite her commitments at the hospital, she found time to oversee her daughters' lessons. She made them read, calculate, go the distance. Just the one more page, one more sum. 'You'll never get anywhere,' she said, 'if you don't go the distance.' And Ruth was clever. Much cleverer than her sister. Her star-chart was always full.

Then Mungo would return. Both girls would rush to him and he was strong and golden and swung them both high. Then he'd laugh and unwrap gifts for them. For Ruth some impossibly delicate piece of beadwork; or a pottery scene with figures that would smash if you breathed on them. For Laura it would be a little hat with mirrors on, a red tasselled shawl, a pair of moccasins still smelling of deer. Things that she took to bed and stroked. Things that he held against her, slipped over her head, her feet. His big hands caressing her body. Ruth's things were hard and brittle. It can't have been deliberate. He must just have stood in the markets visualising Laura, how she would look in this or that, his pea in a pod, his abundant girl.

None of it would have mattered if Bridie had remained hers. If, when Mungo returned, the star-chart had continued

46

to dominate the wall of their lives. But when her man came, Bridie changed. Different things mattered. The bond with the girls broke. She took to her room with her husband. They lay together for hours. For days. Or so it seemed to the sisters, standing outside the door, not daring to knock.

'I want a drink,' Ruth had screamed, one baked August afternoon. 'Get me orange.'

Laura was on the stairs, her blonde hair unbrushed, heavy and wet against her neck. She watched her sister with frightened eyes. 'Hush,' she whispered. 'Hush.'

In the room there was the noise they often heard. That of animals fighting, panting, snarling, crying aloud. 'Orange,' shrieked Ruth, sobbing above the sobs of her parents, their moans and thumps. 'Orange! Orange! Orange!' Then, in desperation, 'Please, orange.'

The grown-up sobs subsided, but the door remained closed. There was an air of hot indifference.

Ruth didn't see Laura retreat, softly padding downstairs to the kitchen. She didn't hear the oomph of the fridge being opened or the drag of a chair over flagstones. The cupboards were high. But still Laura managed, brought her elder sister a small glass of orange on a tray. Got it to the top of the stairs and didn't spill a drop.

Ruth looked at Laura, at the orange, at the door.

'I hate you,' she screamed, and dashed the glass to the floor.

Mungo came then. Opened the door and stood, charged and indolent, in the doorway. 'Clear it up,' he said, 'Now.'

And they did, Ruth and Laura, for they'd felt the flat of their father's hands before. Did it carefully, licking the pads of their fingertips so that they could pick up each tiny, sparkling shard.

Ruth opens her eyes. Alan is back beside her now in his

chair that faces the wrong way. He is dozing, a yellow grin of ice-cream about his mouth. Ruth picks up the spent drink with its bright straw. She sucks hard, a baby ravening at a mother's breast.

Her mouth fills with tepid water.

# 7

This is the seal story my grandmother says does not exist. This is the story I did not read, with my back pressed into the glass, at the window-seat in her drawing-room.

In a time that is yesterday and tomorrow and eternally present there lived a hunter, whose son was so evil that his father took him to an icy crag and cast him into the sea. It was so cold that winter that even the bears shook beneath their fur, but the father carried the child naked to the cliff and threw him naked into the air. The wind was chill beyond imagining and the child lost all breath before he touched the water so that, though he had swum like a porpoise in life, he sank then without struggle, his white body gleaming in the depths. The fish of the sea were as famished as the men of the land that winter, and they showed the boy no mercy but stripped all the flesh from his bones and were glad of it. Then there was nothing left of the boy but the bones and the memory of the bones, which the sea itself swallowed.

But the child was not forgotten. Each dusk his mother came

to the seashore to keen for him. For in her mother love she saw no evil in the child and had she seen evil she would have loved him yet. The howls of the mother were fierce and bitter. 'Oh, my baby,' she called, 'my darling, my boy.' Her cries were carried in the throats of sea-birds and her tears were the spray of the ocean. Then it happened that the same chill wind that had borne her son to his death lifted her grief-bitten song to a faraway rock where a seal the colour of moon milk lay. And though the seal would not have it so, for the shore-mother was not of her kind, the woman's wailing was so savage and so tender that it entered her soul. For the seal was a mother too. And though the seal slipped from the rock and swam hard and long, seeking the silence of the deep, the music remained ever with her. 'Oh, my baby, my darling, my boy.'

So it was that, haunted by an anguish that seemed to turn as sharply in her as if it had been her own, the seal-mother determined to find the child and return him to his mother's embrace. And thus began a search of all the oceans' most far-flung, fathomless places. For so loud was the drumming of need in the seal-mother's heart that she knew she must find every bone of the boy or perish in the attempt. For a year she swam without rest, circling the globe, surfacing only to hear the lament of the wind that was the woman's lament. The seal grew lean but not frail for she fed on joy with each bone that she found, a rib, a carpal, a shin. And still the shore-mother keened, 'Oh, my baby, my darling, my boy.'

On the second anniversary of the boy's fall, the seal-mother returned to her rock. She had found all that she sought, carried each bone in her mouth, brought it home. She laid them out on the grey slate and began her final work, sculpting the white frame of the boy, his beloved skeleton. Then, when the last bone was in place, she began to sing. The song was low and silken, a thread of notes strung from her heart to the heart of the boy who had been. She breathed in and out the starlight air, so that there seemed to be, over the bones, a bright veil, which grew denser and more milky white the louder and longer she sang. For she was singing him flesh, sang all night and the following day, the taut, clear notes of muscle and sinew, and the continuous bass line of blood. At the end of the second day the boy was whole, his skin as radiant naked as the day he was born, a million silk black hairs curling from his head. Then the seal-mother ceased her song for she was exhausted. It was dusk. The shore-mother took up the refrain: 'Oh, my baby, my darling, my boy.'

Then the child opened his eyes, which were bluer than the heavens in summer, and he smiled. And the seal-mother loved him then. Loved him with the power of the song itself, with each of the thousand thousand breaths she breathed him into being. For his flesh was part of her flesh and his blood had drummed in her veins. Oh, my baby. My darling. My boy.

Then the seal-mother knew she could not relinquish the child. Not yet. Not now. She would needs have the boy, just for a while, for one glittering day. For hadn't she deserved such a day after all her pains? So she kissed the boy softly, putting her mouth so close to his lips that some of her sea-breath entered his lungs. Then she called to the child, 'Come, dive, swim.' And they slipped from the rock together. And he swam as he had in life, only deeper and more joyously, for he found he had no need to surface, but could breathe as the sea creatures breathed. So the two of them swam with the whales and played tag in caverns of ice. But the child was never cold for he had the seal-mother to warm him. Dusk came all too soon and the seal would not have the boy return to the rock so she called to him softly once more, 'Dive, my baby, dive.' But the boy was tired now and would rest so, because she loved him, she carried him to the surface on her back. In the chill air was the voice of the shore-mother, keening.

'What noise is that, Mother?' asked the boy.

'It is the lament of the wind, my child,' answered the seal.

Then the oceans shook and from the briny depths rose the sleek-backed Silver Mother, greatest of all the seals. Then the moon milk seal trembled for she knew she had offended, though some part of her heart could not understand how or why.

The Great Silver One spoke softly, but the weight of the sea was on her words. 'Take the boy back. He is not of our kind.'

Then the seal-mother wept, for hadn't she created the child, wasn't he flesh of her flesh and blood of her blood?

'O Great Silver One,' cried the seal, 'hear my plaint. For without me what would this boy be? Just scattered bone. Didn't I search for him, find him, breathe him anew? And don't I love him now as my own? Just one more day. That's all I ask.'

Then the Silver One relented, for she was a mother too, though something that felt like mourning passed through her as she did so. 'It is as you say,' she said. 'So be it as you ask. But at dusk you must return the child to his rightful mother.'

Then the seal-mother dove for joy, breathing once more into the lungs of the boy, folding him to her for the night and day that was theirs. For what was dusk? The turning of a planet away. And so, no longer weary, they swam again, the seal-mother and her darling, two sinuous creatures dancing in water, tumbling and spinning together, hand in fin and cheek to muzzle, two flying fish who thought their game would never end. But the planet turned. It was dusk. And the voice of the Silver Mother boomed through the depths, 'Return the child.'

Then, slow as the coming of spring when the winter is at its darkest, the pair rose to the surface.

'Just one more minute, beloved,' said the seal, and took the boy to the rock where her song was strongest.

Over the sea came the sound of a woman wailing, 'Oh, my baby, my darling, my boy.'

But the seal-mother heard only the wind for the fury that suddenly whipped in her soul. For they would take the child from her! They would steal him away from her, who had, with pain and joy, sung him into being. For what was he without her but scattered bones, dry and lifeless white? Then rage and anguish fought in her so violently that she began another song, one too terrible to name.

'Return the child,' cried the Great Silver One. 'Return the child to his rightful mother.'

'I am the mother,' sang the seal. 'I am the mother now.' And she sang her savage song over the naked boy. And the notes were so wild they flayed the child, stripping the flesh from his hands, his feet, his stomach, his face. And he howled as the wind and the music tore into him. 'Oh, my baby, my darling, my boy.' Deaf to the wind and deaf to the boy, the seal sang on. For the only thing she could hear now was the anger, for they had done her wrong and she would be revenged. The boy was quieter now. The blood had stopped in his heart and the breath gone once more from his lungs. When the seal-mother looked again, there was the boy: a pile of bones on a rock.

And there came from her then a sound that had never been heard before in day or night, a howl to crack the ice of mountains. For she knew she would give her blazing soul to have him live again, even to live all his life upon the shore.

And she opened her mouth to sing again the song of breath and blood and flesh, but she found it was no longer inside her. The only noise that came from her throat was a chill lament: 'Oh, my baby, my darling, my boy.'

Then the shore-mother thought she heard, at last, an answer to her cry, and echo of care. She quieted then, strained to hear. But maybe it was just the wail of the wind or the cry of the ocean itself. Or the sigh of waves. For they do sigh, as they breathe, in and out, on the coasts of the world.

I have written this story word for word as I remember it. But they may not be the right words. Which is why I still search, scour my grandmother's shelves, peek in her dark places, for the hope of the story, which, one day, I know I will find.

For the bones of it are in Bridie's house.

# 8

It is eight fifty p.m. and the dusk has begun to get in Ruth's eyes. She should replace the paving slab, go inside and wash her hands. The weekly conference call begins at nine thirty and she needs to be prepared. But her hands are deep in the soil, the mud packed under her finger-nails. Besides, there are some things that won't wait.

She closes her fists around the bulging sumac root and pulls. The mother sumac tree is ten foot tall now. It was here by the studio when they moved to this house when Grace was five. In spring it has dense green fern-like leaves, with candles of brown seed, which darken to scarlet through the summer. Just as the leaves turn yellow and vermilion in late autumn, so that the tree looks as if it's suddenly burst into flame. For years she had thought the tiny baby sumac trees, which grew between the cracks in the paving, were gifts of the birds or the result of soft puffs of summer wind. Each July she would take her bone-handled garden knife and slice off the three-inch shoots of hopeful green. But now she realises, though it must have been plain to see for at least a year or two, that the pavings are being lifted. That the mother does not drop her seed, but sends out strong roots, thicker than a finger, which push their way along in the dark until there's a gap in the concrete and they sense light. Then they begin to surface, to grow strong knots of life, to force their way into air and sun and rain.

Ruth has one of the knots in her fists. She is pulling against earth and dark and the adjacent paving slab. Six dead babies already lie behind her. But this one is larger than the rest, its subsidiary roots deeper, and the whole of Ruth's weight lifts the knot barely an inch. Ruth feels the tension in her arms, the muscle pull of her leg, braced against the plant. She could make the job easier, follow the line of the root, lift a second paving stone. But, she realises, she's enjoying the struggle, the spit of soil on her lip, the pitting of living thing against living thing. The more the root resists her, the more she grits and twists. For she will have it, tear it up, tear it apart. Thock! One root gives. A slim, moist, bright white arm pulled from its sleeve of dirt. Ruth reaches down and touches the wet white. Simon Trevor. Another enquirer has come and said that Simon Trevor, finance director, has put his hand on her white breast. Where Ruth touches the root it muddies. Her hands are earth now. She wipes an arm against her brow.

Such a little root. This enquirer is not a cheap, scrawny blonde like Adele. This enquirer is lush. Her flesh is rosy young, her eyes downcast. She looks as if she needs to be protected, as if she's somebody's daughter, an innocent, a nubile child. She stutters over Simon's name, cannot say the word 'breasts', but points instead and says, 'It was here.'

Ruth should go in. She should wash her hands. On the Pacific Rim, Howard Kan will be getting up. He joins the conference call at five a.m. his time on behalf of Pharmakon International, Asia region. She stands up. Through the studio window she can see Alan. His hands are also dirty. But he is not making longtoms, although the fortnightly order is, again, not yet complete and the delivery van is coming tomorrow.

They once had dinner with Simon Trevor and his wife. Marie. A pretty, vivacious woman who had stayed at home to look after their two sons. Now Simon touches breasts and Alan makes eggs. Yes, that's what her husband has been doing for the last two weeks. Making pottery eggs. The light of life is in 'los ovarios'. That's what Grace has told Alan. She read it in a book. One of the books that Grandma Bridie gave her for her birthday. 'Eggs as creation myth, all life from this tiny beginning.' How can he say this to her, how can he dare? 'I'm only repeating what Grace told me,' he says. Her boot is on the root, holding it down.

Of course, just because two enquirers mention the same fact does not make that fact true. This is what Gloria Beckenhauer, Supreme Corporate Ombudsperson, New York, will remind the ombuds team tonight. 'One must always keep in view,' she will say as Ruth raises her issue, 'the possibility that Simon Trevor is wholly innocent and the enquirers are, for whatever reason, fabricating evidence against him. What,' Gloria will continue, 'is your own view of Mr Trevor?'

Ruth's view of Mr Trevor is that he's clever, charming and overweight. She cannot imagine him wanting or needing to touch enquirers' breasts. Alan has a small tool in his hand, which looks like a scalpel. He is using it to inscribe one of his eggs. He will write things that nobody but he will understand. Like he used to write on the inside of the golden pots with breasts. Love poems to himself. Ruth releases the root. She has not time any more for its labyrinth. She will give it one clean cut with her secateurs. Snip. The root back to the mother will wither and die. Won't it? Won't it! It can't continue to thicken and spawn. At least the forward root will die. She will pull it from the earth herself, shake and scatter the soil. She snips. She pulls. The thick white blood of it is on her hands. She doesn't want to talk to Howard Kan about Simon Trevor. She doesn't want to talk to Gloria Beckenhauer in New York about Simon. Or to Rory Forrest in Perth or Sam Chatterjee in Bombay.

She wants to walk into Pharmakon International, look Simon Trevor straight in the eye and say, 'Is it true?' And she wants Simon to say, 'Yes,' or alternatively, 'No.' She doesn't care what the answer is. She just wants there to be an answer. She wants the white limb pulled out, exposed. She wouldn't call it truth, for she has long since given up on anything as simple as truth. But the darkness is hurting her eyes. She stands up. There isn't time now to replace the paving. That's a delicate job. You must level the soil, remove loose stones, lay the slab once, remove it to see where the mud is flat, where the stone has touched earth and where not. Then there has to be a raking, a rearrangement, a realignment. And she hasn't time. Because she has to see Alan.

She lifts herself into the brightness of the studio. For a moment she can see nothing and then there he is, threading beads and feathers on to pieces of wire. Tribal things. Like the ones her father Mungo brought for Laura.

'What are you doing?' she screams.

'Beads,' he says, 'feathers. To decorate the eggs.'

'We have to tell her,' says Ruth.

Alan twists gold wire tight about a feather shaft. 'We've been through this,' he says.

'She has a right to know.'

'Had a right.'

'It'll come out. She'll find out.'

Alan takes an egg and holds it in the palm of his hand. It nestles there. 'Isn't it time for your call?' he asks.

# 9

She calls them his eggs. But they are not eggs. Not exactly. Though they began that way, when he coiled the clay around the kernel of space. A small, swelling shape, which he smoothed with a wetted finger. The ridges of clay flowing at last under his hand – at last – being stroked into sinuous form. Then the holding of the egg between the palms of his hands. Such slight pressure. For he had to flatten the curve, just a little. Then his fingers stroking once more, over the belly of the piece, its taut abdomen.

It is, Alan thinks, to do with Carl. Carl has come into his house and touched his girl. His daughter Grace. Grace lies in her crop-tops in the drawing-room, in her bikini in the garden, the curve of her stomach exposed. Of course Alan does not wish to touch his daughter. But he does want to touch. He wants to remember how a warm peach felt when he plucked it straight from a tree in Sicily, how it filled his hand, brushed its sun-gilded flesh against his. He wants to remember how he could push his thumb in the throat of a pot and raise the clay up, bring from his wheel a vessel to hold water. A jug from which to pour love. How he could mould nipples and breasts by touch alone.

Carl is an ugly man, Alan thinks. An ugly boy. He is large and graceless, solid and shiny white. His hair is black and lies on his head in greasy strips the shape of his motorbike helmet. He laughs and grunts and fails to wash his clothes. He has huge hands, the nails bitten and the creases stained with engine oil. It is these hands he has put on Grace.

There are seven slightly flattened eggs on the workbench in front of Alan. Four are already burnished. Alan takes the fifth. The clay is leather-hard and the slip of iron and manganese oxide dry. He presses his forefinger into the hollow of the metal spoon and circles its convex back against the egg. The movement is small, constant. Where the spoon and the force of his hand pass, the surface of the egg buffs. It shines.

Ruth was at work when it happened. Grace was sitting on the grass, reading. She had that absorbed, complete look she used to have as a tiny child, when she was threading beads of clay she'd made herself or staring out of a night-time window, watching clouds scud over the face of the moon. They came through the garden gate. Adele and Carl. There was the roar of the bike, the sudden sputting silence, a call, that grunting laugh and Grace rising to them, to slide the bolt. He saw it all above a rim of the invoice. An order for garden pots.

Carl had a large, proprietorial hand on Adele. He slipped it from her waist to the slim mound of her buttock, began to massage, round and round, because he thought no one could see. Or maybe because he thought someone could see, his large hand on his possession, round and round, closer and harder. Ruth does not like Adele. Objects to her cheap flagrancy, her sluttish smile. But Adele does have an attraction. Sharp. Lemony.

'As for Carl,' Ruth says.

They stood talking on the grass. He could not hear what they said, only the rise and fall of it, the excitement, their plan. Carl had his thick face close to Adele's, nuzzling her, a big dog drooling. Then Grace said something that made him laugh. He turned, lifted a hand towards her cheek. Carl's pudgy, engine-oil hand on Grace's flawless cheek. But no, it was not her cheek. His hand fell short, rested at the hollow of her throat, at the bones' divide. His hand was there, so large that the heel of it was almost at her breast. He was touching her small, swelling breasts. His tongue was between his teeth, Alan clearly remembers the pink tip pushing through. Then the hand dropped, just glancing the rounded flesh of Grace's abdomen as it fell. Adele laughed, Grace shrugged. The moment was over.

Round and round the back of the spoon goes on the egg. Round and round. Burnishing.

Grace left with Carl and Adele to return, some hours later, alone. He did not ask where she had been or what she had done. He did not say, 'Why did you let him touch you?' For she did not let him. Carl touched what was not his. He just stretched out his hand and took.

The egg is finished. Alan lays aside the spoon and picks up a stone. It is a small white pebble worn smooth by the sea, the attrition of rock and sand and salt. It feels good in his hand, it fits, belongs. If he lifts it to his cheek, it is cool. He found it in his desk drawer, dry like a bone. Did he burnish the breasts of the vessel women with this stone all those years ago? Did he golden their nipples with this bone-white stone? Perhaps he did. He takes the pebble now, between forefinger and thumb. Rubs stone on clay. Hard rock on malleable earth. There is something he wants. Wants terribly. The clay shines.

The egg is not yet finished. The egg is barely begun, but Alan gets up and leaves it. He walks out of the studio and across the darkening lawn and into his lighted house. Ruth is on the phone. The phone-call lasts from half past nine to half past midnight. He stands in the doorway of the study and looks at his wife's back. It is a quarter to eleven. Only the desk light is on and she is in half-shadow, her head is inclined and her concentration absolute. She is not aware of him standing there, loving her. Dark hair curls at the nape of her white neck. She reaches up a hand to scratch that neck, a glancing touch on her own flesh. She's not using the headset tonight, but cradles the receiver against the cheek he cannot see. 'It is more intimate,' she says, 'to use the receiver.'

He wants to touch her. It is this simple. He wants to touch his wife. He wants to trace the line of her jaw, stroke the pure length of her throat, kiss the bones of her neck, bury his head in the oil and fragrance of her hair. If he touches her, she will let go the receiver and turn to him. She will fix her surprise on his mouth, taste the clay of him as she used to when she came late to the studio to find him among the fruit bowls.

When she cried for him to take her in the light of the evening, against the curtainless glass, for who should care if two people were in love?

He cannot wait until midnight. There are some things that won't wait. Moments pass. He moves towards her for he is, after all these years, still in love with the girl of her. The girl he saw beneath the stiff business suit the night of the Pharmakon Show. That suit just a dead case on the rippling girl. He could see beneath, through. Knew her immediately as you know kin, recognise blood. Touched her then on the breast of that suit, as he passed to show her his pots, the golden pots with nipples. Of course, there were many people there that night and all standing too close. Just a jog. A mistake. But she knew. He heard her breath.

'Yes,' says Ruth, into the phone. 'Simon Trevor. Finance director.'

She's not aware of him now, though he is very near. Near enough to reach the mute button. He does not, of course, wish to embarrass her. She will understand, she will remember how they lay naked together, before garden pots, before Grace, knowing that their arms had been made by God for just this circle, laughing at how their bodies belonged, became one.

Because she is hunched over her work, Ruth's right breast is close to the desk, close to the phone and the mute button. He can touch both together. He reaches out, he touches.

Ruth startles, cries, 'Oh!' She wheels in her chair. Her appalled eyes look down at her breasts as if she saw not a hand but a large black spider sitting there. Of course he must say something, do something, do it quickly. But what? What is there to say? He is fifty-four years old and he should have known better? He pulls away his hand. But the spider remains. And so does his need. For the truth is he doesn't want to know better. He wants his wetted finger on the ridges, his thumb in the hollow of the spoon. He wants to be given, or if not to be given to take, what he remembers as his. His touch of clay. His joy of his wife. To hold in his arms the woman whom he loves beyond speaking. The woman who sits hugging the spider in front of him. He is backing away. He is almost out of the door.

'Sorry,' he says, though he does not know if his mouth works, if any sound is coming out.

'Sorry,' he repeats, 'my mistake.'

Then he rushes back into the room and releases the mute button.

'Ruth? enquires Gloria Beckenhauer in New York. 'Could you run that past us again?'

'I . . .' says Ruth. 'Excuse me one minute, I . . . I'm going off line.' She presses buttons then seems to fall down into herself, lets go a second soft cry.

He stands in the doorway, looking in on her.

'How could you?' she says.

He lifts a hand as if it might stretch towards her, but it does not.

'What were you thinking of?'

And, of course, he can't say that they used to make love in the light and now they make love, if they make love, in the dark. He doesn't want to say that because it might make it true.

'I'm so sorry,' he says, and he creeps away. He lingers a moment in the passageway. Perhaps she will get up and cross the hall and let him hold her. He waits. He hears a nose being blown and then the tap of buttons again.

'Hi. I'm back. Sorry. A noise. I thought it was a burglar. No, no, I'm fine. Nothing at all. Just my imagination. Where were we?'

It is quite dark outside now. Alan wants to be outside. He moves slowly into the night. The air is wet, though it has been such a hot day. The chill of it is good on his face. He wishes it was not just dew but rain. Torrential rain. He would take off his clothes and let it beat him, pound his flesh, drench his hair. There would be so much rain he would have to wipe it out of his eyes. He wouldn't notice then if, among the raindrops, there were tears on his cheeks.

But it is not raining. Alan hears a noise like sobbing and puts his fist in his mouth. He walks to the studio and turns on the light. He will stay here with the clay and the dirt and the burnished eggs. He will sleep on the sofa. She will expect him to, won't come to check. After the phone-call, at twelve thirty, she will ascend the stairs to their bedroom, get into their bed, knowing that he will kip in the studio. That's what the sofa is for. For if he's working late. If he doesn't want to disturb her.

'Did you sleep well?' she may ask him in the morning. Or she may not. For he often sleeps on the sofa these days. It is nothing to remark on.

But he doesn't feel tired. He knows he will lie on the sofa and feel every spatter of hardened clay. He will pull the dusty rug about him and stare at roof slats, at the broken window-pane. So he's not going to bed. He's going to fire the eggs, even though it is senseless. He takes them tenderly, places them in a basket as if they were real, as if they contained life. Then he switches off the studio light.

The dark seems softer now and his eyes are soon accustomed to the shadows. Ruth has been lifting paving stones for some reason. There is one slab she has failed to replace. It is here that he will site the dustbin which is to be the furnace. It will be safe on the earth. He puts down the eggs and goes to fetch the metal bin. But the soil is not level. There is some root in the way which makes the bin unsteady. When he tries to stamp the root down, it springs up, though he can see it has been cut, bears the white bleed of a knife. He lifts an adjacent paving stone. The root can be clearly seen now, a strong spur from the mother. He takes the penknife from his pocket and hacks it through. Now the soil can be levelled. He rakes it flat with his fingers. The bin sits squarely. Alan begins to line it with fine sawdust.

The eggs should have already been biscuit fired. They should have sat in a kiln at seven or eight hundred degrees and then been allowed to cool. Smoke-firing them blind, as Alan intends to do tonight, is ill-advised. The eggs may shatter. There may be nothing but shards in the bin tomorrow morning. But Alan wants to take this risk. In fact, he wants to increase the risk. He will add small shreds of paper to the sawdust. These will burn faster than the sawdust increasing the likelihood of thermal shock. He knows where he will get the paper from.

He returns to the house. Perhaps he hopes that Ruth will, in fact, have finished her call. She is, after all, leaving for New York in two days' time. The worldwide ombuds team is meeting to discuss – whatever it is they discuss. Pharmakon secrets. So surely they can curtail their conferencing now. But it's not just that. No. He hopes, perhaps, that she's signed off because of him. Is wondering where he is, what he is doing, why it is that he came to love her in that one particular moment. That she is, even now, just about to seek him out. Find him.

'No, Sam,' he hears her say, 'I don't feel that.'

Sam Chatterjee lives in Bombay. 'He thinks as I do,' Ruth says.

Alan is very quiet now. The shredder is in the study. The company have not bought this machine for Ruth. She got it second-hand. 'I just want to be really sure,' she said. 'You can't be too careful, you know.' They send the bills for her office phone to her home address. These she shreds, he knows. What else she shreds, he does not know. Though the blue bin-liners are often full. The shredder drawer slides noiselessly out. He lifts the small plastic sack from its metal holding rim. Inside the paper is curled. He wants to take a handful of the paper and crush the ridges of it against his palm. But that might make a noise and he doesn't want any noise now. So, softly, he shuts the drawer, softly he withdraws.

Outside he pours a little more sawdust into the dustbin and then he opens the blue plastic sack and empties out Pharmakon's secrets. They flutter down, blue and pink and white. At least, these are the colours he imagines the secrets are, for only the white is stark in the darkness. Then he stirs. The sawdust and paper is deep now, it comes up to his elbow. It reminds him of the bran tubs he would put his hand into as a child, seeking a wrapped gift at the church fête. Only this is not a bin to take something from but one to put something in. Something to burn. He takes the eggs one by one from the basket and buries them. He tries not to know whether he places them by paper or shavings, what their chance of survival is, how many will make it through the night. It will be a slow burn. This much he does know. He presses down his tinder, firms it. Then he takes a match and touches it to the surface. It catches, smokes. He must put the lid on, but not yet. He wants to stand and watch, to see his fire smoulder.

It's then that he hears the noise. Or perhaps it's just the pattern of darkness shifting about him. Shadows changing inside the studio. As if someone was there. Watching. But no one could have passed so close to him and him not notice. He puts on the lid of the smoke-kiln. Already the heat is building. There it is again. That particular clink. The fall of fired pottery on a concrete floor. Someone brushing too close to the drying shelves, unaware of the stack of fire chips he uses when loading the kiln. Someone making for the sofa but not wanting to switch on the light.

She has come.

His magical creature has come. She's been smoked out, risen from the ashes. She's created herself from clay, come fully formed, golden nipples burnished with his bone-dry stone. She moves in his workspace, her silhouette dark against the glass. He can see her now, though she wears some covering, a coat perhaps, as though she has something to hide. The sofa is close to the curtainless window. He remembers how they lay there with their drapery of stars. Now she sits again. Takes off the coat. The bony outline is quite distinct. Sharp. The nipples erect.

Alan, reaching the studio door, turns on the light.

# 10

It is eleven thirty p.m. and I have come from the stone. The wide grey shale and the river running by. When I sit there on a summer night I am part of the meadow and the water and the rock. This is my place and I go there alone. Though my father came with me once, when I was a child. It was he who told me the plate of flat grey was shale.

'Look,' he said, lifting a thin layer of stone with his penknife, 'you can see how it was made. Laid down. Just mud, clay. Compacted. Like slate only less solid, softer.' He brushed away the loose chippings with his fingers. Then he spread his hands wide on the slab, palms down. It was summer then, too, and the stone was warm.

He might have grown there, I thought, looking. Or maybe I thought this before or afterwards. No division between him and the rock, though the outline of each was distinct as earth is distinct from sky. My father the rock, the tree, the meadow and river. Not a man who travelled in a landscape but a man who was landscape, clay and lichen and cold water. And if he belonged I belonged too, because we two were one, father and daughter, and also three, father and daughter and rock. Though he never came there again and it became my place. And is my place still.

So when I rise from the evening stone and cross the dewy meadow, which swishes wet against my bare calves, when I tread the night-hot concrete and ascend the roaded hill towards my house, it's as if I know that, though late, the lamp in his studio will be lit. That my passage from dark to light will be eased. That I can come back and come in.

It is not that I'm going to say anything particular to my father. He is not, in any case, a man to whom you say things. Questions bewilder him. Conversation bores him. But he has a way with silence. He can share it. My blood is stiller when I'm near him. As if his being tempers mine. I will sleep more soundly for the few minutes I will first spend with him.

So I am confounded when I slide the bolt of the garden gate, my hand reaching over and in, to see, against the lighted glass, not one but two figures. This midnight moment is mine. And yet, it seems, my father already has a partner for the dance. Something hot licks about my face. They are moving together, the figures, making a slow circle of touch. To see more clearly I would have to be closer and I know, with a sudden miserable detachment, that I should not go closer. I should turn my back, walk across the lawn, enter the cool house and ascend quietly to my room, tapping the fruit bowls as I go. But I've already taken several steps forward. I am drawn by the dance and also by the white motif of my father. He is naked. His body loose and tranquil. His hands are open and he holds in his wide palms the breasts of his partner. I am near enough now to see the pale blue veins that fan from the nipple. He strokes with his thumb and then moves one hand from the small mounded breast, down the line of the stomach, the abdomen and then over the hip to rest out of sight on the white buttock of Adele.

It may, of course, not be happening. I may have made it up. I do make things up. People say this about me and I know it is true. It began when I was ill, the winter I was four and a half. I

68

lay down to sleep in the snow. I don't remember doing it but they said that I did. Just went out and curled up as if the snow had been a blanket. I do remember the hospital, the white of that. And waking, of course. To the singing. The notes came down a long tunnel towards me, a song that seemed to be both reaching for me but also emanating from me, as if my bones and blood were an instrument that someone else could play. It was a woman. She was there when I opened my eyes that first ever time. So of course I thought I knew her, though afterwards they said I had been raving. The drugs, the pneumonia, the shock. And I think they were right, for later it came to me that I had dreamed that woman before. That she was just an icon, a composite image. Blonde like my father, dark-eyed like me, yet with the look, the smile, of my mother. The song was less easy to delineate. I remember it forcefully but without clarity. Too fierce for a lullaby and yet it soothed me. More exhilarating than any music I've ever heard and yet without a tune. I couldn't hum it, couldn't play back the notes in my mind. Yet the pulse of it is with me still, strong as a heartbeat.

Then there was the car. It followed us for a year, I think. Until we moved. I don't think my mother was aware of it at first and I didn't tell her. I'd begun to be afraid of my imaginings. It was a small red car. I tried not to look at the driver though I knew it was a woman. I felt her eyes on me but refused to return the gaze. I suppose I thought that if I saw her face then I would make her exist even if she didn't. Looking the other way kept her in negative. Of what was I afraid? That she was the woman at the hospital? Or, worse, that she was not the woman at the hospital? That, every day, reality was becoming that much less sturdy?

Then, as we returned one Saturday from the weekly

supermarket shop, the red car pulled out too suddenly. Mummy looked in the mirror.

'Jesus,' she said. 'Jesus.' And she stamped on the accelerator.

Even then I didn't ask any questions. Perhaps I was too young. Perhaps I didn't want to know the answers. Perhaps she wouldn't have told me anyway. The moment passed.

After that we switched supermarkets, our loyalty never lasting longer than a fortnight. In fact, all our habitual driving patterns changed. New mothers were asked to collect me from school, our route to the swimming-pool altered and so did the time we swam. I was encouraged to play more in the house. Forays outside, even those to the small enclosed garden that backed our London house, were accompanied.

In the kitchen, my mother and my grandmother talked in low voices. When I approached there was silence. Though I did hear the name 'Alice Watling' more than once. 'That child Alice Watling.' Alice was another being without proper substance. A penumbra around my shadowy core. Only I would have liked to have claimed Alice. I felt a kinship with her and not a little curiosity. She gave me some courage, though not enough to question my mother. My father's response was to put a hand on my head. I remember it there, heavier than his silence. Then he sighed and said, 'Alice Watling is just someone who died a long way back.'

Shortly after then we moved. It may have been planned a long while and my parents only thought to tell me the morning the packers came. But it seemed sudden to me. I cried for the whole of the two-hour journey south. My mother said to hush up, I would like the new house, it had a larger garden and a special place for Daddy to work, he would be able to be at home all the time. And I did like the new house. The whispering stopped and there was no red car.

But even now I retain this lack of belief in my own eyes and ears. Which is why I think my father is not making love to my best friend. They have gone now anyway. Possibly they have simply disappeared below the back of the sofa and I cannot see them any more. But, just as likely, they were an hallucination, a wisp of smoke rising from this dustbin beside me. After all, this smoking bin is new. It didn't exist this afternoon and will probably not exist tomorrow. I reach out my hand to touch it. It burns me, which proves at least that I am here. It is only the tiniest of taps but it still flattens the whorls of my index fingertip. And it hurts. I put my finger into the wet grass. This cools but does not console. And I need consoling. There is only one place I go when I am in need and that is Adele's house. I shall go there now. And Adele will be in.

I know she will.

# II

It is a quarter past midnight and most of the lights are out in Caldicott Road. The flats opposite Adele's house are completely dark. Nothing moves behind the dirty blinds, and the white hospital railings are barely visible. Of course I know now that light does not confer safety, nevertheless my heart sings to see that the one house ablaze in Adele's terrace is Adele's. The drawing-room light is on, and so are both bedroom lights – Julie's and Adele's. What's more, the gate to the house is massively blocked by Carl's motorbike. I lean down to the bike. I kiss it, smear myself with a little grease from the steel engine ribs. The engine is cold. Carl has been in the house some while.

I walk down the path, jingling my keys. Adele and I swopped house keys many years ago. Sometimes, even now, Adele comes to my house in the early hours of the morning and creeps into my bed. Sometimes I wake, occasionally she deliberately wakes me, but usually I continue to sleep and wake to find her beside me in the morning. She is the only person I have ever shared a bed with except, perhaps, my mother when I was a tiny baby. She kisses my cheek and calls me her virgin. My innocence amuses her. These soft morning times are when she whispers about sex to me, advises me what to do with a man, if I ever get one. I think I was thirteen when she first told me about oral sex. The darkness covered my horror but my voice must have betrayed me.

'You're shocked, aren't you? You are. You are!' Delighted, she reached over a hand and idly tickled my stomach, beneath my pyjama top. She pretended she'd had hundreds of men by then, though I don't think it was true.

I arrive at the front door. It is open, at least it's ajar. Carl, I imagine. His sort of slackness. He should take greater care, it's not, after all, as if Adele has a hall. The door to the street is the door of her sitting-room. One small push and I'm in. Downstairs there is an eerie, abandoned silence. But then, of course, I don't have to catch the mirror's eye to know that everyone must be upstairs. Even in the kitchen it would be impossible not to know that the front door was open, to feel compelled to come and pinch it shut. I close it softly. Now the darkness is outside.

I make for the stairs, listening for the usual throb of music from Adele's room. But the only noise upstairs is a rickety sort of movement and punctured breathing. I climb quietly, I do not wish to disturb Adele's mother. Julie often has male admirers with whom she 'talks' at length. 'I'm just going to talk with Paul.' Or Steve or John or Pete. Sometimes they take up coffee and they do talk. Sometimes they row or watch a movie with the volume turned up. More often they fuck. I don't like the word 'fuck'. Adele does. 'Sounds like what it is,' she says approvingly. 'In yer face.' She laughs. 'Among other places.'

Adele's door is open. Just a crack, enough for light and silence to leak on to the landing. I'd normally knock, but tonight I don't. With one swift kick, I have the door wide. The room is empty.

No Adele.

And no Carl.

It is such a small room, there can be no mistake. Besides, I know the place so intimately I can tell at a glance that, if Adele has been home tonight, then it can have been only for a minute, for she has left no print of herself in the room, no trail of powder, no tangle of jewels, no crumple of bed-linen. Yet I still drop to my knees and look under the bed. Still click the lock of her thin white wardrobe. Search for her, will her to appear. Adele, be here for me. Please, Adele. My Adele.

But she is not here. I sit down, taking care that my back is to the mirror. This means I have to sit on the bed facing the cucumber poster. 'Cucumbers,' the poster screams over the picture of a large green organ, 'are better than men because they are at least six inches long, stay hard for a week and never ask, "Am I the best?" ' That's when it starts. The thick assault of my eyeballs, the penis that walked like a pole past my face. I was just twelve years old and sitting under the cool of a bridge by the river. Lizzie was with me. It was a hot day and we'd cycled for miles. Being under the bridge was stillness, tranquillity, earned repose. The water slap, slapping against the brick bank, the distant call of a duck, the proud ache of limbs and the certain knowledge of dusk and supper and bed. And then the penis, a huge pushing stump of flesh, bobbing erect at the level of my nose. A man just walking past, through the dark of the bridge and out the other side, into the sunshine.

For a moment we said nothing at all, stunned mute, holding our breath, perhaps, in case he should return, walk back the other way. Then I took courage. 'My God,' I finally spat out. 'Oh, my God.'

'What?' asked Lizzie.

'What?' Now I looked at her. She was picking at a twig, dreamily stripping bark. 'You didn't see?'

'What?'

'The man.'

'The man what?'

'Flashing' was not something that existed in my mind or my vocabulary then. So I had no words for it. Couldn't describe the penis, the size and throb of it. Its assault. Its violation. And Lizzie hadn't seen. I burst into tears on the river-bank.

For weeks, months, after that, all objects were phallic to me: a stick of rock, the handle of a broom, the cigarette in the lips of the Marlboro cowboy, the lollies on the side of the Wall's ice-cream van. If I shut my eyes the penis was still there, reddening the inside of my eyelids. I could no longer look at any part of a man but his face.

I told no one. Certainly not my mother. My father. I even

brushed it off to Lizzie, who was my best friend at that time. I talked about being unreasonably tired, headached by the sun. It wasn't long after that that Lizzie took off with Fiona Mackintosh. Or so it seemed to me then.

And so it seems to me now. Engorged before my eyes. The thick prick of the stranger under the bridge and the thick fingers of my father, five of them, ten of them, prising apart the flesh of my best friend. The images, which I can't stop now, sticking their heads in my mouth, running their lurid film past my eyes, stuffing up my ears, prodding fat against my neck, so I can't swallow, can't breathe. And the noise too, which seems (seems, seems, seems) to be coming through the thin walls of Adele's house now, that hot grunting, that squeezing and shrieking and pulsing, the cock and the cucumber and the pole the width of a bridge. All of it beating me, again and again, the warm hard slap of the penis against my thighs, my stomach, my mouth. I've got my eyes closed and my hands over my ears but I can still see and hear and feel them all, Adele and my father, Julie and her man, humping and bumping and throbbing and moaning and pushing their bursting thickness down my throat. Then I hear Julie's rising scream, 'Yes. Yes. Yes!'

And finally – finally – I scream back, 'No!'

There is silence then. And zipping and scuffling and hissing and panting. Of course it is Carl who emerges first. He is large and pale and sweaty in his black leathers. He doesn't look at me but thumps down the stairs pulling his motorcycle helmet over his head as he goes. Julie doesn't bother to dress. She stands in the door-frame in a matching set of peach satin underwear, which has gone grey in the wash.

'You filthy little wallflower,' she says, and she lights a

cigarette. I watch her suck on the tiny red-tipped penis. 'Get out of here.'

# 12

Ruth is packing. It is a swift, efficient operation requiring a minimum of thought. Travel has always been part of the Pharmakon job, now as ombudsperson and previously (when Grace was just a baby) as a troubleshooter in Communications. Now, as then, Ruth travels mostly to Headquarters in New York, though sometimes also to conferences in Toronto, or to outlying parts of her 'European' empire; to Lisbon and Cairo, to Moscow and Lausanne. It is over twenty years since she learned the value of a second wash-bag, already packed with a clean flannel and a new razor, with anti-perspirant and a tube of Lancôme Progrès, with a second Oral-B toothbrush and the correct mint-flavoured Sensodyne toothpaste. You can't get Sensodyne in all countries of the world and Ruth has sensitive teeth. She doesn't have to look in the wash-bag to check everything is there because she checks on her return, replenishes, keeps the bag at the ready. Nor does she have to think where to put the bag in her small international suitcase. Because it goes where it has always gone, at the bottom on the right-hand side.

Her flight this morning is to New York and she will be gone for a week. The international ombuds team, or ombuddies as they call themselves, are meeting to discuss

Goals for the End of the Milennium and to attend a series of workshops and seminars on Addressing Conflict. A week does not seem such a very long time now that she does not have to put the yellow stickers with 'Mama leaves' and 'Mama returns' on the calendar in the kitchen. Of course, Ruth thinks, as she briskly interleaves her navy suit with acid-free tissue paper, she was hardly abandoning Grace all those years ago, not with Alan such a full-time, committed parent. Alan with baby Grace alongside him in the workshop, the pair of them dipping their hands in clay, barely noticing whether Ruth was in or out of the country.

'Has she asked for me today?' Ruth would query long-distance. And there would be a pause and Alan would reply, 'Yes,' in that vague, maddening way of men who cannot delineate precisely the defining moments of life. But Ruth knew how things stood. In the nights after she returned Grace would wake and call for her father: 'Daddy, Daddy, Papa.' And if Alan slept stolidly on, which he did, still the child would call for him. And Ruth wouldn't go to her, though she ached to, for that only made Grace's tears fall harder: 'Go away. Go away! I want Daddy.' So she would lie and wait until, eventually (perhaps it was only ten minutes) her daughter called, in a choked, disappointed tone, 'Mama.' Then impatient Ruth would leap to enfold her, graceless in her need, her yearning all elbows. For there was a time, of course, when she never thought to hear the word 'Mama'. Grace was so long in the wanting, the making. And then, when she finally came, so very slow to speak.

Mama.

She will remember it always. Not those first babbled mamas, the streams of delighted but non-specific sounds. But the first real Mama. They hadn't lived near the sea then. She was based at Pharmakon London, before the relocation. But, of course, they came to see grandmother Bridie in Newick and took their daughter, sometimes, down to the Brighton sea. Grace had been thirteen months when they parked by Eastern Terrace, spotting a thin ribbon of sand edging the resolute rocks of Brighton's beach. Low tide. If there'd been such sand before – and there must have been – they'd never seen it. A flat, gleaming strand, beckoning in the dusk. They were supposed to be on their way home, just passing the seafront to look at the coming lights of pier and promenade. Not stopping. But they stopped. Climbed in the wrong shoes over the fisted pebbles, arrived at the sand. Ruth removed infant Grace's summer socks and stood her on the shore. The sea was on the turn, the crests of water soft and white as they breathed on to the beach. The smallest of waves lapped over Grace's feet. She screamed. She stood rigid. Her eyes molten terror. A second wave combed quietly in, but now she moved, a wild, flailing body in Ruth's long skirt, a mill of desperate arms and legs, clawing her way up to safety.

'Mama.'

For of course Ruth lifted her, pressed her baby to her breast, felt the tiny arms encircle her neck and the gulping sobs vibrate her throat. If it was the baby crying now.

'Mama. Mama.'

'Look,' laughed Alan, 'she's afraid.'

But Ruth was not looking, Ruth was feeling, the flesh of the child flush with her flesh, no division between them, the warmth and power and intimacy of motherhood, for Ruth would confound the sea to protect the child and the child knew it. Grace had spoken and made her sufficient. The infant for whom all had been given had finally returned the gift. The child validating the woman.

The memory, though sixteen years old, is so vivid and consuming that Ruth does not hear the approach of her daughter who is suddenly in the doorway, screaming, 'What are you doing?'

'Doing?' Ruth is startled and defensive. She clips shut the metal clasps of her case. 'Leaving, of course.'

'Leaving!' shrieks Grace.

'Grace . . .' Ruth stares at the contorted, panicked girl in the doorway. This almost-grown woman tilting at some invisible skirt. What is she to suppose? Ruth tries to gather herself. She has not been concentrating these last couple of days. Not on Grace anyway. She has been locked inside her head with Simon Trevor, with white breasts and purple liver spots. If there has been anything else on her mind, it has been Alan, the shadow of him. For they haven't spoken directly, not about 'the incident' anyway. They have discussed whether it is more sensible to lift paving stones and fail to replace them, or to leave smoking bins in unexpected places. But the issue of physical contact during Pharmakon phone-calls has not been raised. She has allowed Alan's clumsy fingers to dissolve into Simon Trevor's liver-spotted hands, her own breast to be covered by the polyester blouse of the first enquirer. She's been busy tidying up, putting away.

'Oh,' says the child in the doorway, some tension leaking, 'New York. You're going to New York.'

'Of course,' says Ruth. 'The ombuds conference. Where did you think I was going?'

Then Grace laughs, a high, twisting, fluted laugh.

Where has Grace been these last two days, since the Pharmakon call? Ruth assembles some tableau, a seven a.m. breakfast, a dusk glass of wine on the patio, kitchen chores, an hour of reading after supper. Grace does not figure in any of them.

'Are you all right?' she asks.

'All right?' repeats Grace. 'Of course, why shouldn't I be?'

'I'm sorry,' says Ruth, 'if I've been a little . . . absent these last few days. I've had a lot on my mind.'

'You have?'

'Yes.' Ruth smiles. 'Business, you know.'

Grace does not smile, but she lingers as if she wants more, although Ruth feels at a loss to know what this 'more' might be. Besides, there is only twenty minutes before the car comes for her. And Ruth's leaving button has already been pushed. She's in exit mode.

Grace sits down on the white satin edge of her mother's bedspread and waits. Ruth checks her handbag for tickets, passport, dollars.

'Is there an issue we should be surfacing here?'

'No.'

Ruth lifts her case to the floor.

Silence.

She sits down on the counterpane beside her daughter.

'Well, why don't I tell you what's on my mind?' Of course she cannot be specific, cannot allow her need, or her daughter's need, to interfere with the Pharmakon Promise. Nothing is more important than confidentiality. But sharing intimacies was what used to make her feel close to Grace. Having Grace come into her bedroom to sit, or even lie, on this bed and talk about Lizzie Bolton, for instance.

'Lizzie's so easy with boys,' Grace would remark casually, explaining the rather sudden cooling of their friendship.

Or: 'Fiona Mackintosh crowds Lizzie. I couldn't stand that.' Hurt and pride intermingled.

And Ruth, careful not to lecture, as Bridie might have done, on the importance of loyalty, talked instead of the ebb and flow of friendship. Mentioned the fickle nature of Linda Taylor, a schoolfriend of her own, and how Linda's professed maturity actually ended up with a pregnancy at seventeen and a job in Woolworths.

I can, Ruth thinks, speak generally. Disguise the individual case. She takes her daughter's hand in hers and feels it strange and dry. Besides, a youthful view on Simon Trevor might be useful.

'How would you react,' Ruth asks, 'if an older man made it clear he had designs on you?'

'Designs?' repeats Grace, as though she doesn't understand the word.

'Yes, if he made advances?'

'Advances?'

'If he put his hands . . .' That wild flare is back around her daughter's eyes. Ruth can hear her breathing. 'If he put his hands,' Ruth fumbles, 'on you?'

Now Grace doesn't pause. 'How old a man?'

'How old? Well, about the same age as your father.'

Grace utters a little cry, pulls away from her mother. 'As old as Dad?'

'He's not Methuselah,' says Ruth.

'A man like Dad,' repeats Grace. 'And someone my age?'

'Yes,' says Ruth. 'Say Adele, for instance.'

'Adele.' Grace stands up. 'It's disgusting.' Her body is suddenly shaking and she looks like she's going to be sick. 'It would be disgusting. Him so old and her so – young. It would be a violation. An assault. Your father is an extension of you. It would be like – rape. Like he raped me. I could never look at him the same way ever again, never trust him, never be with

81

him. She couldn't be my friend any more and he wouldn't be my father.'

'Hang on, hang on,' says Ruth, for Grace seems to be crying, 'We're not actually talking Dad here. Just any older man and a younger woman. In an office situation.'

But Grace isn't listening, she's sputtering, 'It would be – be – incestuous.'

'Grace? Grace! For God's sake . . .'

The doorbell rings.

'That's my car.'

But Grace doesn't seem to care. Her arms are folded across her chest and she's beating herself and sobbing.

# 13

Hello, Grace, your birthday was a Tuesday, 29/07/80 – you are 6223 days old.

This is the third day that I have come here. Today there is a slight breeze coming off the ocean so there's a bitter, seaweed tang to the pier's warm vinegared chips and freshly sugared doughnuts.

'Not you again,' says the earringed man in Merlin's Astroscope.

Grace, you are a Monkey. The Chinese say: this is the animal that hides in your heart. Charming and adorable, you were born in the year controlled by the Metal element. Powerfully

strong and unyielding as your Lunar sign allows, you will
have trouble letting go . . .

My mother, uncertain as to what I was to let go of, suggested
that I write a letter. Addressed to her, maybe, the week she
was away. Putting pen to paper, she said, can help put a
problem in perspective, clarify feelings. She took time with
me to say this, an arm around my shoulders, a hand on her
suitcase, the engine of the Pharmakon car running downstairs.

'Dear Mum, your husband is playing away with my best
friend. Cross out, delete, expunge. Ex-best-friend. Love
Grace. PS It might not be true.'

Beneath me the water rhythmically slap, slaps against the
pier struts below me, suck, sucks on the pebbles of the beach.

'Three arrows a pound, pierce the gold to win a prize.'

I found her on Archery that first day, in the dark slit
between the two pleasure domes. Employees of the Palace
Pier Corporation have to wear yellow T-shirts, with their
name badge-pinned on to them. Adele chooses a shirt a size
too small for her and sticks her 'Adele' on upside down.

'What can they expect for three pounds sixty an hour?'

She can expect the men to leer at the breasts beneath the
tight cotton. She can expect the supervisor to reprimand her
about the badge and then be won round again by the swing of
her hips, the flick of her wet tongue in her mouth. She could
not have expected me to be one of her punters, to take a
heavy wooden bow in my hands.

I watched them from an oblique angle. Of course I did, the
filthy little wallflower observing the stall girl and her
rapacious audience. Men lifting the bow and taking steel-
tipped arrows from her fingers. Slotting the flights into

the string and pulling back hard, to show her the flex of their upper arms, the power of their taut bronze muscles. Twanging, laughing as the arrows buried themselves in the red or blue.

'You wait,' they said. 'Next time.'

Adele collecting the arrows, running her fingers over the tips, showing her teeth: 'Next time.'

One man taking a different aim. An older man with skinny arms. Adele not looking. So old. Why should she?

Why should she?

Thock!

The arrow whistling across the ten foot gap and embedding itself in the neck of a Dalmatian.

'Blimey,' says the man. 'Those ain't spots. Those are wounds.'

She pulled the arrow out then, stuck her finger in the wound, rearranged the stuffing and refluffed the fur. Business-like but tender too, finding the nap, stroking it flat. Adele, whose tapered fingers have also stroked the nape of my neck, traced the hollow of my throat.

'I'm sorry, Your Honour, I can't think how I missed the target. I'll never forgive myself. Will she really be scarred for life?'

The Chinese are right. I am a monkey and I have a metal heart.

The second day was Western Astrology.

Grace, your Sun sign is Leo, the fiery flamboyant 5th sign of the zodiac, you hate anything underhand and say so in no uncertain terms . . .

That day Adele was on Frogs.

84

'Place your rubber frog on the catapult and give it a whack! A prize for evey one that lands in a lily-pad.'

Unlike the archery booth, the frog stall is circular. A punter can come to any one of twelve catapults. To observe without being observed meant that I had to move with care between the tumescent helter-skelter, and the dark entrance of the pleasure dome. I didn't take my eyes off her once. Perhaps I wanted her to feel watched. To experience that discomfort, that dis-ease, is there really someone there or is it just my imagination? Perhaps I thought I could bring her to admission, emission. Rub, rubbing until she reared up and betrayed herself. Yes, it was me that night in the studio with your father.

My *father*.

Perhaps the fiery Lion was just biding her time until she had the words to say what she wanted to say in no uncertain terms: '*Adele, your prince is a rubber frog. I saw him upstairs, fucking your mother.*'

Be calm. Today I plan a different consummation.

'Left-handed or right-handed?'

'Right.'

The Astroscope man takes my palm and places it on a dark screen with a luminous handprint drawn in red pinpricks of light.

'Space your fingers on the dots,' he commands.

And I do and, for one millionth of a second, the computer considers Adele's destiny. The printer buzzes and whirs.

'There you go.' He hands me a flimsy sheet of paper. The computer setting is draft, the letters dot-matrix fuzzy.

There is one space left on the white slatted bench where the old people sit doing word-search puzzles. I sit down and read:

*General Outline:*

Choosy in your choice of friends. *Potential and Talents*: Highly imaginative. *Pronounced Positive Traits*: loyalty, trustingness. *Personal Responses*: a tendency to obsessive introspection. *Pronounced Negative Traits*: Grace, you seem to have difficulty translating ideas into action.

Oh, do I.

I am not in disguise, that would be absurd. But I am wearing shades and a baseball cap turned the wrong way round. I've pulled a bit of mousy hair through the gap at the front so it looks like I have a fringe, though of course Adele knows I don't have a fringe. Otherwise my clothes are the usual dun, shorts and a T-shirt, what anyone might wear on a hot August day.

The first arcade is clear. Adele doesn't like to work this end of the pier and she has made her view known to the management. She particularly hates the 'Odds You Win, Evens you Lose' giant teddy-bear stall.

'The next bloke who draws a six and turns the ticket upside down for a nine is going to get my fist in his mouth. They all think they're the only one who's ever done it. It's pathetic.'

I move through Archery, Penalty Kicks, High Basketball and Darts in Cards. Above my head gulls scream, or perhaps it's the squeal of the ratchets on the centrifugal Ranger, or the shriek of humans being belted inside.

Hot indoor air pumps from pleasure dome two. But I'm not concerned with this slot-mouthed darkness. The only workers here are cashiers and they don't allow the casual labour on the tills. So I skirt the pulsing palace and check the Giant Spinning Tea-cups and the Dolphin Derby.

Blank again.

All that's left now are the big rides. The climax, the end of the pier. I check the Turbo Coaster, the Sizzler Twist, the Dodgems, the Space Loop, the Crazy Jungle.

No Adele. But I know she's here, I can smell her.

At the carousel I accost yellow-shirted Jorge.

'Do you know which booth Adele's working today?'

He looks out at me from Scandinavian blue eyes. 'I student,' he says. 'I Spanish. I don't speak English.'

Behind him is a magnificent red and yellow charger. The horse has flaring nostrils, a turbulent mane of wood, a flying tail. His name, painted gold at his throat, is Lysander. I touch his carved stillness, run my fingers over his monumental solemnity. Then I see her, have her. As rank and close as if she were astride Lysander, her hands around his twisted pole, squeezing his red and gold.

She's working the Roller Ghoster. Framed by Lysander's pole, I watch her pull a lever and jerk three children through double doors into blackness. Above her are eight gleaming skulls. Their grins crack an electronic threat, sing-song, idiotic: 'Yee-es, the fright of your life.' I take my hand from the horse. I'm so calm I might be a person whose heart pumped ice. In the kiosk Adele's hand hovers over what I imagine must be the skirt-lifter button.

'It's great that. I've seen it take people's tops off.'

I look for her victim. A blonde girl who can't be more than four is about to exit. She's accompanied by a burly man. He is walking, she is staggering from the cart. I'm too far away to see her expression, but her body is all clutch. Suddenly Adele jabs at the button – perhaps because the man is overweight and his T-shirt loose. But it is up the child's legs that the violent jet of air whooshes, ballooning her flimsy dress over her face, exposing her bare stomach and pink knickers. She screams. The man lifts her up and laughs, holding her so that his large hand rests on her bottom.

I get tokens then. Push my pound into a machine and wait for it to spit brass. It will be impossible for Adele not to see me. The Ghoster has a turnstile. I will have to put the tokens into her hands. But, for the time being, I have surprise on my side and I want to keep it that way.

I try to blend in. In front of me in the queue is a group of babbling Japanese, behind me foreign-exchange students, from somewhere east, Slovakia, I think. I'm not dark enough for Japanese and have no camera so I lean my mousiness towards the Slovaks. A green plastic rucksack is part of the uniform. There is one at my feet. I edge towards it. There are so many Japanese Adele is having trouble getting them through the turnstile, explaining that only four of them may ride in any one cart.

The Slovaks are getting impatient now, they begin to push. The boy to whom the rucksack belongs takes my attempts at appropriation as a cue to glare at me, swing the bag over his shoulder and shove past. A girl, who clearly wishes to have the fright of her life in the same cart as him, barges after him. Now I am part of the group.

I'm also close enough to see that Adele is tired. She's getting flustered. She has to be in two places at once, inside the kiosk to take the tokens and pull the starter lever, but also out on the track ensuring the carts are kept close and the safety rules obeyed. Her hand is held out for money but her eyes are on the last of the Japanese.

'I said only four, you fuckers,' she yells.

The Slovaks drop their tokens on the desk and push through the turnstile.

And now, at last, it is my turn. I take off my dark glasses. I take off my baseball cap. I shake my mousy head. And then I wait. I have waited a long time and I can wait some more. It will begin so very softly. I see it all already. Just me and her and a single word.

Why?

'Jesus.' The fifth Japanese man has once again got out of the second cart and climbed in front with his friends. With no regard for me or the mounting queue, Adele slams out of the kiosk and angrily manhandles him back into the second cart where the Slovaks now sit. This infuriates the man but not as much as it appears to enrage the girl behind me who, I realise too late, is clearly also maddened by my apparent patience. All of a sudden her elbows are at my back, the hard edge of her rucksack in the hollow of my knees. I buckle, lose balance, the strap of the rucksack caught round my legs. And as I fall she falls too, the two of us leashed. Together we crash on to the turnstile, which bursts open under our combined weight flinging us both towards the second cart. The girl pulls herself up, dragging me with her as she attempts to scramble into the front seat with the obviously popular Slovak boy. This leaves me, hanging, just outside the back with the screaming Japanese.

'Right,' says Adele. 'Right.' All at once she's back in the kiosk, both hands on the lever. 'That's it.'

The double doors swing open and, with a crack of static, the carts take off as if possessed. I try to get in, the Japanese tries to get out, the Slovaks roar as Dracula rears out of the darkness. I'm afraid for my left hand, which seems too near the track. Five polystyrene tombstones pop open and five disembodied heads flash and grin. But what's frightening me is the speed, for all of a sudden we are descending and the wheels are turning pell-mell. With my uppermost hand I grab for anything and locate the shirt of the second Slovak girl who screams, though she might be screaming because of the patient who rises from the operating table streaming blood. We twist and bang into something solid. Doors – which open to send the cart shuddering through. Finally the standing Japanese falls, but I have my left hand inside at last. It's under his buttocks.

'You have crossed the divide,' intones a ghoul. 'You are now on the other side.'

There's a jerk and the Japanese and I disengage. He is hysterical. Again we twist back on ourselves and then begin to climb, but the speed we have picked up on the downward slope drives us on. This time there are cracks of white around the double doors. Bang! We explode into daylight, swoop perilously on the outside of the Ghoster for a moment and then bang back into darkness. The Japanese is weeping. 'Shud up,' yells the Slovak boy, delightedly. 'Shud up!'

A phantom in need of a new coat of luminous paint opens a purple mouth. His lips close on a badly synced demonic laugh. The cart has a kind of rhythm now and I know what the black block ahead signifies. A last bang and we are out, gliding towards Adele's kiosk.

She isn't there.

The kiosk door swings. It is shift-change time. Some new T-shirt has arrived. The others get out of the cart. I watch the door swing, back and forth, back and forth. Like a pendulum it loses momentum and I wait and wait, wanting it to close. But it doesn't close. It remains ajar. Then, very slowly, I step out of the cart. The weeping Japanese is back with his friends, they are all shouting now. There is going to be a scene. But all that seems a long way away from me. Because of the doors. Swinging open and swinging shut. Remaining ajar.

Not Carl at all, of course. But Adele. Coming home and finding Carl's bike parked up by her house. Entering the house with pleasure and anticipation. Finding no one downstairs but hearing movement upstairs. Talking, perhaps. Ascending the stairs. Seeing the door of her mother's room shut. Her own door open. Open wide. No Carl.

No Carl.

The sudden realisation sick in her throat. Her hand on her mother's door-handle, frantic to know. A pause. Frantic not to know. Unable to turn the knob, but turning anyway, her heart banging in her chest. And there they are, a tangle of sweating flesh, pumping, groaning, Carl on top. And she screams then, but no noise at all comes out of her throat. And she would run forward, thrust her gouging nails in the white mound of his moving buttocks. But something stops her. Something keeps her fixed to the door-post. It is a horror worse than the throbbing white slug of Carl. It is what lies beneath. What, at the moment, is hidden. It's Julie. Adele's mother.

And they haven't seen her. They haven't heard her. So intense, so noisy is their passion. So she might not have been there, might never have come upon them, working late as she had at the pier, going on to club as she had told them she would. So all she has to do for it not to have happened is close the door. Adele is a survivor. She's had to be. She knows when it's time to advance and time to retreat. She closes the door.

But then what is she to do? Sit downstairs and help herself to a cup of cocoa? No. Despite her self-possession,

Adele burns with the betrayal. She has to get out. She needs time to think, to plan. She's already down the stairs, across the living-room. It's important now that they don't know she knows. The secret is power. So she doesn't close the front door, in case they should hear. No, she goes softly, leaving the door ajar. A door swinging. Swinging in the wind.

There is only one place of safety in Adele's life. A refuge to which she has her own key. She climbs the hill from the estate. Lets herself into the dark house, ascends the dark stairs. She's done it so many times before, she knows exactly where the boards creak and the treads narrow. It is only a moment now before she reaches the sanctuary of her friend's room. She opens the door.

'Grace, Grace.' Her whisper is hot. She is urgent now. Her fury cannot be lidded much longer.

There is no reply. Adele slides beneath the bedcovers. The eiderdown slips to the floor. The bed is empty. It is cold.

'Grace!' Adele cries.

But Grace is out, she's down at the river.

Where is Adele to go now? She thought she had a victory, but this is beginning to smell like defeat. The studio. Perhaps. Maybe.

Adele in the garden now, a thin shadow moving silently across the grass. Hope fashioning a figure in the night window. Yes – yes! Definitely a figure. Her friend just a breath away, after all. Stretching herself as she comes through the studio door, out of the dark,

Alan.

Not Grace but Alan. Rage and disappointment spiking tears at last.

'Hey,' says Alan, 'what's up?'

A strong masculine chest. Arms for crushing, forgetting. Adele, who has no father of her own, reaching out. Adele taking comfort from a man the only way she knows how.

I let the knife fall then. It's only a slim thing, my father's silver penknife, the one he keeps in his pocket. It slips from my hand to the deck of the pier. I watch it disappear through the slats and drop like a stone to the sea. It doesn't even make a splash.

# 14

Alan sits in the drawing-room and sweats. The french windows are open. It is late enough to be cool, but it is not cool. Sunlight burns in the air. Perhaps, Alan thinks, he should bath. Normally he showers but these last few days he has been bathing, running the water deep and hot in the morning, the afternoon, the evening. The middle of the night. At night he keeps the curtains open and the lights off, as if inviting in the darkness. But there have been stars. There has been an almost full moon. The darkness is white.

His hands are not white, although he has been especially scrupulous with them. He has brushed beneath each nail in turn, scraping out the last specks of clay with a metal nail-file. For his palms he has used a scourer, a metallic one that he thinks Ruth uses for the bath. He wants his life-line, his love-line to be clean. But they don't seem to come clean.

Nothing comes clean. He is stained terracotta. And where there is softer skin, at the base of his thumb, his mount of Venus, or around his wrists, he has made himself red raw with rubbing.

He has also soaped his penis. Lifted it from where it lies sleeping on his groin, fingertipped its head with bubbles, let the water slosh and close about it. Dirty water, made grey with soap, washing over the penis so it can barely be seen.

His studio clothes he has put in the washing-machine. At ninety degrees. The old shirt with the frayed cuffs and the yielding softness, the trousers which so belonged to his body they might have been a second skin. He knew they might shrink, or tear, which they did. The clothes he is wearing tonight he found stiff and folded in the wardrobe on the landing. So now, uncomfortable and unfamiliar, he sits in his chair in the drawing-room. He smells of mothballs and airless spaces, of oatmeal soap and Dettol (he added a small capful under a running tap and watched the water whiten), of Radox and Lemon Fresh and blood. He also smells of whisky. Maybe it is the whisky and not the sun that is making him sweat. He sniffs his arm. He thinks he is oozing whisky, leaking it. He has never liked whisky and yet the bottle looks almost empty.

His wife is in New York. 'Look after Grace,' is what she said as she kissed him goodbye. Yes, kissed. A small peck on the cheek (he doesn't think he's washed this spot) but a kiss nevertheless. His wife kissed him and asked him to look after the baby, just as she used to all those years ago. But Grace doesn't need looking after now. Grace is seventeen. Grace looks after herself. Takes food from the fridge and eats in her own room. Or that's what she must have been doing these last few days. For he hasn't seen her, he doesn't think. But then perhaps he hasn't sought her out, perhaps he's pressed his back against a door when he's heard her footfalls on the stairs. But, if she really needs him, he will be there. She knows that. He's always been there for his daughter. He's a good father. Everyone says so.

He should get up, go to the kitchen and crack ice. The hard, chill blocks would be good in his fingers, good in his whisky, good against his forehead, a cold melt down his back. But he's disinclined to get up. If he moves it should be to go to the studio. There is much work to be done. He peeked through the window this morning, saw beyond the sofa to where Lee was working. Lee and Jerry both making garden pots. His place at the workbench was taken by eggs. Four of seven survived the burning, two cracked in clean halves and one shattered in a thousand pieces. He put his hands deep in the still warm ash to feel for the shards. The hard grains of clay that had dried too fast and burst asunder, forgetting that they belonged together, had been kneaded so, dug from the same pit. Of course, he couldn't gather them, not all of them, grit in the feathery ash, so after a time he withdrew his hands, smudged and blackened, and wiped them on his trousers. The soft trousers that are themselves just threads now, torn from each other.

Of the four intact eggs, three are the colour of blood and one a frail translucent white. He does not remember choosing white, mixing the pale glaze. But there the egg is, white and curved, the perfect fit for the palm of a hand. But he does not hold it in his hand, does not take the beeswax cloth the egg cries for, doesn't buff or polish, round and round, sealing the pores and deepening the gloss. For if he looks at this egg, it no longer seems like the swell of an abdomen, but the slim, white cupping of a buttock. So he keeps his hands away, clasps the cut of a whisky glass instead. Drains that.

It is the shadow he sees first. A slight darkening on the glass that leads to the garden. It is impossible, he thinks afterwards, for someone in a room to obscure the sun outside, to cast an interior shadow. But this is what he sees, or maybe he feels, as he turns to face the intruder and the shiver of the coat runs through him. It is a dark grey winter coat surmounted by a dark head and a darker intent. Of course he has feared this, this bleak expectant return. But not here, not so close, not walking so boldly into his drawing-room as if it had been lodging just outside the door, not an intruder at all, but someone he has opened the door to, welcomed in.

His throat is whisky-dry, he can barely crack his voice through it.

'No. Not again. Not this time.'

'Oh, yes,' says a smooth voice, which is not Adele's. 'Oh, yes. Again and again and again.'

I let the coat slip then, feel the rough wool of the collar chafe against my naked shoulders and the satin lining slide the length of my back and fall cool from my bare buttocks on to the floor. In my shining puddle of grey I am a Venus rising. Not as tall as Adele or as slim but, today, curved and luminous-skinned, my nipples as mottled pink as early summer strawberries. My breasts bob as I stand otherwise still before my father.

'Grace,' he says, 'for God's sake.'

It's warm but I feel the ripple of gooseflesh. I take a slow hand and spread my fingers at my throat, then I trace a sinuous line over breast and stomach to reach between my legs and touch behind. I had not meant to sway, but there is a rhythm to my hips as my hand strokes fore and aft.

'Stop it!' His hand goes up to his face, shields his eyes as if he didn't want to see, as if he could block it all out.

I turn and bend a little, my hand reaching further now, up and over my buttocks. Perhaps he finds me ugly. But I'm not ugly, not today. Today I find myself beautiful, today I am loving myself for him.

'Grace,' he says. 'I'm your father!'

I stop stroking then and turn towards him.

'Oh, no,' I say, surprised by how quiet and cold my voice sounds. 'No, you're not my father. Not now. Not ever.' Then I put my face very close to his, my erect nipples on his musty shirt. 'So it's OK, Alan. You can touch me. It's all OK.'

He's leaning so far back in his chair I think it will swallow him.

'You don't understand,' he says.

'Oh, I understand. I have eyes, Alan.' I'm sitting astride him now. It's as Adele says. It all comes naturally once you start.

'Get off,' he pleads. 'Grace, please get up.'

I begin to rock to and fro, feel the prick of excitement between my legs just as Adele always said I would, just as she must have done when she pushed against this man, when he pulled her close.

'Grace . . .' He looks so small now, like a frightened child. I lean forward, stroke his cheek, move towards him as if I would kiss him on the mouth. He can no longer shrink from me. He has nowhere left to go, so low is he already. Our noses touch, our eyes are just an eyelash apart.

'Grace. Grace!' He finds something then, a terror, a horror, and he pushes the flats of his hands against my breastbone. I feel his gritty palms, his malty breath as he forces me violently from him. And I stagger, but not from the blow. Not from the blow.

His eyes are blue.

They are blue. Blue. Blue as my mother's eyes. Blackbird egg blue.

A noise I don't recognise comes from my throat, a kind of crushed sound, a stillborn sob.

'Oh God,' I whisper, and my heart suddenly seems a piece of tissue paper I'm about to tear in two. 'Oh God, oh God.'

I grab for my coat, which I fumble and pull and belt about me. For this is it. The thing that I have always known and not known, the thing that has been hidden all my life but from which I also have been hiding. This blue thing that I can no longer avoid, for it's staring straight out at me from the centre of Alan's eyes.

He begins to stand, to move towards me. I feel the tower of him, see the lift of his hand. But he's not a man to hit, he just wants silence, he wants me not to say it. But I'm already saying it, it's spilling out of me.

'It's you, it's you, isn't it? You're really not my father. You can't be.' So simple. Just fourth-form biology: two blue-eyed people can't make a brown. And my eyes are such a deep, such an obvious brown.

'Grace,' he says, 'Grace . . .'

I'm backing away. But he's following me. He's after me.

'Grace . . . I am your father. God forgive me.'

Then it's me who doesn't want him to go on, who stands and wills him not to open his mouth a second, a final time. But this is the time, the moment for him to say it and for me to hear it. Even though, of course, I've been aware of it every hour of every day since I turned in the womb.

'It's your mother,' he says, 'who is not your mother.'

# NIGHTFALL

# 15

I take the train to Essex. My destination is marked on my ticket. But I try not to know the name of the place towards which all my life is now headed. I suppose I think about it the same way I thought about the woman who followed us in the red car. I cannot quite allow it, cannot let this place, this woman, assume too much importance. Separately they were dangerous enough. Now they are co-joined. If I don't tread on the cracks it may never happen. If I pretend the station has no name, just an identifier, say the number seven, then it may never happen. But I'm too old to play games now. The station does have a name. And so does the woman.

I've bought a map, of course. Or, rather, a town plan, though it is clear to me immediately that this place is not a town but a village spread spaciously around a tight market centre. The station is on an incline, and the land undulates away, clusters of houses between August golden fields, a stream, a hill, a wide blue sky. I think the walk to Greenbury Lane may be forty-five minutes but, of course, being afraid to arrive, I have no reason to hurry.

I set off down the main street, slow as you like, observing the timbered shop-fronts, the Afternoon Tea House, the old-fashioned sweet shop with what I imagine is a jangly bell, where I might have come, aged five, with my sixpence to buy

Black Jacks and sherbet flying saucers. Only I didn't come here. I peer in and the white-haired lady behind the counter looks back suspiciously. If I belonged here, she would wave, she would call out my name. She would smile, having known me all my life. But she doesn't know me. How, in any case, can you know someone who's just a shadow with skin round?

The remainder of the high street is chains and multiples, Woolworths, Waitrose and Top Shop all crammed into buildings clearly designed for other purposes. It looks like a layer cake, bottom layer modern glass, top layer fourteenth-century beams, with the jam in the middle a mish-mash of lurid logos and planning-law restrictions.

I'm glad to turn off into Woolcombe Road. The town thins out rapidly here and it's only a hundred yards or so before I'm passing a low-lying and rather shabby building marked 'Scout and Guide Hut'. I always wanted to be a Brownie. Ruth said there was 'no local pack' where we lived in London. The word 'pack' still makes me catch my breath, still holds for me a fervent, a reverberant longing. Dressed in brown and yellow I would be as the others. Like them, indivisible from them. I would belong.

But Ruth said there was no pack. Ruth, my mother.

Beyond the Scout hut is a police station. Or, rather, a small, brown gravelled home with a neat blue sign outside that says 'Police'. Is it only me who cannot tell by looking what is solid and what is façade? Perhaps behind these ordinary walls there really is a police station, with real officers and files and computers and criminals in cells with locks and keys. Or perhaps it is just a home, or used to be just a home before national cost-cutting meant Bert the Bobby had to transform his front parlour into an ops room and stick a police sign on a post outside. Perhaps the whole thing is no more than a joke, the sign raided one student rag week. I could knock on the door, enjoy the humour.

'Good afternoon, Officer, I've just been burgled.'

'Right, Miss. Come in, sit yerself down, 'ave a cup of tea. What's been taken?'

'It's a bit difficult to say, because I think the theft's been going on all my life but I've only just noticed.'

'Oh, I see.' Scratching head and writing in spiral-bound notebook. 'Take yer time. No hurry.'

'It could be my identity. Or my soul, I suppose. Some part of it. My childhood, perhaps. Trust, certainly. You see, they all lied to me.'

''Appens all the time. How long did you say it's been going on?'

'Seventeen years.'

'Ah, well, that's that, then.' Shuts notebook. 'There's the six-year rule. Six years to lodge a complaint. After that – well. You've missed it, luv. Can I see you out?'

Beyond the police station are four or five boxy sixties houses, with large unkempt gardens. It's the weekend and it's hot so there are children playing outside, dogs barking and the smell of sausage fat sizzling on barbecue coal. In one house three generations are gathered, a youngish couple, their two children, the toddler sitting on her grandfather's knee. A family. Joined together by blood. Laughing, chatting. No one missing. No shadow on the lawn.

I always wanted a sister. More than I wanted to be in the Brownies. Because if I had had a sister, I wouldn't have needed to be in the Brownies.

'You're fine as you are,' said Ruth.

'No, I'm not, I want a sister.'

'You might get a brother.'

'Well, all right, then, a brother.'

'How would you like a dog?'

When we moved from London, Dad got his studio and I got a dog. A bumptious yellow Labrador puppy called Goldie after the one on *Blue Peter*. Six weeks later she was dead. A floppy piece of fur under the front wheels of someone else's car. I buried her in the earth near the studio, in the place where my father later built a patio.

'I should have got a sister,' I said. 'They don't die.'

'Oh, don't they?' said Ruth. My mother.

When I was wiser and got to be about ten, I asked Grandma Bridie why she never got a sister for Ruth.

'I did,' Grandma exclaimed, and then she checked herself, chop, chop, chopping at the onions. 'Only she died.'

No pictures of the dead child in Grandma Bridie's house. No little shrine. No photograph of Ruth and her once-alive sister. That should have tipped me off. But I was a child and they were adults. What did I know of 9 Greenbury Lane?

Greenbury Lane. I have arrived. It is a rutted place, a rough track up a hill, the clay mustard-coloured and dusty. I look ahead, but there is nothing to be seen because the track curves. I begin to climb, to follow the dried-up tyre marks to the left of the central camber. The mud is in hard ridges and sudden troughs and there are huge embedded flints. I should be looking at my feet but I'm looking at the numbers, an iron-wrought one, a gateposted three, an overgrown (cow-parsley and nettles) five. At seven I stop. I still can't see ahead. There is yet another curve, another bend. Like a horizon that looks like the edge of the world but isn't. Yet this is my horizon, my edge of the world. My flat plate of a place where the last step is over the precipice.

But I step on. Of course I do. I make myself concentrate on the road. What it would be like in winter, how the troughs would fill with ice. How my sisters – oh, yes, I have sisters. Two of them. Two sisters. Two brothers. A whole pack of siblings – would put on woolly hats and skid to school, laughing as they fell, picking up snow, balling it to throw at the boys, while my mother shouted (yes, my mother), 'Be careful of the flints. Mind the flints.'

Then, all of a sudden, I am at the gate and the gate is open. The first gate in Greenbury Lane to be so open, so inviting. Come in, Grace, you are expected. We have thought about you a great deal these last seventeen years during which we haven't contacted you once. It was for your own good, we were only thinking of your happiness.

On closer inspection I see that the gate is open because it's wedged that way. The top hinge is pulled from the post and the gate has fallen under its own weight into the mud where it is now stuck fast. Anyone can enter. All comers welcome. No one can be kept out, shut out. Just a matter of calling across the lawn, 'Hi, it's me.'

The only trouble is there's a girl already on the lawn, dark-haired and lying in a deck-chair. She's about fifteen, her body one long relaxation. Leisurely she turns the page of her book. She has the rhythm of home, of belonging. I see her but she doesn't see me, outside the gate, hiding in the nettles. Her name, for what it's worth, is Sadie.

Laura I don't see for another moment or two, because she's background, standing at the far reaches of the garden where the chicken run and the orchard are, though orchard is a rather grand word for this higgledy-piggledy abundance of fruits. There's a crooked line of greengage trees, which hum with wasps, there are currant bushes, red and black, gooseberries overgrown with grass, tall raspberry canes and espalier pear trees loosely tacked to a wall. But Laura stands by none of these. She and her basket are beneath a huge Victoria plum tree. Her back is to me so I see just her mouse-blonde hair, her floral print dress and the strings of her apron. She is reaching, lifting a bare, brown-fleshed arm upwards towards the laden branches. The fruits are plump, yellow and blushed rose, deep pink and speckled red. She picks them one or two together, giving each a tiny tug and then letting it fall ripely into her hands, transferring fruits from hand to apron, apron to basket. She will make pies, I think, or jam. For there are too many fruits here for a family to eat, even a family of six.

Bridie said I should not come. She begged me not to come. Not without warning, without conversation, without preparations. Without Ruth. She wept, my grandma did, as I took the address from her. And now I see what she saw. A snake about to walk into the garden of Eden. A venomous, unwanted thing in a place of natural harmony. Yet here is Laura.

Laura, my mother.

She does not turn. She picks, she harvests, she gathers in her crop while Sadie reads and flicks flies on the lawn. Of course, it is not really an idyll, it is only my place in the nettles that makes me think so. The house is quite poor, just a bungalow of peeling paint, unkempt, sad at the corners. The garden is unkempt too, overgrown, a little wild. And, yes, the jealousy floods for the wildness too, for the apparent simpleness of it, for the part of this garden which is like my father's clay, something to put one's hands deep in.

And still she does not turn. Laura, my mother. And I know there will never be a right time, so why not now?

I come out of the nettles, I step through the gate. They do not see me, either of them. They do not hear me. Where the gravel is not weedy my shoes crunch loudly but their absorption is complete. I am not a snake in their world. In their world I am not even visible. I am almost at Sadie's outstretched feet before she lowers her book and looks at me.

'Yes?' she enquires, as if I have bored her already.

I say nothing for I just want to look, to see and study her face, the darkness of it, her black hair, her small defined chin, her beautiful angular cheekbones, her shadow-brown eyes. And then, as I look, she looks too and her expression changes.

'Oh, Jesus.' She shuts the book. 'Mum,' she shouts. 'Mum!' She stands up. 'Looks like the river has returned to the sea, after all.'

And it's not the flatness of her irony that turns my stomach to water, but that one word, so casually shouted across the garden: Mum.

Mum turns then. She squints across the lawn at us, her daughters. The sun is in her eyes but so are we. She sees us. Her head swings, one to other, other to one.

'Grace?' she calls. 'Grace!' Between the two words is an intake of breath I can hear all the way across the garden. High, fluttery, panicked. She drops everything as she begins to run. Plums fall from her hands, her apron. She is a woman raining plums.

I watch her coming down seventeen years. She runs like me. Leaning slightly to the right, ungainly, determined. She's running so hard I think we should get out of her way in case she can't stop. But she does stop, stands face to face with me, her eyes the level of my eyes, for we are precisely the same height.

Her eyes are brown. They are my eyes. Not the uniform brown of Sadie's but the soft, hazel brown of mine. It is like looking at myself in a mirror, only she is older and she is crying.

'Grace. Grace.' Her arms come out towards me. She cannot stop herself. But I don't move, either to accept or refuse the embrace. I just stand there like a block of stone. Then she falls, she collapses, her face at my feet. 'Oh, Grace, oh, my darling, my darling, my baby, my girl.'

And still I say nothing so it is Sadie who has to speak. 'Oh, for Christ's sake,' she says.

# 16

They have locked me in here with a book. Well, it's not really a book, rather a pink folder with thirty sheets of foolscap inside, each page densely written in black ink. The hand is gracious, wide and sloping, but there is very little space between the words. I feel like one of those spaces, hemmed in and surrounded. Of course, they haven't really locked the door, I could just walk out. But I won't. For outside, where Laura and Sadie are, there are expectations. I am required to react but, as yet, I am without reactions. I am moving through time and space like a figure in a dream, observing myself but that is all.

They want me to read this text and I will. But not just yet. It is called 'Testament'. Perhaps I have shut the sluice gates because I'm afraid that if I open them just a crack all of me will simply pour away. It was Sadie's idea that I come to this room alone and I'm grateful to her. The rest of the family, my brothers Michael and Toby, my second sister Manda, they are not at home. Of course not. They are twenty-six, twenty-four, twenty-two, so Bridie advised me. Why should they be at home? 'If you'll only warn them you are coming,' Bridie pleaded. But I am glad that they didn't know, didn't all gather here to greet me. Inspect me. It is enough to see the blood between Laura and Sadie. More than enough.

A second mother. Two brothers. Two sisters. Sisters. My family. My pack. You could drive yourself mad in a room by yourself thinking. Thinking. I have thought so much and so often over the years, but I have not thought this. All I could imagine has been less than this. Greyer. I want to stop thinking. My head is billiard balls in collision.

I will concentrate on the room. It is square and dark, despite the brightness outside. There are two windows, one small and the other tiny. Someone has pulled the curtains across the small window but the tiny window is high and bare. From it issues the one seemingly solid thing in the room, a plank of yellow light. At the bottom end of the plank is me, at once held down and also connected up to the sky above. Of course it's not a cell. That's just thinking (thinking). Besides, there is a clock, a huge one screwed to the wall. Tick tock, tick tock, tick tock. It's a quarter to four in the afternoon. I could open the curtains, open the window and jump out. There are no bars and it's a ground-floor room. I could run away.

The testament is addressed 'To Grace' and dated the winter I was four and a half. It begins 'My darling'.


My darling, I have just come from the hospital and I am so

angry I can barely breathe. She left you in the snow. Just opened the door and pushed you out. Abandoned you. Returned to her warm bed. Slept well while you were gone. An hour? Two hours? The ice melting through your thin jumper. An inadequate coat for a pillow, your shoes wet through.

Of course Bridie didn't say why when she rang, didn't say how. 'Hypothermia,' she said, 'pneumonia.' And, of course, I didn't question, glad enough to be called, to know where you were. To be, for once, allowed. Just got on a train, drumming with impatience, unable to bear any station not yours, delayed, of course, thinking, thinking, fearing it was all just another phantasm of my brain, that I would arrive, as I arrive every night in my dreams, and you not be there.

But you were there. A white face, a piteous dry cough, a drip straight into your tiny veins. But you were there. There. I could reach out my hand. I could touch you. You were warm. I wanted to rip you out of that place, hold you for ever against my breast. As they wouldn't let me hold you that first ever time. 'She's cold,' the midwife said to Ruth. 'Wrap her in a blanket.' When you should have been next to me, flesh to flesh, as God intended. Oh, my darling, what have I done?

You have grown so much. Even limp, even barely conscious, the heart shines out of you. You are so beautiful. Still with that halo of brown-blonde hair, that fragile, perfect skin. And your eyes. How much I wanted to look into your eyes. But your eyes were shut. I sang to you. I would have spoken but I didn't know what to say. Didn't know where to begin. And what would you have thought, if you had woken, to find a stranger talking? I sang you the songs I sang Michael, sang Toby, sang Manda, sang you in the womb. That you might hear from far back, that your blood might beat with the rhythm of my blood, that you might take life again from my life. You stirred but you did not wake. Then they came, my mother and the one who calls herself your mother. They shouted. I begged them not to shout near my baby, for I feared they would drive you further out, deeper in. I left you then, so that they would leave you. Didn't cry loud enough for you to hear. But whispered. Did you hear me, my darling? I think you did. For it is in a river's heart to flow to the sea.

Sometimes I think nothing has been real since the day you were born. That it all started then. Sometimes I think it began the day I conceived, when I lay in that upstairs room with the dogs barking and the fireworks exploding and my brain repeating, 'She has raped me, my sister has raped me.' But now I think it began with Mungo and Bridie, that the seed of it was there and that Ruth and I together watered it, together made it germinate.

I loved Ruth so much I wanted to break with loving her. They say the children of lovers are orphans. Ruth and I were not just orphaned once but many times. As many times as our father came and went. For we were our mother's darlings until he came and then we were nothing. Ruth, who was always Bridie's favourite, suffered, I think, the greatest continual loss. Of course I didn't see that then, only saw the crushed look of longing on her face, recognised the corners of her exclusion, which was my exclusion too. And while I tried to be so nice, so good, so perfect, I would be readmitted to the inner sanctum, Ruth just stamped outside the bolted door. Because she stamped, I didn't have to stamp. Couldn't stamp, put my younger arm about her shoulder.

Why couldn't I stamp? I could stamp now. I could scream and rage. I could also put my strong hands round Ruth's neck and wring life from her as I'd wring life from a chicken. To let you fall, slip into the snow, sleep there. A real mother couldn't do so. The bones of a real mother cry with her child. Even Bridie, who knew nothing, understood that. I remember how she pulled me back from the snow the winter Mungo left. When he packed his bags that final time and walked out never to return.

'I'll follow him,' I cried, my hat and scarf and wellingtons on.

'You won't,' Bridie said, behind me in the clean fall of snow. 'You can't. He's not the sort to leave footprints.'

For weeks I went every night to the back door, slid the bolt on winter and blew my goodnight kisses into the dark. I imagined them floating warmly on the chill night air, finding my dada as the wind would find him wherever he walked in the world. For a couple of months Bridie humoured me, then she locked the door and hung the silver key up high. I watched its steely swing. After that I had to blow my kisses through the keyhole. Ruth stood and watched.

'They'll be too thin, now,' she said, 'they'll never reach him.'

I imagined the kisses stripped by the metal keyhole, flayed into thin lines, the divided strands too light to hold their direction in the air. Wisps of hope drifting, drifting. Coming close to my father but never close enough, passing him by. I stopped my vigil then. Ruth was my older sister. She understood things.

I took to my bed with the rabbit skin Dada had given me. A white pelt flecked with black, an endlessly stroked supple thing, smelling of leather. I wound it round my fist and lay to sleep on my hand. In the bunk bed above me, Ruth sobbed. She said she was afraid of the dark. I was nine then, clever with a needle. I took my pocket torch and sewed it inside a face of felt. I cut a hundred lengths of yellow wool for hair, attached the strands one by one. This was my happy face, I told her. If she was frightened she had only to push the back of my head and my nose would light up. Every night she pushed my head. Above me in the dark were cracks of yellow. Eventually the battery ran out. She flung the face from the top bunk.

'You're stupid,' she yelled, 'you stitched it all up. It won't open.'

I unpicked the stitches, replaced the battery and sewed on a popper at the join in the neck. But it didn't work again. The bulb was broken.

Sometimes I lay awake at night, waiting for Bridie to come and make it all better. Sometimes I shouted for her. Sometimes Ruth did. But she never came.

'Once my children are in bed,' I heard her say once, 'that's the way I like them to stay.'

But it wasn't that, I don't think. She didn't come because she wasn't there. Not in any real sense of the word. Physically she was there, apparently reading, working, drinking, but she wasn't there if you spoke to her. Her eyes were down long, long corridors. You could never quite get there, attract her attention. It had been like that, I realised later, even when Dada had been home, in the two years after the enquiry when there was 'trouble at the hospital'.

'You leave Alice Watling out of this!' she'd scream at him.

'No,' he'd yell back. 'You leave her out of this.'

I knew nothing about Alice Watling except she was dead. Sometimes I wished it was me who had died, because all our troubles seemed to stem from this one death. I was the same age as Alice Watling. The connection seemed so obvious. She had died but it should have been me. None of them would have minded if it had been me. So part of me flattened myself against walls so as not to take up Alice's space. Part of me tried to fill the space that my mother's absence had created. Only that space was too big. It left me rattling and cold.

I'm not sure if any of this is relevant. I don't know why I go over and over it again. I think I'm still trying to understand why I said yes that day. 'Yes, of course I'll carry a child for you.' Just like that, over the phone, the first time Ruth asked. Didn't ask for twenty-four hours to consider it. Didn't ask for five minutes. Didn't say I'd just discuss it with Thomas first. Just said yes. 'Yes, Ruth, I'll give you a baby,' as though I could sew it up like a nightlight.

It took Ruth three years to arrive at this point. One year trying to conceive, two years having tests. Eventually they decided she had pelvic inflammatory disease as a result of using a certain sort of coil. Her tubes were an impassable block of adhesions, and her ovaries, for no obviously discernible reason, were also malfunctioning. Her chance of having her own baby, the consultants told her, was less than one per cent. She was thirty-three years old.

What did I feel about her infertility? Part of me, I'm ashamed to say, felt she deserved it. Or rather it deserved her. You see, she'd never really wanted children, not actively, passionately, like I had. She was horrified when I had Michael, aged twenty-three.

'What about your career?' she said, in a tone that made her sound just like Bridie. Because that was what was important to Bridie too. What we did with our minds. Our bodies were just cases, things to be dragged along after us, a result of poor design, an inconvenience. But when I first saw Thomas, I knew I wanted his babies. I knew nothing else mattered. I didn't expect praise from the family. But I didn't care. If Bridie had taught us anything it was that we should go out and get what we wanted. This was what I wanted. Just two years after Michael, Toby came, two years after that Manda. We were poor, but I always knew we would be. Thomas chose osteopathy and I chose him. It was never going to be a path to riches and that was fine by me. Nor did I want to work myself when the children were young. Not even part-time. That was the bargain I made with myself. I was going to give my children a childhood of presence. That was to be my gift, the thing I'd learned, never to shut the door on the children, never to retreat down those long corridors. Not to be Bridie.

Of course she resented it, implicitly, explicitly. Why wouldn't she? I was a living criticism of her mothering. She revenged herself by phoning to inform me which continent Ruth had just left for, how much Ruth's last raise had been, what holidays they could afford, how Ruth was justifying all that education which I, by implication, had thrown away. Wasted. I didn't say I had learned different things. I don't think I could have said it. I don't think Bridie could have heard it.

And then there was Ruth herself. Questioning three children, thinking of overpopulation, of the constraints on the planet.

'Another one?' she said. 'Three? Oh, my goodness. Laura!'

So when she began to want, when she began to need, when she saw that all her brains and all her money and all her ambition couldn't bring her a baby, then, yes, I felt some kind of justification. At last, I thought, she is discovering what really matters. And, yes, I felt unkind, but I also felt gladdened, for when she had her child (and I never doubted that she would, somehow, get herself a child) then we would be brought back together again. Then we would be able to share again, swap secrets and knowings, feel each other's blood beating again as we did before in the bunk-bedded dark. She would, at last, be returned to me. My sister.

Is that why I said yes?

Or was it finally Bridie? The shadow of her over me. Thinking now, at last, Bridie will value me. That finally Bridie will have to stick the largest star on my chart.

I don't know. All I know is that Ruth rang, one glittering September day. I was doing some baking, dropping scones on a griddle, she was sitting in her garden with the mobile phone. There was an article in one of the Sunday newspapers about two American sisters, how the younger one had carried a child for the elder one.

'Would you do it for me? she asked.

'Yes,' I said. 'Of course.'

That was it. The beginning and the end of the conversation. That night I informed Thomas. He was furious. Who was to be the father?

'Alan, of course.'

Thomas's mother was also furious.

'That's my grandchild you're planning on giving away.'

I brushed them all aside. That was the Bridie in me, I suppose. Stubborn, determined, knowing best. I thought Thomas and his mother old-fashioned. And why not? They hadn't been brought up in a feminist household like mine. They hadn't had the first woman anaesthetist for a mother. They hadn't had a father who had run away and left the women to it. They didn't know how I felt about my sister, how we had had to be as close as twins. How, though younger, I had stretched out my arm to her, because of the lack of older, stronger arms. And, yes, God forgive me, I wanted Ruth to have a baby. I wanted her to know what I knew.

118

Eventually, because he is a good man, Thomas agreed. We had finished our family. Three was all we wanted and all we could afford. We didn't think of our own children, the impact on them. They were too young, we thought. We were the adults, we knew what we were doing. It was a sacrifice but it was going to be worth it. As if on cue Bridie rang. 'You've made me very proud,' she said.

There was just one thing Thomas insisted on. He wouldn't, he said, he couldn't, be in the house when conception took place. As it happened, my next fertile period was due at the beginning of November, around Guy Fawkes' night. We loaded the kids into the battered estate and drove to London. At home fireworks night was special. Thomas always bought a box of small, cheap fireworks, but each child was allowed to choose their 'own'. Michael would have rockets, Toby fizzers and fountains, for Manda (who was only two then) we selected Roman candles and catherine wheels. At the end of the garden display, the boys would put on gloves and draw their names in coloured sparklers. I hadn't known it was a tradition until Ruth suggested she take the children to the display in the local park. The children were keen, Thomas was keen, it would get him out of the house. Alan could 'do his thing', as Ruth put it, and then join them. I would stay at home with my legs up. Ruth had read the books. She knew that after an insemination it was best to rest, to enlist the support of gravity.

I think I knew it was wrong when the children left. When they put on their coats and hats and faces of excitement and kissed me goodbye. When the house was so terribly quiet all of a sudden and the thought flashed through my mind, This is what it will be like for this new child, a ticketed fireworks party in the park, not an intimate family experience at home.

The thought was absurd. I tried to rationalise it. It was just, I argued with myself, that I had never missed an occasion with the children before, had taken them, been with them, for every birthday, Christmas, school play, dental appointment, every important date in their lives and now I wasn't there. I was in the house alone with Alan.

I like Alan. He seems a gentle man to me. I thought perhaps it was Alan who was keeping Ruth centred, Alan who, perhaps, was playing the role in Ruth's life I used to play. Alan who stretched out a hand and cared for her. Why are there some people who care and some who are cared for? I have never been able to understand this. Why don't the carers care for each other? Then they could be loved back.

Of course Alan was embarrassed. Didn't look at me at all that day. Not when we arrived, kissing me with the blind flat of his cheek; not when we spoke nothings at lunch, as though it was an ordinary day, just families meeting; not as he helped to mash potato for the children's tea. But then my eyes were elsewhere too. I remember the indentation of the lino in the kitchen where Ruth's chair must have scraped back a thousand times, the scratched hollow, the brown scuff marks. I remember the feel of the thick pile rug by the fire in the drawing-room, how I teased the strands with my fingers, fiddling the green nylon under my finger-nails. And I remember the bedspread.

'You must use our room, of course,' said Ruth.

Hers was a much bigger room than the guest room, warm and light, with a view over the backs of the houses beyond, the park in the distance. When she suggested it, I thought it just a courtesy and complied willingly. Only later did I think, That's where she wanted it, in her bedroom, on her bed, as if she had really conceived herself.

She had planned everything. Given me a turkey baster, a long plastic pipette with a bulbous rubber end she'd found in a hardware store.

'It's really for drizzling oil on a bird.' She laughed.

To Alan she gave a see-through plastic cup.

'Lots more where that came from. You can only buy them in twenty-fives.'

I don't know where Alan masturbated, though a *Playboy* was left on the linen basket in the bathroom. I just lay on the virginal white lace bedspread and waited. Outside, in the gathering dark, children were shouting. My children among them. I could hear excitement and see a bonfire lit. The flames made a lick of yellow against the night. Inside the house there was no noise except the beat of blood in my ears, which might have been the knock.

Knock, knock, knock.

Alan knocking on his own bedroom door to gain entry to parenthood. He didn't really come into the room, just stuck his arm round the door with the cup outstretched.

And I said, 'Thank you.'

Thank you.

That's how it was done. The sin polished over with politeness.

I sucked the liquid out of the cup with the turkey baster. Hardly any liquid, viscous, already slightly congealed and with a smell that made me retch. A smell that I must have known and loved in Thomas but which here seemed sickeningly thick. Dirty was the word that screamed around the room. Dirty. Dirty. Dirty. Revolted, my flesh crept, it goosebumped, but my mind grasped that rubber bulb and squeezed. I swear I felt the emission cold inside me. Then I lay back on the stiff white cotton. Outside, over the park, a huge firework exploded. A star that rained fantastic gold for a few seconds and then burned out. In that moment I knew I had both created and lost a life. And I wept. Oh, my darling, how I wept.

Each month of the pregnancy Bridie sent Ruth baby clothes, booties, vests, Babygros, white knitted cardigans.

'It's difficult for her,' Bridie said, 'to see you pregnant.'

But Ruth didn't see me. I returned to Essex and hid. I hid from myself, from Thomas, from the children. I couldn't hide from the mothers at school.

'When's your new baby due?' they asked with delight.

Early on Thomas asked if I wanted an abortion. But how could I have killed a child half mine? All mine, as it felt now.

After seven months Thomas said we would keep the child, if that's what I wanted. He would be a father to it, make no distinction between this child and his own. How I loved him for that. And hated him also. For there was Ruth, waiting for this child, which I had promised her, which was my ultimate gift to her. 'Oh, you're expecting,' they said to me. But it was Ruth and Bridie who were expecting.

'You could not let her down now,' said Bridie. 'It would kill her.'

When the time drew near it was high summer, the corn beginning to ripen and turn gold. I will go in the fields, I thought. I will give birth under the sky. Nature will let me take the babe and hold her close. For what other morality can there be but that which is pure and simple? From the earth we come and to earth we return. There is nothing else.

'You have other children to consider,' said Thomas.

'Are you going to give me away too?' asked Toby.

Michael, Toby, Manda, they were all late babies. I was not expecting the sudden tightening that began you, my adored fourth child. But there it was, that early grip of pain and me just in the middle of a phone conversation with Bridie. Afterwards I thought Bridie a witch, that she had sent that pain so that she should know the start, so that she in turn could call Ruth.

It was to be a home birth. Each of my deliveries had been easy. Michael and Toby had been there to see Manda brought into the world. This time I didn't want any of the children near me. I didn't want them to see what I was going to do. It is only obscene things you can't show a child.

The room was prepared, the downstairs bedroom where Manda had been born. I cleaned it thoroughly, laid out sheets and fresh towels. When the contractions were five minutes apart Thomas phoned the midwife.

She arrived at the same time as Ruth did. It was a Friday. Ruth had come straight from the office, she was wearing a cream suit and cream high-heeled shoes. Though she'd driven in the heat with Alan, 'Ninety miles an hour up the motorway,' Alan said later, she looked utterly cool, composed. I was sweating, groaning and in pain. I'd never had so much pain at a birth. Then the contractions stopped. They didn't just decrease in ferocity, or become more widely spaced, they simply stopped. Stopped dead. As if there was no birth expected. No longer a baby.

At first I thought it was her, Ruth, standing there in the room all ugly, grasping need. All cream control.

'Has it stopped? Has it stopped? Oh, my God, make it start again.'

But you can't make babies start. They start when they want, come when they want to. And that's when I realised that it wasn't Ruth at all, but you. My darling, darling baby. You had decided to come ahead of schedule because she wouldn't be here, because we could be alone. And now she was here, you were not going to show. You were going to hold your breath, refuse to be born. Because she was there, standing, waiting to catch you and take you away.

'It's all stopped,' I said. 'It's all gone away. You might as well check into a hotel.'

'A hotel!' she shrieked.

'There's no room here.'

'I'll sleep on the floor,' she said. 'We'll sleep on the floor, won't we, Alan?'

For four nights she slept on the floor. On Monday she phoned the office to say she wouldn't be in until after the birth. She sent Alan home for more clothes but she wouldn't go herself. He came back with crisp navy linen, with pure white cotton.

And still you waited, my darling. I should have been strong then. Should have taken myself to that field. But I was weak and beginning to bleed.

It was Tuesday. Tuesday's child is full of Grace. You came then, angrily, fighting all the way, not a large baby, but flailing, angular, difficult.

'Push,' said the midwife.

'Push!' yelled Ruth.

All of my body was birthing you. Wave after tumultuous wave forcing you out. I was crying. But not with the pain, though there was pain, but with the loss of you. For every muscle of me would keep you in, would hold you for ever tight in my womb. I refused to expel you, but expel you I did.

And you cried as she reached straight down and put her cold hands around your stomach. Even the midwife said, 'Wait, I need to cut the cord. I need to clean her.' But she couldn't

124

wait. She snatched you up. I looked at the blood on her cool white shirt. I hadn't even held you, looked into your eyes.

Later she did let me suckle you. You wouldn't fix. Your lip trembled, you fell away. Years afterwards someone told me that early babies don't suckle so well, they take a little time to learn. But at the time I thought you were rejecting me. And I thought that I deserved it.

Ruth stayed in the house a week. I begged her to go to a hotel then. Told her that I couldn't bear to hear your cries as she bottle-fed you, my milk spurting, soaking my clothes.

'I thought you wanted to be close,' she said.

Just the once I had you alone. Thomas and me together, looking at your fluff of pale hair, your deeper than knowing eyes.

'Miranda,' Thomas said. 'She looks like our Manda.'

I cried then and he held me. Held us both.

An hour later Ruth put you in a car seat and drove you away.

I set down the manuscript then. I don't know whether I have fed on it or it has fed on me. But I am full up, surfeited, choked with it. I go to the window and throw it open for air. It's a small window but I am small too. In a moment I am up and out. A crunch on the gravel and then I'm running. Running. Running.

But whether I'm running away or running towards, I don't know. I've lost my sense of direction.

# 17

Alan walks in a tube of glass. Below him is the traffic of the city's periphery, and above him, beyond the glass, a blue arc of sky and a blazing August sun, which does not blaze here in the cool cylinder of glass. He thought he knew why he'd come. He imagined, as he rose from the clanging depths of the Seventh Avenue subway, that he had something to say. But now that he walks in the shining corridors of this palace of commerce, he is not so sure. The tubal people, who understand this brisk, chill, air-conditioned world, move easily among the lights and the mirrors. They have bright coins in their pockets and they know where they are going. Alan does not know where he's going. He's just following signs: World Trade Center; World Financial Center, Tower 3. He thinks he has traversed Tower 1 of the castle, but he cannot be certain. His princess resides in Tower 3. Will she let down her hair from floor 202, Pharmakon International, and allow him to climb up? This picture is not quite clear. He arrives at Reception, he declares himself. And then what? They ring the ombuds suite: 'It's Alan. Your husband Alan. Yes, here. Yes. In New York. He has something to say that couldn't be said on the phone. That couldn't wait. Do you have a minute?'

Of course, it is insane. He is insane. He is walking on a drawbridge of glass. He'd like to take a brick and throw it through the glass. He'd like to reach his hand through the jagged gap to touch the elements beyond, to see if they still exist, if he still exists. He is a piece of clay desiccating for lack of air. He has only walked in the sun once since he landed in this place. Took a baked-tarmac breath at the airport as he waited to board his bus for Grand Central Station. Since when he has been surrounded, hemmed in, by concrete and rubber, silica and steel, neon, fluorescence and the smell of cleaning fluid. Yes, hemmed in, despite the spaciousness of his surroundings, the huge structures, the public curves.

How will he tell her?

How can he stand in front of his wife and say that, five thousand miles away, her daughter knows the truth? Her daughter who is not her daughter.

'Why didn't you tell me?' screamed Grace.

He'd wanted to. They'd both understood how incredibly important it was to tell their daughter the truth.

'It wasn't easy,' he'd said. 'Not with Laura . . . the way she was.'

Laura so impossible, so needy. So dangerous. Besides, it hadn't really been his place. He was the father. He had so much less to lose than Ruth. Somehow he'd let it slip.

'And we did try.'

'You did?'

'Yes. Yes, we did.'

Or Ruth did. 'It would be better,' Ruth had said, 'if I told her. Better coming from her mother, don't you think?' And, of course, he'd agreed. So when Ruth informed him that an opportunity had arisen and the deed was done, Alan had believed her. That's why, many years later, when it became clear that Grace did not know, he kept his own counsel. Chose, perhaps, to believe that Grace had forgotten. Things were as they were. But it was also why, when Ruth finally came to him needing to tell, bursting to tell, that he'd said, 'No. No. I forbid it.' For by then it was too late. It was also, he'd thought, dishonest. 'You just want to get it off your chest,' he'd said. And: 'It will hurt Grace terribly and for what?' Why, he asked, did Grace need to know? Didn't there come a point when happiness was more important than truth?

'Why did I need to know,' screamed Grace, 'that I have a mother, another mother, siblings, a family? Why did I need to know?'

'Ruth created you,' Alan said solidly. 'Her desire, her motherhood, she made you happen. Ruth, your mother.'

'Ruth created me?'

He had come to this idea, had not seen it at first, when the two sisters plotted together. When they came to him and said he was to be a father in a plastic cup.

'Yes,' he'd replied. 'Yes. OK.'

Is that all? That was all. He wanted to be a father and they would make him one. It did not seem immoral. The child was passionately desired and would be passionately loved. He did not know then – for he was not then a parent – quite how passionately loved. The women, so they told him, were doing the difficult, the giving thing. By comparison his part was small. All he had to do was trust them and retire to the bathroom.

Ruth provided a copy of *Playboy*, left it on the linen basket. He did take a small, a discreet, revenge then. He put aside the shiny pictures and imagined Laura instead. He had, in any case, never been a man to fantasise in laminate. He liked his women real, even in his imagination. He liked them so real he could see their eyes and put his tongue in their mouths.

He was accustomed to touch, the supple feel of clay and flesh. He liked to trace outlines, discover curves, to lick and smooth and stroke. When Ruth was away on business, it was her body he always masturbated to. But that night it had been Laura's. It was Laura's child so Laura should be fucked, that's what he said to himself as he grasped his red, rod-hard prick. Perhaps it was anger that made his penis swell so, made it throb and jerk as it spurted against them, these women who were using him to make their child. When he took the cup to Laura he didn't look at her, as you wouldn't if you'd just fucked your wife's sister.

The tube is at an end. It has delivered him into a vast atrium, floored in giant squares of salmon pink and grey marble, ceilinged in spans of steel and arcs of glass. Set rigid in the floor are the trunks of twelve seventy-foot palm trees, their high green heads nodding towards the sky they will never feel or breathe. Where the sea of marble ends, the real sea, beyond the glass, begins. Moored in the harbour are huge white yachts with names like *Excalibur* and *Entrepreneur*. Alan stands, for a moment, at the top of the mighty marble steps that would sweep him down to the concourse below. He observes the stiff steel benches placed back to back where a few late-afternooners read or eat take-out from brightly coloured packages. He looks at the organised sprawl of Parisian cane-backed chairs that pretend to be the atrium's *al fresco* café.

And then he sees her.

She's in her navy suit with the shoes that have narrow, steel-tipped heels. She pushes back her café chair, puts money on the table, closes her briefcase, stands up. She looks thin, grey-haired. Brittle. His Ruth. The woman he loves. The woman with whom, above all things, he wanted to have children. She shakes her male companion by the hand, makes adieus. She's coming out of the café, walking on the marble floor. She can ascend on one of the two escalators or she can come up the steps.

Why did he do it?

Why did he say so brutally – straight to his daughter's face, 'Your mother is not your mother'? Was it because she denied him, screamed, 'You are not my father'? Could he have been so very vulnerable, his fatherhood built on such sand that he needed to demolish Ruth to buttress his own foundations? Or was it just that Grace knew a different truth, knew about him and Adele? That what he was doing, quite simply, was heading her off?

Ruth is coming up the steps. The man is going up the escalator but Ruth is coming up the steps. Alan should move. He should hide. He is not prepared. But there is nowhere to hide. There is glass and marble and space. Besides, his feet are tombed in the stone.

'Oh, my God!' She has seen him. For a moment she stands rigidly still and then she laughs, a high, sharp 'ha', her hand flying to her mouth. He doesn't respond. He doesn't move. So she smiles. 'I'm so sorry. It's just that you look incredibly like my husband.'

'Ruth,' he says.

'Ha!' Now the gasp is higher, gulped, a touch hysterical. She is just a step beneath him, her face uplifted. 'Oh, my God,' Ruth, his wife, says. 'It's Grace, isn't it? Oh, my God, it's Grace. She's dead, isn't she?' Ruth's face is twisted white. In the atrium people stop and stare. Her anguish is bouncing off the glass.

'Tell me,' she screams. 'Tell me!'

'She's alive,' says Alan. 'She's fine. She's gone to Laura's.'

Ruth collapses then. She folds in two, falls on to the hard white marble steps. At once Alan is down beside her, making a pillow of his lap. He cradles her head.

'It's fine,' he says. 'It's all fine. It's going to be fine.'

He puts his hand in her grey hair, strokes his wife's beautiful scalp. He smooths her forehead, traces the exquisite line of her cheek, puts the gentlest of fingertips on her red lips. She is breathing, he feels real breath. He leans down in the huge public space and kisses her.

Telling his wife about Adele, the other reason for his journey, suddenly doesn't seem so important any more.

# 18

At the bottom of Greenbury Lane I stop running. I can go left, back towards the station, right down another rough residential track or straight on towards a hill at whose foot there seems to be a small bridge. I choose the hill, thinking if there is a bridge there may be water and if there is water I may yet be cool.

As I get closer I see that this is a ford, the road that curves up the hill currently running dry over the stream. A large white and black measuring stick nailed to a post makes it clear that, in flood, the stream may rise as much as six feet. As I walk on to the three-planked bridge I think I am like this stream, the trickle of me in sudden flood. To my right, the water runs fast and clear, broadening into a cool pool before disappearing along the green edge of a golden cornfield. I would descend here, I would put my hands in the water, find cold pebbles for my face, my neck. But my place is taken. There is a child who squats here with a net and jam-jar. She's dark and lithe and full of darting concentration. I lean on the metal railings, watching her hands sudden among the weed. She is catching tiny brown fish. The jam-jar is quick with them.

Is this the child who might have been me? At her age, six or seven, I was never out alone. My mother (my mother) did not like me unaccompanied even in the garden. I felt followed everywhere. When the red car stopped pursuing us, Ruth began. Watched me on my journeys to the studio, liked to know I'd arrived. Her eyes long from the kitchen, high in the bedroom. That's when I started my tapping, I think. If I tap here, she won't follow me. If I touch here before she sees me, I'll get away. I'll be free.

I can barely imagine being this fish-girl. Out by herself with jam-pot and dreams. Would Laura have let me be so? Would I have walked across this ford with Manda and my brothers to school, the four of us laughing and joking, the boys swishing sticks, Manda taking an ear of corn to share with me on our way? And what, then, of the return? Laura our mother coming to meet us with Sadie in the pram and a pocket full of plums, the juice already spilling down Sadie's fat cheeks? And if it had been so, who would I be then? Who would I be now?

Who am I now?

The girl has seen me. She squints up at this stranger, this intruder. I smile because I want so much to be allowed to be here with her.

'What are you catching?'

'Minnows,' she says, as if all right-minded people should know this.

'What do you do with them?'

'Put them back.'

'So the fun's just in the catching?'

'I guess so.'

She goes back to catching and I return to leaning and watching. After a while, when it's clear I'm not going away she says, 'You don't live here, do you?'

'What makes you think that?'

'I haven't seen you before.'

'I might have done.'

'What?'

'I might have lived here. I was born in a house not five minutes from here. Greenbury Lane. Do you live up there?'

'No.'

She wants me to go now, to leave her alone.

'What's your name?' I ask.

'Beth,' she says without looking up.

'Mine's Grace. Grace Thomas. Or Grace Alder. One or the other.'

'What?'

'Either Grace Thomas or Grace Alder. Or Miranda. But there's already a Miranda Alder. Manda. Which is why my mother, who's not my mother, flipped out when I asked to be Grace Miranda when I was your age.'

Beth collects her jam-jar and net. 'You're weird,' she says.

'Yes,' I say. 'But I could have been you.'

' 'Bye,' says Beth. She has at least been warned about people like me.

'You don't have to go.' I get off the railings. 'I'm going.'

'I've got tea,' she says. 'I have to get home.'

She tips away the fish and walks off briskly in the direction of the town centre.

I am alone now but I no longer want to put my fingers in the water. It is not my water any more. Besides, the eyes of my mothers are on me. They regard me, from outside and in as they always have. These adults who have made a child of me. Who have created me. Made a dirty secret sin of me. Something too horrible to speak of.

I see them all around a table, drinks and cards in their hands, smoke rings in their hair. Ruth and Alan and Laura and Thomas. Discussing me. Discussing terms. Deciding what will be and how it will be. On the middle of the table is the little sin, only the size of an orange, all pale and curled up, its eyelids sealed. They wager and barter and put their bids in envelopes. There are sideways looks, tense drumming of fingers, but they know what they want, the four of them. It is only a matter of time, of negotiation. Suspicion gives way to smiles. The price is agreed, the pact concluded with blood cut from their wrists. They stand up and shake hands, slipping the sin with its pale budding limbs into a bag. They have done it, achieved it. Laura passes the bag to Ruth. In the drawstring darkness, the sin would shriek but it doesn't have a mouth.

I'm going to run again. When I run my lungs have to take breath, my heart has to pump. I'm away from the bridge in an instant, skirting the pool, tracking the edge of the cornfield. I run on the small hard strip of earth that divides the cultivated land from the wild green of the riverbank. I could go either way. I could crash through the green density of bramble and dock, elderflower and nettle. I could scratch and tear myself there, trip on roots and send stones scudding into the water. I could fall and lie where I fell, keeping my mouth shut on thorns. But I won't. Not any more. Nor will I run for ever on this hinterland, this brown edge of my life.

I turn into the field. The corn is almost up to my neck, a million neat, straight, civilised golden rows of it. I stamp it down, in front, behind, beyond. I am wild but not random. I'm working against the grain, against every one of the field's billion grains and the men who planted them here. I pull at the wheat heads, my fists spurting hard seed and golden chaff. I'm thrashing and flailing but I know where I'm going. I'm going to the heart, to the centre of it all. I am destroying what they would make.

For I am the whirling act of God, I am lawless nature returned. It is me screaming and shrieking and stamping in this ordered, this man-made field of corn. I am the swollen seed, the milled and the threshed, sown by two and reaped by two, kneaded and shaped and set to rise in flames of fire. Well, now I am risen.

But I am not what they thought. They must have left me too long in the fire. I am burned hard.

# 19

Bridie is methodically unpacking the chest in the drawing-room. She has taken the orange tree in its green majolica pot and placed it, where she always does if she needs to open the chest, on the black tiles of the hearth. And now she's emptying, stacking. There is a small mountain of brown-paper packages. Some are tied with string, some stamped with Christmas stamps, others with stamps that still carry amounts in halfpence, eight and a half pence, twelve and a half pence. A random collection of the parcels sent over thirteen years. The ones she didn't open.

To the right of the packages are the books. Three different editions of *Rumpelstiltskin*, one – a lavishly illustrated retelling – annotated in black ink. A paperback *Rapunzel*. Also annotated. *Moon Tales from Argentina. An Anthology of Loss*. And many, many more. Behind these are the shoes. A pink satin first-size pair of ballet shoes, with long pink ribbons. Small Christmas boots with a light-up nose on the appliqué Rudolf the Reindeer. Summer sandals decorated with hand-drawn yellow and blue seaweeds.

The piles look neat and orderly, even the one that contains the assorted personal mementoes, an old T-shirt of Manda's, a favourite toothbrush, one of Toby's gifts, a collection of shells and rocks from a holiday in Norfolk. But things that look neat and orderly, Bridie thinks, may not be so. As she takes things out of the wooden chest she feels as though she is taking them from her own chest, reaching through her ribcage, stripping out her internal organs and placing them tidily on the floor.

Lub dub. Lub dub. Lub dub. This is the sound she heard so very often at the end of her stethoscope before the death of Alice Watling. Lub dub. Lub dub. The beat of a healthy heart. Today she doesn't hear this sound. She hears lub shlub, lub shlub. A whistle that tells her trained ear that a heart valve is leaking.

The more she has emptied the chest, the louder the noise has become. But she must continue emptying the chest because there is something she wishes to find. A brown envelope, right at the bottom, which contains the letters, the ones from court and the ones from the hospital.

Of course Mrs Watling was at the inquest.

'Having sticky-out ears,' said Mrs Watling, 'ruined Alice's life and now they have cost her her life.' And she burst into tears.

Bridie remembers going to see Alice the night before the operation. The child was alone, reading, no parents allowed on the ward in those days. What she recalls is that she could tell Alice only from the name on the notes hung at the end of her bed, not from her face, from her apparently hideous ears. It wasn't until she began to chat to the girl and Alice turned her head that her hair flicked away revealing the three layers of plaster that strapped those ears to her skull.

'Tomorrow,' said Alice, 'is going to be the happiest day of my life.'

Lub dub. Lub dub. Lub dub. Alice smiling. Her heartbeat strong and regular.

Now Bridie has reached the dresses. Some of them are still in polythene wrap, though each one has been exquisitely, laboriously worked by hand. There is the Red Riding Hood dress, the green shift with the drawstring cape of red velvet; the summer party frocks with beaded smocking or white and yellow embroidered daisies. There is also the fairy dress, a bodice of silver satin with a skirt of sequined gauze. With this dress came wings, a silver circlet, a spangled wand. These at least, thinks Bridie, I passed on. These and some of the other neutral, seemingly innocent things – like the books. Gifts that would not arouse suspicion either from Grace or Ruth. Though she still worked hard at concealing their origins, giving them as from herself or leaving them lying in her own house for her granddaughter to chance upon. But it was Laura who didn't play fair, who began to ink her anger on to the stories. It had taken Bridie a little while to catch on. The picture of Rapunzel in her tower: 'This is the glass prison they have you in. But one day you will know the truth.' Well, now Grace knew.

Bridie feels her breathing shallow, quicken. It is not doing her any good. And she did try. Had always tried, done her best. Just as she tried to do her best for Alice Watling. There was no pre-med in those days. Normal, analgesia, excitation, anaesthetic. That's how it was, how it had to be. The litany. And the nurse who wheeled Alice down on the trolley was a good nurse, Barbara, Barbara MacKinnon. They called her Mack.

Bridie had put on her green theatre dress, slipped the cotton bags over her shoes, made ready the mask. She was waiting in the ante-room. Lub dub. Lub dub. Lub dub. Mack checked it was the right patient.

'Yes,' Bridie had said, looking at Alice and thinking of Laura who was the same age to the month, 'it's the right patient.' Alice's hair was tied back, her ears unplastered.

'It's only gas and air, really,' said Bridie, holding the black rubber mask above Alice's face, 'puts you in a nice deep sleep. And when you wake up, hey! Happiest day of your life.'

Alice smiled, wide as a sunbeam. Her mother never saw that smile, Bridie thought afterwards.

Of course she struggled. Everyone did as you pumped the halothane gas down the tube. It was expected. That's why it had a name. Excitation. Mack gentled her, pinioned her arms.

'No!' Alice was shouting into the black mask. 'No! No! No!' She coughed, she cried. Bridie pushed down the plunger, increased the halothane level. She quieted then. Anaesthetic. Mack released her.

'One down and four to go,' Mack said.

Lub dub. Lub dub. Lub dub.

They wheeled the little body into the theatre, banged the

Boyles machine against the swing doors as they entered. But that hadn't mattered. Not at all, they'd said at the enquiry. It was written in the judgement, in the paper in the envelope at the bottom of the chest. The paper that exonerates Bridie. The paper she must find.

'Gran! You shouldn't leave doors open. This is a bad, dangerous world. You never know who . . .'

The voice is behind her. Bridie, on her knees, turns, her heart lub dub, dub dub dubbing.

'Grace!'

Grace has stopped in the doorway. She is a statue of herself caught in mid-step. She has seen the piles on the floor, the shoes, the dresses, the books, the parcels addressed to herself in black ink, in a sloping hand with no space between the words. Grace, Grace Thomas, Grace Alder-Thomas, Grace Alder. My daughter.

'Jesus!' Grace cries.

She unlocks. She begins to come in. Bridie puts up her hands to protect herself. Lub dub. Lub dub. Lub shlub. And then no breath. Alice Watling is pale. She isn't breathing. They are barely into theatre, the surgeon chatting to a junior. Bridie takes a peripheral pulse, her fingers on Alice's wrist.

'Where is it?' Grace is down among the books already, her mad hands pulling, tearing, flinging. 'Where is it?'

'What?' says Bridie. Lub shlub.

'The seal book. The seal story. Where is it?'

No pulse. Alice Watling has no pulse.

'There isn't a seal book. Never was a seal book.'

'Liar!' screams Grace.

'No, it's true. There were other books. But not that one. You made it up. Made it all up.' Her fingers on Alice's neck, feeling for the carotid. Nothing. Panic. Panic. Call out. More oxygen. Squeezing the bag, squeezing the bag. Can't breathe. Can't breathe. Like now. Shallow. Quick. Lub dub. Lub shlub. Lub . . .

'I didn't make it up.' Grace in a frenzy, her hands in the air. Wild, flailing things. 'I don't make things up. You make things up. All of you. Liars. All of you lying to me for seventeen years. Stop it. Stop it. Stop it!'

But Bridie can't stop it. She's in a dark place, despite the bright lights of the operating theatre. There is no resuscitation team now, just as there wasn't then. There is no heart massage. Just the noise of Grace's shouting and the darkness and the feeling of her fingers searching for the envelope, which she thinks she may have in her hand, the one that says she didn't do it. That she wasn't to blame when, after fifteen minutes, they gave up on Alice Watling. Lub dub. Lub shlub. All of them gave up on the child but her. Bridie was screaming as she squeezed that oxygen.

'Alice. Alice! Hold on, Alice!'

But Alice died. They wheeled her along to the mortuary and shut her in a drawer like a lump of meat.

'I curse you,' cried Alice's mother at the inquest, although the coroner had already threatened to eject her if she couldn't keep quiet. 'I call on Almighty God to deny you grandchildren as you have denied me. For as long as I live I will never forgive you. An eye for an eye and a tooth for a tooth and a life for a life. Alleluia. God is just.'

So what was Bridie to think when Ruth couldn't conceive? A life for a life, was what she was thinking when she made that call to Ruth: Ask your sister. Let her carry a child for you. Not to deny Alice, to forget her, but because it was all her fault. It is so dark now, tunnel dark, that Bridie can no longer see her fingers. The brown envelope, if it is the brown envelope, has slipped away.

'Gran?'

She cheated God of Grace. So God took Michael. He took Toby, Manda and Sadie.

And He took Laura.

Lub dub.

Her beloved daughter.

Lub shlub.

'Gran!'

Lub . . . lub . . . lub . . . lub . . .

# 20

It is rush-hour and the traffic on the M25 is heavy. Even in the fast lane Laura is moving slowly. They want to prevent me even now, she thinks, drumming her fingers on the steering-wheel. She imagines arriving at her mother's, at Bridie's house on the outskirts of Newick.

'Give me my daughter's address,' she is going to say. 'Give me Grace's address or I will kill you.'

To have had Grace come at last, to have had her so close, to have been able to touch her and then to have lost her yet one more time. Even Sadie had understood.

'Go to her,' said Sadie.

At last her crawl has brought Laura to the exit for the M23. Ahead the traffic is almost at a standstill, but to her left, to the south where she is going, the cars are moving. As she pulls off she can see space on the motorway below, clear road. She weaves, takes risks, puts her foot flat to the floor. She will never forget going into that room. Of course it was right to give Grace the testament, for there were no words in her own mouth that day but 'Sorry'. 'Oh, my darling, I am so sorry.' Right also, Sadie's idea, to give Grace privacy, to let her read alone.

But how impossible to sit outside that door. To wait and wait as the pages turned. To lock Grace away when, just an hour, just five minutes before, she would have torn down a tower of stone with her bare hands just for a glance at her daughter. So what had she done during the wait, during the time that was longer than all the seventeen years before? She'd sat at the kitchen table and stared at plums. She had no idea why she'd picked the fruit, why the jam pan was on the stove, the sugar out of the cupboard. She'd reached out and taken a plum, held it, pressed a finger-nail into the soft flesh, needing something to yield. Pressed until her finger reached obstinate stone.

Grace.

It was not a name she would have chosen for the child. But the child was Grace. Grace incarnate. That face! Such a face as an angel would have had if God himself had seen to the work. The lines clear, the skin smooth over the bone, the lips with the lift of a smile. A slender faerie creature with dark eyes and a bright ring of hair who moved not as Ruth did, stiff in her body, but lightly, as though she belonged. As if she had kept faith, as if her blood still sang the song of her birth, and her soul remembered the lullaby Laura had wept so fiercely over her as she lay, barely conscious, in the hospital.

Vivid with this fabulous, dancing child, Laura had jumped from her chair. She'd thrown herself through Grace's door. At first she hadn't been aware of any absence. She'd placed

Grace in the room. Observed the angel sitting on the bed where she had been born. It was only when the curtain flapped, letting sunlight into the room and revealing the open window, that Laura had seen, with throttling horror, that the room was empty.

Laura had screamed. Screamed as she had as she'd given birth. Screamed as she had when Ruth had tucked the baby into the car seat and driven away without so much as a backward glance. Screamed for the seventeen lost years and also for abandonment, hers of her daughter and now, her daughter's of her.

Sadie, because it was a small house and the noise loud, had slammed shut the door. Paint fell from the hinges. When the noise didn't stop, she left the house and didn't return until supper-time.

Laura had not left the house. That was her mistake the first time. She'd run away, slept out in cloudless cold summer nights. Been woken dew damp and exhausted by Thomas. Once, he'd found her in the cornfield by the ford. When he'd lifted her up, the crushed print of her body remained, a stain of red between the broken stalks of her legs.

'It's not right to bleed this long,' said Thomas. 'Is it?'

Of course her sister had promised to let Laura see Grace. And Ruth and Alan were only in London then, just an hour and a quarter's drive away.

'You know I can never, never thank you enough,' said Ruth. 'Never repay you for what you have done. Visit any time you like. As an aunt. Open house.'

But when she held the baby, Laura shook. For the child's eyes, which were her eyes, cried out, 'Why have you done this? Why have you forsaken me?' To be an aunt was not enough. Not nearly enough.

'You're forgetting,' said Thomas. 'Alan is the father.'

'Does that mean you won't take the child back?'

'No. It means what it means. You are the mother but he is the father. He also needs his baby.'

'My baby.'

Bridie rang.

'It's the baby blues,' she said. 'You'll get over it when your hormones calm down.'

But she hadn't got over it. The shaking got worse. She wanted to snatch up the child, run out of the house and never return. And Ruth knew it. Alan knew it.

Thomas opened windows and tins of paint. He flung primrose white at the room in which the baby had been born.

'Freshen things up,' he said, rollering the ceiling, splashes of white in his hair.

She stood in the doorway and watched. Beneath the window-ledge was a runnel of paint that dripped into a tear and, after a day or two, set hard.

'When are you going back to work?' Laura asked her sister.

'It's not decided,' said Ruth. But it was. The date was marked on the calendar in the kitchen.

'It might be wise,' said Bridie, 'if you postponed visiting for a little while. Might be better for you. Better for the baby.' Better for Ruth, her favourite child, Bridie did not say, but Laura was not fooled.

Then the adoption papers arrived. Ruth had been obliged by law to wait nineteen weeks before applying for custody. She had waited a year. 'Out of kindness,' Bridie said. 'Respect.'

'I won't sign. It would be like putting my hand to a death warrant.'

'Sign,' said Thomas. 'And leave be. For God's sake, leave be.'

Later, as the documents sat on the kitchen table, he'd said, 'If you want another baby, we'll have one.'

She was sick as a dog during that pregnancy. Not just for the first twelve weeks but for every one of the nine months. She had signed the papers but she had not let go and her body knew it. It was in rebellion. Her flesh cursed her as she cursed it. Sadie was born early and small, just skin and bone. Laura had chosen to deliver in hospital, though she hated hospitals, so as not to try to replicate Grace's birth. In a white room, between antiseptic sheets, she gritted her teeth. She would not scream. The labour was mercifully short. When she took her newborn in her arms she burst into tears.

'It's all right,' said Thomas.

'It's not,' she replied.

Ruth sent flowers to welcome the new addition to the family but she did not come in person.

'Grace has a cold,' Ruth said. 'I thought, for the baby's sake . . .'

That set the tone for the next six months. Requests were denied, politely but firmly. It wasn't convenient, Grace had a party, she was in quarantine for chicken-pox. A photo Laura had been promised 'got lost in the post'. It was then that Laura drove to London and banged on the door of her sister's house.

'Yes?' Alan said, not moving from his threshold of his home.

'Where's Grace?'

Alan paused, he sucked in his lower lip. 'At nursery school.'

'Which one? Where?'

'Laura,' said Alan. 'I'm sorry . . .'

*I'm sorry.*

Laura hadn't meant to pursue Grace, to follow her, to lie in wait, intimidating the child, putting her in fear of kidnap – as documented in the later legal proceedings – but what was she to do?

Sadie went on all those journeys with Laura, sitting in the back of the car, mournfully sucking her thumb. She was a quiet child then and easy to forget, though Laura only actually forgot her the once. She'd parked out of sight of the main nursery gate, as she always did, and just left Sadie – locked – in the back. Afterwards she found her mistake difficult to understand, especially as Sadie was always an asset, allowing Laura to move easily among the mothers, 'Yes, I'm picking up Grace Thomas today. Do you know her? Is she in your daughter's class?' Perhaps it was because Jack and Jill's was the fourth nursery Laura had tried and, as there were only five registered in Ruth's vicinity, she was excited by the prospect of success. Yet the mothers shook their heads. There was a Grace, but Grace Pallister, they thought. Was that the one? Laura had hung on, maybe if she could see this Grace Pallister . . . By the time she returned to her car Sadie was screaming and a crowd had gathered. Someone had called a policeman.

'You wouldn't do it to an animal,' said one old man, yanking at the leash of a fat sausage-dog. 'Quiet, Caesar!'

The policeman raised a very quizzical eye at Laura's excuses, the child had been asleep, Laura was pregnant again, absolutely had to find a loo, nowhere to park, couldn't just go on the pavement, had it really been so long?

Once in Laura's arms, Sadie quieted immediately, fat tears drying on her cheeks.

'Lovely lass,' said the policeman. 'Have you got others?'

'Yes,' said Laura. 'Four.'

'Blimey,' said Caesar's owner. 'I'd want to forget one if I 'ad four more.'

The policeman gave her a ticking-off but waved her away genially enough. He had five himself, he said, sighing.

That day Laura was late returning for the other children. It was not the first time. Michael's teacher had a word with her about it. 'Michael and Toby are restless boys,' smiled Mrs Tidmarsh. 'They're beginning to play up.'

Had Grace been told the truth?

Laura needed to know this in the same way that she needed air in order to breathe.

At night, Laura dreamed about the birth. Time and again the child slithered from her body. Time and again she reached down to catch it. But there was nothing there.

'You're torturing yourself,' said Thomas, when she awoke sobbing. The fourth time she roared herself upright, he just held her and said nothing.

Then Grace was ill. They let her snow-frozen body lie in the hospital for three days before they thought to phone her. And then it was Bridie, not Ruth, who made the call. Why? Laura wanted to think it was because Ruth was ashamed. But Ruth was not ashamed. Bridie made the call because she believed Grace might die. And Bridie, unlike Ruth, obviously thought Grace's mother had the right to know this. Afterwards Laura wondered just how and when Ruth would have let her know if there had been a death: by phone, by post, by advertisement in the local newspaper? No, Laura thinks, doing eighty-five miles an hour on the M23, she has not forgiven. How could she?

The lawyer's letters were a response to anger, to grief.

'Are you saying,' the greying, dapper little solicitor had asked, 'that Ruth Thomas is an unfit mother?'

147

'No,' she had replied. 'Just unfit.'

But Michael Goringe hadn't understood this remark any more than he had understood why Laura needed Grace to know the truth.

'It is only the welfare of the child that is taken into consideration,' he said. He also said that, after four and a half years, the uprooting of Grace from everything she knew (and, he implied, loved) would be difficult if not impossible.

'I want to go the distance,' said Laura, shocked to hear herself use that cold phrase of her mother's, the one that was always used to praise Ruth.

Michael Goringe talked about precedents and cases and realistic expectations. But he did send letters. And letters came back.

'You know . . .' said Michael Goringe. 'Maybe . . . a small irregularity, a loophole? The original adoption order . . .'

Laura went to the library. She studied Rayden and Jackson, volume two, appendices, familiarising herself with legal language and points of law. She photocopied The Adoption Act 1958, The Children Act 1975, The Adoption Act 1976. She devoured The Surrogacy Arrangements Act 1985, and The Human Fertilisation and Embryology Act 1990, even though Michael Goringe told her repeatedly that the law was not retrospective. She brought books home. Contacted organisations. Was on the phone for half an hour to America, speaking to the chairwoman of the Coalition Against Surrogacy. Michael and Toby knew better than to interrupt her while she was working. They made sandwiches for themselves in the kitchen. Only Sadie tugged at her skirts and said, resolutely, 'Owinge. Owinge juice. Sadie want owinge.'

Manda took Sadie away. She made her sister a beaker of orange squash, which Sadie flung against the fridge.

'Naughty!' Manda said, 'Naughty girl!' and thrust a stinking cloth at the toddler. 'Clear it up. Now!'

'What's this?' asked Thomas, of the sticky floor.

The children told him.

Thomas went into the drawing-room and slammed shut the book his wife was reading. He threw it on the floor. He threw all of the books, one by one, on the floor. The spines of the red books broke in two. Sadie ran and hid behind a curtain. None of the other children moved.

'That's it. That's the end. If you persist,' he said, 'I will leave you. It is as simple as that. And I will take the other children, your other children, with me.'

'You wouldn't. You can't,' she said, bringing her husband into focus. He looked worn out. He was haggard and grey when he had always been young, fresh, happy-go-lucky.

'I will claim,' said Thomas, 'that you are obsessed. That your obsession has led to systematic neglect of the other children. That you are the unfit mother.'

'But I love them more than anything in the world!'

'Do you.' said Thomas.

That night in the mirror she saw a monster. Studied its fixated face. Saw what Thomas saw, what the children saw. A creator turned destroyer. Traced the ugly, hardened lines. So this is what she had become. She was astonished and ashamed. How could love have brought her to this? Thomas was right. It had to stop. And, for the sake of her husband and her other children, Laura would stop it. But Grace deserved one final appeal.

Laura, passing the Gatwick turn-off, remembers the day she made this same journey twelve and a half years ago. She only wanted what was just, and Bridie was a woman who believed in justice.

'I'll take the children,' she said to Thomas, intimating that he might like to stay behind, have a day to himself. Then she'd belted them in, Michael, Toby, Manda and Sadie and driven south for Sunday lunch.

It was March and very cold. The pristine snow in Bridie's garden was crunchy. The children put on boots and coats and scarves and went out to build a snowman.

'We could make one lying down,' said Toby. 'And call it Grace.'

The windows of the kitchen were steamed up from the cooking. Bridie placed two crystal glasses on the table. 'You must halt legal proceedings,' she said. 'It will destroy the family.'

'I'm already destroyed,' said Laura. 'Don't I count as family?'

'You have to think of Grace,' said Bridie, pouring sherry.

'Thomas says I think of no one, of nothing, else.'

'Laura, it was an accident. A mistake. She went out to play in the snow. That's all.'

'She was four and a half. Someone should have gone with her.'

'You're not out with Sadie now and she's only two. You can't be with a child all the time.'

'Sadie's with her brothers. Her sister. I can see her through the window.'

Bridie drained the carrots, put them in a warmed dish in the oven. 'You know it will never happen again. Ruth's learned her lesson. She's a good mother, Laura.'

'Ruth is not a good mother. She's not even a mother.'

'She has cared for Grace every day of her life. Got up to her in the night, kissed her grazed knees, nursed her when she was sick, read to her, been there for her. That is what a mother does, what a mother is. What else is there, Laura?'

Laura's grip tightens on the steering-wheel. As if she hadn't wanted to do all these things for Grace, as if she wouldn't have given her life to do them! But that long-ago day Laura had been controlled. She'd had a plan and she'd needed to be careful. So she hadn't vented her anger against Ruth, nor had she simply said, 'Where does that leave your motherhood then, Bridie? You who shut the door on your children when your husband returned?' No, that winter day, mindful of the monster in the mirror and of Thomas's ultimatum, Laura had issued an ultimatum of her own, saying it softly, as if she'd given in, 'I will withdraw the case, if you promise me you'll make Ruth tell Grace the truth. Tell her who her mother is.'

'Her genetic mother,' said Bridie briskly. She'd sluiced fat over the roast potatoes. Pierced one with a knife. Laura waited, she'd waited so long she could wait some more. Bridie replaced the potatoes in the oven, straightened her stiff back. 'All right,' she'd said. 'I agree.' And then, so quietly it might have been Laura's imagination, 'Thank you, Laura.'

'So she doesn't know,' breathed Laura. 'I thought not.'

'As you said, Laura,' Bridie had retorted, 'she's only four and a half.'

Laura stood up. 'And as soon as she knows I intend to visit again.'

'No, Laura.'

'Yes, Mother.'

'No. And no again.' Bridie wiped her hands on her apron, turned so that she faced her daughter directly. 'I didn't want to have to say this, but you force me. The visits ended because you couldn't cope. No . . . don't start, don't say anything. Just listen for once. However much you want to believe that Ruth stopped you coming, it's just not true. You stopped yourself coming because you couldn't cope. You could have had a role in the child's life –'

'A role!'

'A role, if you had just allowed Ruth to be mother. And she is mother. I'm sorry, Laura. But that's as plain as I can be.'

'I have rights, Mother. I have duties.'

'And Grace also has rights. Rights that supersede yours, and Ruth's too for that matter. Not least the right to grow up in peace. Loved and unconfused.'

'And do you think,' Laura had said, very quietly, 'that Grace's rights are best served by letting her know that she has another mother, a blood mother, and then allowing her to believe that that mother doesn't care about her, doesn't even want to see her?'

Bridie had been silent a while then. 'Grace is a child. I think it can be put in a way that will make sense to her.'

'Tell her some lie, you mean.'

'No. Not a lie. Though if a lie, I'm not so sure that it really matters – not as much as Grace's security and happiness.'

'It may matter to Grace!'

'Well, that's for time and Grace to tell.'

And that's when the crevasse opened. The huge gaping crack between now and then, the black wedge of time that Laura would have to wait before her own child was old enough to seek her of her own volition. Somehow Bridie had snatched victory from defeat. 'Why do you always take Ruth's part against me?' she'd yelled then. 'Put Ruth's happiness above mine?'

'I don't,' said Bridie, and she'd gone to the window and banged for the children to come in.

Their gloves had been dank and their coats streamed ice. They shouted and jostled as they washed and warmed their hands and came to the table.

'Tell us about Grace, Gran,' eleven-year-old Toby had said, unfolding his napkin. 'I want to hear about my sister.'

Laura had stared at him. It sounded so innocent, so sincerely meant. Though, at home, he was all irony, all disinterest, bottled anger.

'Another time,' said Bridie.

'I want to see a picture,' said Manda, aged nine. 'I want to see if she still looks like me.'

'The subject's closed,' said Bridie, lifting out the lamb with its garlic and crackling sprigs of rosemary. 'I'm sorry.'

'The subject's closed?' said Laura. 'What's that supposed to mean?'

It meant, apparently, that Bridie had paid a price for her disloyalty to Ruth. Incensed by Bridie's revelation of Grace's hospitalisation, Ruth had told her mother that if she ever again passed on any information of any sort about Grace to Laura, then she would lose Grace. Ruth would ensure that Bridie would never see her grandchild again. There seemed to be tears in Bridie's eyes as she recounted this.

'Do you know what you are saying?' demanded Laura then. And she'd dragged her children from the table where, idling with their knives and forks, they were warm at last and eagerly awaiting lunch.

'We're going,' she said.

'Going?' said Bridie.

'Do you think you can have your grandchild,' said Laura, 'but deny her to her brothers and sisters? To Michael, Toby, Manda, Sadie? Deny her to me? Is that your idea of fair play, "happiness"? Or is it just your own rights superseding everyone else's? Well, two can play at that game. Come on, children, get up. Get up, I said!'

And she'd taken them. Left the lamb and the roast potatoes and the carrots and broccoli steaming on the table. Bundled and pushed the children back into the car for the long drive home. Impervious to their protests, their yells, their desire for a McDonald's.

'Laura, Laura,' Bridie had cried. But Laura was gone.

Later Thomas said, 'I understand why you did it,' and he shook his head.

No more than she had shaken her head at herself. Her implacability shocked her as did her inability to be generous when giving had been the motif of her life. But how could she sit down to eat with someone who had promised to divide her from her child? She also resented being wrong-footed, being made to feel the aggressor, the unreasonable one, when they together – Bridie and Ruth – had transgressed not just against her but also against nature itself.

'It's as though they want to punish me for not sharing,' she told Thomas. 'Like, I have so many children, why would I miss one? Can't I spare one? No one would say that if one of your children was killed. "Well, never mind, you've got four more."'

Thomas had understood that too. That's what had helped her remain firm. It was twelve years since her mother had seen the children.

Coming to the T-junction, Laura takes the Newick road. Six months after Grace left hospital, Alan and Ruth moved. Parcels meant for Grace were returned, marked 'Gone Away'. Laura – secretly now, for she cared about the feelings of her husband and the four children at home – went to the London house. It was locked and empty. She peered through the drawing-room window. There was soot in the grate and the carpets had been taken up. On the bare floorboards were some scraps of newspaper and the plastic arm of a doll. Laura laid her head on the window-glass. A passing stranger stopped to ask if she was all right.

Laura rang her mother.

'Tell me where they've gone.'

'No,' said Bridie.

'If I put the phone down now,' said Laura, 'I'll never pick it up again.'

'I'm sorry,' said Bridie, Laura's mother.

In twelve years Laura had heard nothing. Not how tall Grace was, how she was doing at school, what she was good at, what made her smile. Or whether she'd ever been given any of the thousand gifts Laura had packed up and sent via her grandmother. Brown packages for Grace's birthdays, for Christmas, for Easter, for Valentine's Day, for no reason at all except to let her know she was loved, that she remained one of five children who were considered each and every day. Parcels sent not so much to shame Bridie but to reach out to Grace, for the river would, as rivers must, return to the sea.

Turning into Bridie's road, so near the end of her journey, Laura sees the leylandii. The trees are so tall now that the house is obscured. My mother is still trying to hide, thinks Laura. But nothing can be tall enough or dark enough to shield Bridie now. Laura parks. This is the end of the road. Justice, truth, fairness, morality, happiness, all of them demand Grace's address. Bridie will give it to her. This time, at least, Laura will ask and Laura will receive.

She rings the door-bell, her foot on the top step, the toes of her shoes flush to the door. If the door opens so much as a crack, she will be in. She expects to have to wait. Bridie is an old woman now, she will move slowly. But barely is her finger off the bell when the door is flung wide. It is pulled and crashed open. In the hallway stands a wild, agitated figure. She bursts into the sunlight.

'I didn't do it. God help me, I didn't do it!'

Laura looks at the river of her daughter.

'Of course you didn't,' she says.

Grace falls then, sobbing, into Laura's arms. And Laura holds her, pulls the whole of Grace's gulping body to her, folds her in, tighter and tighter until, beneath the racking chokes, she can feel something bigger, something stronger. The beat of her daughter's heart. Her hand goes to Grace's head then, stroking the soft hair as she has stroked all her babies' hair.

'Of course you didn't,' she murmurs again. 'My darling.'

# 21

Ruth trembles as she puts the key in her door. Maybe, she thinks, I've not come home at all. Maybe this is just a house. For if Grace is gone, if Grace is still at Laura's, there will be a hollow chimney-breast where once there was a roaring fire.

'I left the lights on,' says Alan, indicating the glowing kitchen at the back of the house, 'against burglars.'

But there is nothing now to steal, thinks Ruth. She has tried to forgive her husband: for informing their daughter when she was a thousand thousand miles away; for having those tell-tale blue eyes ('Just think,' said Alan, 'she could have guessed years ago'); for not calling her at once, putting Grace on the line. But, then, what could Ruth have said except 'Sorry'?

'I'm so sorry, my darling.'

She had never intended to conceal the circumstances of Grace's birth. In fact, it sometimes seems to her that she has spent the last seventeen years trying to find ways of telling Grace the truth. As she lifts her case into the porch, Ruth remembers that first steamy bathroom attempt. Grace had been nine months old. Naked, her daughter was a voluptuous, a glorious creature. Ruth soaped her not for cleanliness but for the pleasure of running her hands over her daughter's limbs. She washed her face not because it was always dirty, but because when she touched Grace's lips, the child made delighted Red Indian warbles against the flannel. Everything enthralled Grace then, the sponge, the soap, the flannel, the little tea-cups drifting on their plastic saucers.

Grace even laughed as she was lifted from the water, taken dripping to a warm towel and snugged in. Ruth kissed her toes, raspberried her navel, stroked the nape of her neck, peep-boed her, whispered in her ear. The telling, Ruth thought, would be just another whispering, some other piece of love Grace shared with her mother. Ruth had even decided the words, 'You are my beautiful,' she was going to say, 'my most beautiful, my best-in-the-world surrogate baby. I adore you.' But that nine-month night, when she held Grace cheek to cheek, full of intentions and hope and the powdered fragrance of babyhood, she just couldn't do it. Said, 'You are my most beautiful . . . baby,' and burst into tears.

I'll wait till after the adoption, she'd thought then. I don't want to tempt fate, tempt God. I mustn't be hubristic. I'll wait. Just a little bit longer. Until it's settled, until it's safe. And wait she had. A whole year before she even sent the papers. It was July when she'd finally sealed the envelope, stuck on the stamps. All of it seemed dangerous. Actions, like signing a kidney-donor card, designed to court disaster. If the mouth of the post-box had been any wider she would have thrust her arm inside to retrieve the ticking bomb.

Four weeks went by, time in reverse, each day slower, each hour an elongation. Then the buff reply dropped through the letter-box. Alan had to open it, Ruth clinging to his arm, impeding him.

'She's ours,' Alan cried. 'She's ours!' Ruth had never seen her husband weep before.

Ruth hugged Alan and the papers. The euphoria was so intense she thought she'd burst with it. I'll do it now, she thought. I'll tell Grace right now! But she hadn't. Some part of her still resisted, the part that wetted her finger to see if Laura's signature was real, if it was made of blottable ink. Besides Grace was still so young, so vulnerable. Too young perhaps, maybe it would be better to wait until she was older, more able to understand. There was no question of keeping it a secret.

Grace's second birthday came and went. Ruth composed a few casual references in her mind. Then Sadie was born. Post-natally depressed, Laura started following them – in cars, on foot, she knocked at their door. It would be one thing to tell a small child that she had a second mummy, quite another for her to see such a woman striding madly at the edges of her life. Frightening for her. Those long, dark hands stretching. Time passed.

Then came the incident at the hospital and the suddenly launched, vitriolic custody case.

'Tell Grace who her genetic mother is,' said Bridie, 'and Laura will drop her claim. She will. She's promised.'

'Tell Laura to mind her own business. To leave us alone. Leave Grace alone,' Ruth shouted back. 'And tell her she'll never get custody!' That's what Ruth's expensive lawyer had advised.

'Maybe not,' said Bridie, 'but she could get access, visiting rights. Weekends, part of the summer holiday . . . Besides, we don't want it all through the courts.'

Later Bridie had changed tack. 'Talk to Grace and I'll help you move. You could come and live near me. It's an easy commute.'

As it happened, Pharmakon was just about to open a branch in Brighton, an association with the university. Ruth could apply for a transfer.

'There you are, then,' said Bridie. 'It's obviously meant to be. And we could build Alan a studio. He deserves a studio, don't you think?'

Ruth and Alan could be the disappeared. Laura would never know where they'd gone. Where Grace had gone. Grace would be safe.

Grace would be safe.

'All right,' said Ruth. It had always been her intention to tell her daughter in any case.

Grace was four and three-quarters. It was the Sunday before Easter. They had spent the afternoon painting eggs, Ruth piercing the shells with a needle and blowing the globular white and the sudden yellow into a Pyrex bowl. Ruth had sponged patterns of red and black, edged them with gold. Grace had painted a face with a lopsided smile, the blue eye dripping a little, the paint too dilute.

'He's crying,' said Grace.

'And smiling,' said Ruth.

They'd set the eggs to dry and cut a branch of apple blossom from the garden. Ruth put the blossom in a vase of blue glass. She cut lengths of yellow wool and threaded a blunt embroidery needle.

'Look,' said Ruth, 'we'll knot the wool. We'll thread the eggs and hang them here. We'll make an Easter tree.'

Alan had come in to see the eggs hanging, turning, twirling amid the pink-white blossom.

'Oh,' he said, 'how beautiful.'

'I did it,' said Grace. 'With Mum.'

It had been late by then and Grace had gone willingly for her bath. Ruth had washed her hair, tickled her dry, slipped on her pyjamas with the black Scottie dogs in the tartan collars. She'd taken Grace to her bedroom and sat her on the stool in front of the dressing table, blowing her long gold-brown hair till it was shiny dry. Then she'd put away the dryer and taken Grace on her knee.

'Look,' Ruth said, combing the golden strands of her daughter's hair, 'look how beautiful you are. Have you ever seen anyone more beautiful?'

And, shyly, Grace looked.

Then Ruth, her mouth in her daughter's hair, said, 'Once upon a time . . .

'Once upon a time,' she said, 'there was a mummy and a daddy who passionately wanted a child.'

'Is it a story?' asked Grace.

'Yes,' said Ruth. 'The most wonderful story in the world, because you see the mummy and daddy didn't just want any child. They wanted a really special child. Someone as beautiful as you, Grace. Do you want to hear this story?'

'Yes,' said Grace, snuggling, 'of course.'

'So the mummy and daddy began to look. But such special children don't grow on trees. So the mummy and daddy had to search a really long time. More than four years. And all that time the mummy's longing got stronger and stronger. And do you know what? The longing got so strong that one day it made a little egg, just like the ones you painted today, a little speckledy golden egg.'

'How'd it do that?'

'You can do that with love,' said Ruth. 'You can use your love to create things. And the mummy really loved the baby even before it was born. So the baby said, 'Right, I better be born, then.' But it was only an egg. So the mummy knew she had to find a way of keeping that egg safe and warm, so it could grow and become the baby the mummy wanted and the life that the baby itself wanted. And she thought the best place for the egg would be in her tummy. But there was a problem. Can you guess what?'

'No.'

'Well, she loved that baby so much, she couldn't bear the idea of not being able to see it every day, being able to watch it grow. Then, quite by chance, she met a woman with a tummy made of glass. That's the answer! she thought. So she asked the woman if she could borrow her tummy for a little while. And the woman . . . who was . . .'

'Are you all right, Mummy?'

'Yes. Yes, of course I am. Well, the woman was . . . very kind. You see, she was a special sort of person too. So she said yes. "Yes. By all means, I'll carry the egg for you." So she did. And every day the mummy looked into the tummy and saw how the baby was doing. And every day the baby got bigger and bigger and more and more beautiful. Until one day she was so big and so beautiful that the mummy cried to see her.'

'Why'd she cry?'

'Because she was so happy. Her tears were really big.'

'How big?'

'As big as figs. And one of those big, fig tears landed on the glass tummy and it made a kind of hole, a keyhole. And the baby, who was very clever as well as very beautiful, put her finger in the hole and opened the door. And oh, Grace, when she stepped out the mummy thought she would die of joy. Because inside the tummy, the child had been beautiful but all bunched up. But when she stepped out she was four times taller and four times more beautiful. She had huge brown eyes, just like yours, and the loveliest hair, exactly your golden-brown colour. And do you know what? The minute she was out she walked straight up to the mummy and daddy and said, "Hello, my name is Grace."'

'And that,' Ruth had finished with a handkerchief, 'is how we got you.' In the hall of her own house now, Ruth blows her nose. The story still surprises her, for she is not a story-teller. It was always Laura who, when Bridie turned out the lights, peopled the dark from her imagination. Always Laura, who sang her sister to sleep with mermaid songs and shell chariots and the silver fur of seals. Stories of which Ruth heard the beginning but rarely the end, for they would rock her and she would let herself drift into sleep so as not to be left alone when the singing stopped. If the singing did stop. For sometimes Ruth thought that Laura sang all night, a chain of notes that bound them safe and close till morning came and daylight could take up the refrain.

So, even now, Ruth is not quite sure where the egg and the glass tummy came from. It was not a story she had in her mind when she began, when she sat Grace on her knee that night in front of the mirror. It just seemed to be there at that particular moment, hanging in the air like a spider's web made visible only by dewdrops. And she'd simply recited what she'd seen, described something that already existed, though it had not existed before and might not exist again. When she'd finished speaking, she'd waited for Grace to react, thinking, Now the spell will break. But Grace just looked at her reflection in the mirror and said nothing. So the spell held. She understands, Ruth thought. For now, Ruth thought, it is enough.

Later, much later, when Grace still asked nothing, Ruth began to doubt herself. The story had become dusty, lost its magic. She could no longer trust the story or the story-teller. More than once she wondered whether she had imagined the whole thing, that there was, in fact, no moment of sharing in front of the mirror. Though she had said differently to Bridie. She'd had to. Her increasingly deranged sister had insisted on a statement sworn on Grace's life.

'It's obscene!' said Ruth.

'It's hysterical,' said Bridie. 'But why should you care? Just sign.'

And she signed, but not the duplicate copy Laura had so thoughtfully enclosed for her to keep. That she tore to shreds.

Years passed. Laura receded. It occurred to Ruth that it was perhaps appropriate now to talk to Grace in facts not fictions. And Ruth was good at facts, prided herself on them. She could tell twelve-year-old Grace the truth about the surrogacy as she had, without embarrassment, told her the truth about sex. But somehow the opportunity never arose. By the time Grace was fourteen, Alan said it was too late. 'You want to tell her now,' Alan said, 'not for her sake, but for yours.

Because you can no longer stand the deception. It is only your conscience that wants to talk.'

'Alan,' Ruth cries, in the hall of her house, 'there's someone in the kitchen.'

But it is not someone. She can hear voices plural. There are people in her kitchen. One of them is Grace. Ruth can hear her voice. Grace is there. Grace is home. Grace and . . . She flings open the door.

'Laura!'

The scene is intimate. Her sister and her daugther are sitting together at the kitchen table. They are so close their chairs are almost touching, their hands would be touching but they have their hands round mugs. Grace has an almost finished cup of coffee and Laura a half-drunk mug of peppermint tea. Laura is using Alan's night-sky mug. The one he made himself with cobalt stars. The mug that nobody in the house uses but him. She has it clasped loosely, lazily, as if there is no question that it is hers, that it belongs to her. Her head is inclined towards Grace, as if Grace also belongs to her. As if Grace is her daughter.

When Ruth enters, they both look up, taken by surprise. So deep has been their conversation, they haven't heard the car, the key in the lock, the footsteps in the hall.

'Grace,' cries Ruth.

'Ruth,' says Laura.

Laura stands up. Twelve years have etched lines in her face, made her thick blonde hair thinner, wispier. She is stouter too, though not fat, her curves just more ample, her bosom (Ruth cannot stop this thought) more motherly. It is a bosom to cry on. Perhaps Grace has been crying. She looks as though she has been crying. Her brown eyes are red-ringed. Laura's eyes, which are not red-ringed, are, Ruth notices with shock, precisely the same hazel brown as her daughter's. A spike turns in her heart. The years apart have made the two more similar. Apart, they have grown together. At once Ruth is back where she ever was, on the margins, at the edge. Laura is beautiful still, abundant still. From the floor of Ruth's being, rage and inadequacy well. Looking at her sister she feels what she has always felt: powerless.

Powerless because she couldn't conceive when Laura was so fecund. Powerless because no matter what she was prepared to risk (which was everything) or sacrifice (which was everything) or pay (which was anything) she could not grab control of her own life again, could not make a baby happen, when making a baby was the most ordinary, the most natural thing in the world. Powerless, too, during Laura's pregnancy for, at any moment, Laura could change her mind and keep the baby. Powerless at the moment of birth, when she saw the cord that attached the child to her mother. The cord she wanted to cut herself but couldn't hold the scissors for shaking, so the midwife cut it. Powerless all during that long, long first year before the adoption papers were signed, for Laura could still come to her house, pack up the baby (who was Ruth's life now) and take her away. Powerless when Alan said, much later, 'Look how much she loves you. You are her mother now. The only one who counts.' Because in the secret hurt of her heart she wanted so much to have carried this child inside her own body, to have laboured and given birth to her. And she needed Alan to know and accept this and he didn't.

As hollow as the day Laura – wild with grief – knocked on her door and asked for the child. For the idea that she had stolen her sister's child, which is what her sister's eyes said, was unbearable. Loss, after all, was something Ruth understood.

'Grace,' Ruth cries again. She needs to go to her daughter, for the child has been crying. She needs to put her arms round Grace and make it better. But Grace's tears are dry. Laura has dried them.

'I'm afraid there is some bad news,' says Laura.

But there can be no bad news if Grace stands up, if she walks across the room towards her mother. If she holds out her hands . . .

But Grace is motionless. Her head hangs.

If she simply looks up . . .

'Grace,' cries Ruth, 'I love you.'

Grace looks up. 'Gran's dead,' she says.


# 22


I've never been to a wake before. Never been awake in the wake of a wake. Never woken from one turbulent dream straight into another. I suppose I thought that when I looked in the mirror for the first time and saw my own reflection there that that would be the end of it. That that waking would be the last, that I would henceforth walk in daylight. But I have woken in some other place, somewhere between the vigil for death and the strip of water that churns behind a ship that would pass on by. Awake. A wake. Pass on by. Pass on.

I stand in what appears to be my own garden on an August afternoon. But things are not what they seem. There are people here who shouldn't be here. There is wind in the trees when the forecast was for still air. The groups are simply arranged, the ordinary patterns of family. That's how it's done. The sin polished over with politeness. Or, in this case, the sins buttered over with cucumber sandwiches with the crusts cut off. We are all smiling. We know the rules and no one will rock the boat, because there is a death. Bridie's death. My grandma. Whom I loved.

Laura is standing balancing a cup of tea. To right and left of her, flanking and protecting, are her sons Michael and Toby. Michael is twenty-six, a solicitor, apparently, though he looks more like a farmer: big, blond, outdoorsy. The sort of man who looks you directly in the eye. The sort of boy I'd have adored to have as a brother. Toby is smaller, darker, about twenty-four. He's a driver for some overland-tour operator. He's just returned from five weeks in a bus in Africa. He looks fit, restless and slightly out of place, in his not-quite-smart-enough clothes. Smart enough for whom? For Ruth, of course, through whose eyes I inevitably see him. This is how close I am to the woman who is not my mother.

'Grace,' said Michael, when we were introduced at the crematorium, and he took my hand and crushed it in his, smiling like it was some cocktail party. He held my hand a long time while his wife, Janey, looked on, stiff as starch. Then Jackson, their eighteen-month-old son, whined at his father's leg and Michael swung him up on to his hip and said, 'Hey, little guy, this is your aunt.' Toby just cleared his throat and said, 'Hi,' as if his long trousers had disappeared and his knobbly schoolboy knees had been exposed.

And now we're all in the garden. I say 'all' but Miranda hasn't come. She would have done, of course, said Laura, but she's a student. It's the summer vacation and she's in

Bulgaria, working for an offshoot of the Romanian Orphanage Trust. Manda is taking children from their cots, children who have never been held, and holding them. 'It's her way of "giving back",' says Laura. A remark that Ruth, welded to my side at the time, chose to take as an insult.

Sadie is very much here. Though standing apart, dark glasses on. She is neither protecting nor being protected by her mother. She is just standing. You cannot tell where her eyes are or if she weeps. If I had to guess I'd say she wasn't weeping and her eyes are on me.

Thomas, the man of the family, husband, father, is a tall, angular man. His eyes are for his wife only. Even looked over my shoulder at her when it was his turn to clasp me in the churchyard. Held me like I was some kind of chest pain.

Ruth, scanning the lawn, comes out of the french windows with a tea-pot. All her best china, the white with the scalloped edges and silver filigree, is set on the patio table. The cloth is lacy, old-fashioned. It looks like something Bridie might have had in a drawer. It's been starched and ironed and has the sharp creases of good housekeeping. The tea-pot is the fluted silver one that belonged to Great-aunt Mags. The one we never use, the one that collects dust in a cupboard.

Ruth pours tea for Flo and Bert, for Jimmy and Mrs Orpen, people who walked in the life of my grandmother. They are old, they sigh. It will be their turn next, they think. She offers them triangular sandwiches, plain biscuits and fruit cake without icing. Everywhere she goes she has a shadow. The man who calls himself my father. If she has the tea-pot he has the milk-jug. If she offers sandwiches, he has the biscuits. When she dips her head to hear the aged whispers, he leans too, nods when she does. Smiles her smile. But Ruth is not paying attention, not to her guests, not to her husband. Her sly eyes are on Laura. And on me.

I am standing by myself. Yes, I have got away at last. My back is against the fence, where the garden gate is. I am the mouse at the skirting-board. The eyes of the cats upon me. For Laura looks, too, when she's not wringing her handkerchief. They are watching for any movement. At the moment we are poised, an equilateral triangle, with me at the apex. But if I move, if I shift just a footstep, one way or the other, then they move too. They want to keep the distances equal. It's a dance where I'm not to be closer to one than the other. A chemical compound that can hold its form only if the atomic structure is minutely obeyed. Too much heat and the molecules will ricochet, the solid turn to liquid. To steam.

I readjust my body, shift my weight from my left to my right foot. Laura flutters. Am I closer to Ruth? What can Ruth see that she cannot see? Ruth can see the gate. Ruth knows that I may, at any time, unlatch the gate and walk through. Walk away.

Alan is oblivious to the dance, though close to his wife. So very close. He has his arm about her waist. He has made himself one with her on the lawn. Not a pair, not linked lives, but one undivided whole. The perfect circle that is man and wife. Mr and Mrs Alan Thomas. Faithful unto death. They are talking to the vicar.

The mouse could spoil it all. The mouse could jump across the lawn and squeak, 'Adele!'

But the mouse doesn't. Her mouth is made of cardboard. She's a cardboard cut-out mouse in a cardboard cut-out garden. That's what they've done to me. Made me flimsy. Made me feel that if I stick my whiskers out just a tiny bit too far it will all collapse around me.

Or, worse still perhaps, not collapse. That it will all remain the same. That nothing can make my father my father again, or my mother become my mother, or my grandma rise just one more time from her chair and say, 'Oh, Grace, it's you.' And come slowly – but with such a garland of smiles – to kiss me.

In life she divided us, but in death . . . Laura is standing at the edge of her sister's lawn trying to make sense of Bridie, her mother. She wants to be able to remember Bridie as she was forty years ago, when the woman who is now ashes in a chimney was bright and hopeful flesh. She wants to be able to visualise her mother smiling and feel that the smile is for her. But young Bridie is denied her by old Bridie, the woman she saw sprawled on the living-room carpet, her head askew.

Grace would not return to the room, sobbed quietly in the hall while Laura stood. And stood. Looking. Bridie, whose shadow had been so large, was such a shrunken thing. A dry bone of a person, awkward on the floor. Her head bent back, her hair as thin and gauzy silver as the fairy frock against which she lay. Her eyes open, staring. At her feet a tiny pair of pink ballet shoes. Her flesh, what there was of it, a strange parchment white, as if life had not just slipped away that instant but been gone a long time. A moth person who had closed her wings to hibernate but who had died of the cold anyway. A dusty presence you would pick up in a piece of tissue paper for fear of it coming apart in your hands. This woman, this mother, whom Laura had hated so much.

Laura wanted to feel something huge, something big enough to fill the space where the rage had been. Triumph or relief, perhaps. But she experienced only a thin pity. She knelt to take her mother's hand, forcing herself to feel the bones of the death, trying to clasp something more. But her searching fingers encountered only the ring. The worn band of gold that Mungo had given his wife on their wedding day and which she had never removed, not even after the divorce. Bridie's knuckle was swollen, arthritic, but Laura pushed the ring over it. For the ring was a lie like so many others with which Bridie had adorned herself. And Laura wanted her mother bare of lies, needed to come to something clean with Bridie, something stripped-down and naked. But there was no joy in the act, any more than there would have been in pulling out the crest feathers of a dead bird.

After that she sat by the body willing the tears to come. Dry-eyed, she unwrapped parcels, slid her fingers under yellowing Sellotape and pushed her nails through brittle brown paper. She lifted out yellow bonnets knitted of memory, bluebells pressed dry from a long-ago walk in the woods, a Christening candle which had been Sadie's. She touched again the velvet capes, which had never lain around her daughter's shoulders, and fingered the summer smocks whereon she'd embroidered her dreams. And still it was only Grace who cried. Out in the corridor.

And when she finally emerged to hold her daughter again, Laura thought only this: will Grace's tears fall so hard for me?

In the garden of her sister, Laura fingers the gold ring in her pocket. At the church the Reverend Donald spoke of his parishioner's pioneering spirit, her fearlessness, for she was, he said, a woman beyond her time. Things hadn't always gone smoothly for her, Reverend Donald, who was now in the garden eating egg-mayonnaïse sandwiches, had re-marked. But Bridie had always met life face on. She was strong, brave, loyal. Loved. She would leave a gap. Winnie had blown her nose then, and Flo, and some other members of the congregation that Laura didn't recognise. Ruth had also wiped a hanky behind her dark glasses. Even Alan had looked a little moist about the eyes. Slow, sanguine Alan. But Laura had remained arid as a desert.

So why is it now, as she squints across the lawn in the bright sunlight, that she feels the tears coming? Why is it suddenly so much more than she can bear, these people, known and unknown, chatting and eating and drinking as though they know how to incorporate this death, to make it just one blackish thread in the otherwise gaudy patterns of their lives?

'Gan,' says Jackson. 'Gan!'

'Not now,' she says, and gently pushes the child away. Her own children, Michael, Toby and Sadie, have begun to quip about the other guests. Bantering as they did as teenagers. She does not criticise them. They, too, are estranged, have no right emotions, no accepted role. What are they supposed to do?

'Mum?' says Michael.

'No,' she says. 'I want to be alone.'

She feels cheated, but of what or whom she doesn't know. Maybe just of the mother every child feels she deserves, the one who places her daughter's needs above all others. The sort of mother Ruth had. Maybe it is really nothing so complicated. Maybe she is crying only, and at last, because Bridie is her mother and her mother is dead.

'Hello, Grace.'

For the last half-hour Mungo has been chain-smoking and talking to Winnie. At his feet is a pale scatter of ash. No one can quite remember when Winnie joined my grandmother's household. Sometime cleaner, house-sitter, plant-waterer, cat-feeder and, more latterly, shopper and grass-cutter, Winnie came young and now she is old. Perhaps Mungo recognised her. It is possible that Winnie was around when he was still Bridie's husband, Ruth and Laura's father. Perhaps he has had to speak to Winnie because his daughters are ignoring him. Ruth, horrified to discover her father at the church, issued an icy invitation for him to return for the wake. No doubt she expected that he would refuse. But Mungo is here. He walked out of their lives and now he's walked back in. My grandfather.

'I loved your gran,' he says. He stoops, a big man unused to the weight of years on his shoulders. As a young man, I imagine he might have been like Michael, blond and muscular and very blue-eyed. But now he is bald and, behind his spectacles, his eyes are faded. He walks with a stick, a walnut cane as gnarled as he is. I feel tender towards him, not because of his appearance, but because he has owned Bridie as my gran. He has let just one of my relations belong to me.

'You loved her,' I say, 'and I killed her.'

Alan is in the kitchen making more tea. He has poured water from the filter jug into the kettle, carefully refilling the jug from the tap. He has put the jug back in its place by the bread-bin, but not before turning the serrated counter on a notch so he will know when the filter needs to be replaced. Ruth doesn't always turn the counter, thinks it's a waste of time. But small movements forward, measured advancements, these things are never a waste of time. Alan closes the whistling lid and sets the kettle on the stove. He turns on the gas and clicks the ignition button. There's a hiss and a flare of blue. The kettle is still warm from previous boilings so it is only a moment before he hears the first gurgles and then the metallic fizz and ping of bubbles bursting against aluminium. Steam is already beginning to escape from the closed snout of kettle, but Alan waits. He likes the initial seething of the whistle, its sibilance, the first hum, which rises in pitch and intensity to a crescendo of insistence. It is only when the kettle reaches its third note that Alan switches it off.

Ruth wants a plastic jug kettle. One that's quiet and subservient and switches itself off whether or not you're there. But Alan thinks you should be there.

'I've more important things to do than hang around for a kettle,' Ruth says.

But it is, Alan thinks, getting out the Lapsang Souchong, the being there, the taking time for and account of the mundane that nets and webs the big things, which makes it possible to function, to go on. That's why he's getting out the Lapsang and not the Earl Grey, which Ruth has asked for. Ruth will not notice, but Bert and Flo, for whom this pot of tea is being made, they will notice. They will think, Bridie made us tea such as this. They will smell the smoke and flowers and they will remember, as he remembers, Bridie who is gone.

Happiness. This is what flutters in Alan's mind. His moods come to him like this now, brief bubbles rising from the murk, bursting on him. Tired. Miserable. Baffled. But today – of all days – happy. Not a sturdy happiness, not as massed as miserable has been, just a brief stirring, a flurry. He put his arm about her waist and she let it rest there. Happy. His arm about her waist. Happy.

Alan goes to the fridge and takes out milk to replenish Aunt Mag's jug. He watches the creamy white swirl in the polished silver, swirl and settle. Ruth also let him take her hand in the plane coming home, allowed him to hold her fingers in his. Ruth has double-jointed thumbs. Even at rest her thumbs curve backwards. Alan stroked these curves – just lightly – with his own straight thumbs, while praying that the airline staff would forget the food. That the plane would crash before the stewardess reached him with her trolley and her plastic tray. Or perhaps that Ruth would just smile up at the woman and say, 'No, thank you,' never for a minute taking her hand from his. But, of course, they had had drinks and food and then she'd slept.

She'd tucked her pillow against him, pulled her rug about her singly, shut her exhausted eyes. He'd waited till her breathing had slowed, evened, before he'd reached out again, letting his arm fall across the sleeping curl of her, almost as if by mistake. She didn't stir. So the arm remained and, as he didn't sleep, it was there when she woke and turned towards him. Turned without breaking the embrace.

'If she stays with Laura,' said Ruth, 'I won't be able to bear it.'

'I know,' said Alan. 'But she won't.'

The kettle is boiled. Alan warms the tea-pot, though it is still warm, for the pleasure of pouring in the water and watching it lap and slap against the tannined interior. When the water is quite still he pours it away and then he spoons in the Lapsang leaves. The tea is brewing when Thomas comes in. He is carrying a tray with dirty cups.

'Gosh, it's hot,' Thomas says.

'Yes,' says Alan.

Thomas hovers uncertainly. He's a tall, lanky man with big hands, and arms that seem too long.

'Just put it on the table,' says Alan.

And, gratefully, Thomas sets down the tray. The stacked cups chink.

'Can I offer you a glass of water?' asks Alan. 'Or something stronger perhaps?'

Thomas looks at his watch. It is four thirty.

'Water, thank you. That would be very kind.'

Alan takes two tumblers from the cupboard and fills them with filtered water.

'Cheers,' he says, passing Thomas one and remembering how on the second day of Laura's labour they had gone together to the pub. We should have been friends, he thinks.

'Just go,' Laura had said, from the birthing bed. 'And you go too, Ruth. Nothing's going to happen.'

But Ruth had stayed and the men had gone alone. They'd drunk Caffrey's Irish Stout from tall glasses.

'What did you talk about?' Ruth asked later.

'Politics,' said Alan.

'Politics!' exclaimed Ruth.

It was as they discussed foreign policy that Alan had first observed Thomas's big hands, his long fingers, his beautifully cut nails and perfect half-moons. Clean white hands, not at all like his own tough, terracotta ones. But working hands none the less. Hands that knew muscle and sinew and bone.

After the third round they decided they should return home. Thomas had taken the empty glasses to the bar. When he rejoined Alan at the table Thomas had lifted one of those large hands towards the door in a gesture that might have meant, 'OK, let's go,' but what he'd actually said was this: 'Nearly over now.'

Alan hadn't mentioned this remark to Ruth because he thought she would find it, like politics, insufficient. And though, as he was painfully to discover, it had, in fact, barely begun, he remembered that remark and that lifting of hands as the thing that had carried him on, borne him out of the pub, making it possible for him to re-enter the house for the final hours of that interminable labour.

The tea is brewed.

Alan smiles. 'Not long now,' he says, as he lifts the tea-tray. And then, bearing Thomas with him, he walks back out into the bright afternoon sun.

'The thing with tree poppies,' Flo is saying, 'is that you can cut them back hard.'

'Really hard,' says Bert.

'Just a foot from the ground. They really don't mind at all.'

'So you see,' says Bert, waving a hand at the weeping mass of flowers in Ruth's border, 'you're saved.'

'Yes,' says Ruth.

Bert smiles and picks the last of the crumbs from his plate. He squeezes them into his mouth. There's a pause and then he says, 'Very good biscuits. Did you make them yourself?'

'No,' says Ruth.

'Bert thinks everyone makes their own biscuits. Just because I do.' Flo smiles. 'But people don't have time nowadays, do they?'

'No.'

'Of course, bought's just as good,' says Bert.

'Oh, just as good,' says Flo.

'These are delicious,' says Bert.

'Where do you get them?' asks Flo. 'If you don't mind me asking.'

'Marks and Spencer's.'

'Marks and Spencer's,' echoes Flo.

Ruth wishes there was another plate of delicious Marks

and Spencer biscuits because, if there was such a plate, she would cram those biscuits into Flo and Bert's mouths. Crumb by crumb she would pack their orifices, choking them with oats as she is choked with small-talk, with superficiality. For Ruth, who has waited so long, wants nothing so much as the chance to clean and clear her own mouth, to speak out at last. For there is so much that needs to be said, explained.

'You had seventeen years to explain,' says Grace. 'And you didn't. Now leave me alone.'

Thus has Grace stopped her mother's mouth, cut out her tongue. Left her biscuits and borders and a bleeding stump.

'Please,' Ruth has said, 'I beg you.'

'Sorry. Not interested.'

But Grace is interested in what Laura has to say. This much is clear. Ruth has found proof, a handwritten document called 'The Testament', penned by her sister in vitriolic black ink and sent first-class post. Attached to the paper a note: 'This is yours now, Grace. I want you to have it. It belongs to you.'

'Look,' shrieks Ruth to her husband. 'Look at this! She says I raped her!'

Alan looks. 'Where did you find this?' he asks.

'Never mind where I found it. Look what she says!'

'Where did you find it?'

'On the kitchen table.'

'If you did,' says Alan, 'Grace must have wanted you to find it.'

'Just read it!' says Ruth.

'No,' says Alan. 'That would be like reading a diary.'

'Oh, it's all right for you. You're nice "gentle" Alan. It's me that's the witch. I forced Laura. I raped her. I ripped her baby out of her arms, snatched her away and never looked back. She's the Goody Two-Shoes and I'm the wicked witch.'

'It's all lies,' Ruth has told Grace. 'It's just not true that I pushed you out that day in the snow. Viciously. Deliberately. Why would I do that? How can she say it? It's not even true about the nightlight. Laura broke that. She stood on it. It's a pack of lies from start to finish.'

'Lies?' says Grace. 'You mind about lies? About lying?'

'Look,' says Ruth, 'just give me the same chance as you've given Laura. Just hear me out. That's all I ask. Listen to my testament.'

'I know your testament,' says Grace, going upstairs. 'I've lived your testament all of my life.' She shuts the door.

What is Ruth to do? Annotating the text seems reasonable, fair. She takes a red pencil, one that makes thick, sticky lines like blood. She circles, underlines, scores out. She writes, in dripping letters, *Not true! Rubbish! Liar!*

'How could you do that?' says Grace. 'How could you do it?'

'The same way she did, she has. Laura's been annotating texts for you all your life. My sister and my mother in cahoots, plotting. Rumpelstiltskin. Don't you remember Rumpelstiltskin? "Something human is dearer to me than all the wealth in the world." The wicked, wicked dwarf's words ringed in ink.'

'Did you take away the seal book too? asked Grace.

'But that wicked dwarf had been promised the child. He'd saved the princess's life, you see. So he'd been promised. A willing promise. An oath.'

'The seal story,' repeats Grace. 'Did you take that too?'

'What?'

'The seal story.'

'I don't know what you're talking about.'

'Fine.'

'Grace . . . Grace!'

The front door shutting with a bang.

'Ruth,' says Alan, 'Ruth, my love, be patient.'

'Patient? How can I be patient when my sister has filled my daughter's head with poison?'

'Come on, Ruth.'

'Come on? Come on, what? How can you just stand there? Do nothing.'

'What do you want me to do?'

'Talk to her. She's your daugther too. Why don't you speak to her? She might listen to you.'

'Speak to your father, Grace,' Ruth says, when Grace comes in again, even though it's past eleven o'clock.

'I'm not interested in what Alan has to say,' says Grace, feet already on the stairs.

'Alan?' repeats Ruth. '*Alan?*'

Alan steers his wife away. 'Give her time,' he repeats. 'It is only a matter of time.'

But time has stopped. The clock is fixed at a quarter to four, the time at which Grace was born and not born. The time it was when Ruth crossed the Atlantic by plane, never getting any nearer. The time when she first saw Grace and willed her to rise and she didn't. A moment containing infinity, aeons of time holding nothing. The universe pulled inside out like an octopus.

And now Grace, who will talk to no one, is talking to Mungo. What is Mungo saying, what is he telling her? Grace is inclining her head, she's looking interested. Anger trembles Ruth's hand, she slops Mrs Orpen's tea.

'Sorry,' she says.

'That's all right, dear,' says Mrs Orpen. 'No harm done.'

It is almost forty years since Ruth has seen her father. At the churchyard he'd looked too old a man, too decrepit a man to hate. A bent set of bones in a shirt frayed at the cuff, the flesh of his mouth shrunken around discoloured teeth. But she couldn't hold that old mouth in her mind, suddenly saw only the white teeth and full lips of his youth. The lips that kissed Laura so many more times than they kissed her. The mouth that opened so wide and red in praise of Laura but not of her. The teeth that clamped shut on goodbye when she was only eleven, so whatever she did she could never right the balance. Never make up the deficit of kisses. Never deserve sufficient praise. For the praiser was gone.

And now he is back. Mungo is talking to Grace and Grace is laughing. Grace is getting chairs from the patio, so they may both sit down. And talk.

'Why have you come here?' Ruth had asked Mungo at the churchyard. Brutality, she'd thought, is something he understands.

'To pay my respects,' he'd answered, from vague, clouded eyes. And then: 'I was married to your mother for fourteen years, you know.' There was a gravestone beside him, he'd put out a hand to steady himself.

He's just a harmless old man now, she thought. Am I still to be frightened? His claim was just a courtesy, the dignity of an ending. 'Come to the house,' she'd said, standing tall, standing above him.

But now as she watches her father with Grace she knows he was after something more. The same something that Laura has come for and because of. Blood. Mungo has given himself rights because Grace is his granddaughter. What he is claiming is her. Because the red stuff that beats in his veins beats also in hers. The same red claim that Laura waves in Ruth's face. The same bloody flag run up the same blood-stained pole. Blood. The right to do nothing, to be absent, to care not at all and then to return, sweeping away everything but this. Blood. The one thing Ruth does not have. Cannot claim. The one thing that binds and ties until death and beyond.

For when Ruth is dead that will be an end. For her blood dies with her. Whereas Mungo's blood, Laura's blood, this beats on. And on.

In Grace.

Ruth puts down the tea-pot.


Laura, looking at Mungo playing grandfather on the lawn, thinks, Even now it is impossible for me not to be the child to this man. A child of nine thinking it all her fault. If only I had loved my father more, thanked him more profusely for his gifts, been more grateful for his returns, less traumatised by his goings. If only I could have been good. Really good. If I'd been a good girl, Mungo would never have left.

'You made me want to fill the gap,' she'd wanted to say to Mungo at the churchyard. 'To make amends. To fix the unfixable. To give my sister my baby. It all began with you.'

But, of course, she said nothing of the kind, barely recognised her father, in fact. Just saw an old man standing at the edge. An outsider in a group of outsiders. Someone who, after an interval, ambled up, cleared his throat and said, rather quietly, 'Huhm. I'm Mungo.' And then, when no one had paid him much attention, had repeated 'Mungo?' with a small question mark, as if he wasn't quite sure of his identity himself. And it seemed, when she finally brought him into focus, so very long ago that he had brought her rabbit pelts, that it might have been another life, lived by a different person. And that, as she continued to look at him, she felt no connection, good or bad, between them at all. It was as though she had no emotion left over for him, that they were just strangers passing by. Her and her father.

Laura turns from him. Where is Ruth? There she is on the edge of the patio, tea-pot still in hand. Laura watches the glint of the sun on silver. Mrs Orpen's cup wobbles on her saucer. From the sudden movement of Ruth's hands, the tilt of her head, Laura knows there has been a fumble, a splash. Ruth is not good at tea, at cakes. Laura should be serving. Laura should be playing mother. She thinks this without animosity of any kind. It is just that the sisters have always had roles and Ruth, in the funeral garden, has the wrong role. She will know this as much as Laura. But Laura, because she loves Ruth, will not take the tea-pot from her.

This is the astonishing fact that Laura discovered when Ruth returned from the States. Of course she had imagined what it would be like to see her sister again after all these years. It was impossible not to think of Ruth as she sat at Ruth's table, on one of Ruth's chairs, drinking from one of her cups. As she sat with Ruth's daughter. Who was her daughter.

Yet she had not listened for Ruth's key or Ruth's footsteps so was taken entirely by surprise when Mummy Bear burst into the kitchen with a look on her face that said, 'You have eaten my porridge, smashed my furniture and stolen my child.'

And Laura, who had prepared some sort of speech, a grown-up talk of hope and restraint and sharing and burying of hatchets (she had so much now to lose) had just said, 'Ruth.'

For when she looked at her sister she did not see the icon of pitiless greed she'd held like a mirror in her imagination for seventeen years, nor yet did she see a panicked, middle-aged woman. She just saw a child, a fierce, needy child. The same child she would stand in front of when Mungo yelled, the child she would tidy up after when Bridie was abstracted, or feed when Bridie forgot. The child she sang to sleep at night so that they both would make it through to the morning. Her darling. Her baby. Her girl.

Laura is crying. Ruth has put down the tea-pot and is moving across the lawn to where Mungo and Grace are sitting, talking. Laura moves now too. For one of them, her father, her sister, her daughter, surely one of them will comfort her?

'Come, come,' says Mungo, stubbing out a cigarette.

'It's true,' I tell him. 'I did kill her.'

Coronary thrombosis is what they wrote on the death certificate. They weren't, it seems, that surprised, although Bridie didn't smoke, wasn't overweight, didn't have high blood pressure. Unless, that is, someone raised that pressure.

'I was shouting at her.'

'Ah-ha.'

'I was yelling.'

'Mmm.'

'Screaming at her.'

'And why were you doing that?'

'Because . . .' And then a thought occurs to me. 'Do you know who I am?'

'You're my granddaughter.'

And I am, I suppose, whether Ruth's daughter or Laura's, it doesn't matter. I am his granddaughter. Here before me is a

genuine right-side-of-the-sheets, uncomplicated blood relation. I laugh.

'Take it from me,' he says, 'take it from an old doctor. A
person having a heart-attack isn't too bothered by the noise
around them. She probably never even heard you shouting.'

'She did.'

'Well. I'm sure you had your reasons.'

'Reasons? Oh, yes, I had reasons. Selfishness. Seeing things
from my own point of view. Generally being angry. Ag-
grieved. Forgetting that other people have a right to respect, if
not to life. Failure to remember there is always a morning
after, when it's all just a bit too late.' My voice is going
wobbly. I think I'm crying.

Mungo sighs. 'Bridie's granddaughter and no mistake.'

He's leaning so heavily on his stick I think he means to
plant it in the ground.

'Do you want a chair?'

'I want to tell you something. Something very important.
Look, I know it's not my place. But Bridie, it was the same
with her. Guilt, blame. It doesn't do any good, you understand. You've got to stop. Stop it now.'

I fetch two folding chairs from the studio patio. I place
them on the grass near the fence, their backs to the sun and
the mothers. Now there are two mice by the garden gate.
Two rats. For he is going to tell me something. That's
obviously why he's come today. After all these years. He
hangs his stick on the metal arm of the chair.

'Did she ever tell you about Alice Watling?' he asks.

'A bit.'

Then he lights another cigarette and he starts.

'Alice was a child with sticky-out ears. She went into
theatre for a routine operation and ended up dead. Bridie

185

thought it was her fault. That she could have prevented it, but she couldn't have. There were legal enquiries, hospital enquiries, all of them exonerated her. It turned out the child had had some "growing pains", rheumatic fever probably. Some viral infection not mentioned on her notes. But even if it had been mentioned she'd apparently been clear some three months or more. Bridie thought there must have been some arrhythmia, that if she'd only listened longer, harder, she would have detected it. She would have known. But there are some things you can't know. Some things which aren't there to be detected.

'Why your grandmother couldn't grasp that, I'll never know. In all other respects she was a highly rational person. "What if it had been Laura?" she said. But it wasn't Laura. And that wasn't the point anyway. It was like Bridie had her own undetected arrhythmia that Alice's death triggered. Suddenly she was beating in the wrong time to the wrong tune. Overnight she stopped being straight, fun, hardworking. She just wasn't the woman she'd been before. Not half the woman. She let it crush her. She gave up. While the enquiries were going on she was on paid leave. When she was cleared she just didn't go back. She had a failure of nerve. Said the smell of the hospital alone made her retch.

'I wasn't in the country when the hospital committee finally reported. Had just been posted to Lima. She could have come with me but she wouldn't, of course. Not then, not later. I started to blame myself then. That I should have been there, could have done more, should have forced her on to the plane. But you can't force people and you can't keep blaming yourself. Blaming doesn't help. That's the point. She let it get to her. She let it dominate her life. Both our lives. She wasn't the woman I'd married.' He pauses, coughs.

'So you divorced her.'

He looks up startled, as though unaware that I am beside him, that what started as an explanation has become a reverie and he's been caught in the act of speaking his mind aloud when he thought he was safely locked inside his own head.

'Actually she divorced me. Though I suppose it amounts to the same thing.'

'Then you walked out on your daughters, on your own flesh and blood,' he cannot possibly know what 'flesh and blood' means to me, 'and you never came back.'

'I sent money. I always sent money. But I wasn't allowed back. Once your grandmother made up her mind . . . Well. She could just turn a page. Wipe you out.'

'Like she wiped out my mother.'

'Did she? Ruth? I didn't know.'

'Not, not Ruth . . . Laura.' I stand up then. Both my mothers are coming towards me. My mother Ruth has, for an explanation, a plate of biscuits. Laura has nothing but her outstretched hands and her ungainly, sloping walk, which looks, now I think about it, not unlike her father Mungo's.

'Excuse me,' I say, and I unlatch the gate and walk out into the lane.

'What did you say?' asks Ruth, arriving. There is sweat like a crown around her hairline.

'Say?' queries Mungo.

'Say to Grace. To make her leave.'

'Nothing,' says Mungo. 'We were just talking.'

'Talking,' says Ruth.

'Yes. Talking.'

'About what?'

'I don't know. I can't remember. Oh, yes, I asked her to tea.'

'To tea?'

Laura arrives. She sounds like she's been running. Her breath is sobbing in her throat.

'Hello, my dear,' Mungo says.

'To tea,' says Ruth. 'You invited Grace to tea.'

'Or lunch.'

'Lunch?'

Mungo gets up and gathers his stick. 'I thought repeating things was the prerogative of the old,' he says.

'Get out of here,' says Ruth.

'Ruth . . .' says Laura.

'I said get out of here.'

'I heard,' said Mungo, dropping a lighted cigarette and grinding it in the grass.

Alan is coming across the lawn.

'Goodbye, Laura.' Mungo turns and then turns back again. 'Oh, Ruth, what did Grace mean when she said you weren't her mother?'

Ruth flinches, she cries out. Laura moves towards her. 'Nothing,' says Laura, and she puts an arm about her sister. 'Nothing.'

'Oh,' says Mungo.

Alan arrives. His wife is leaning, her body slumped against the sister she claims to hate so much. 'Vicar's going,' he says.

'Mungo's going,' says Laura.

'Well,' says Alan. 'It has been a long day.'

# 23

There have been three phone-calls. Three that Ruth knows about anyway. And now there is a letter. Another letter. A thick vellum envelope addressed in that distinctive, demanding black hand. It is sitting on the kitchen table. Unopened.

Ruth is in the study. With careful solicitude, Pharmakon International have encouraged her to work at home 'during this difficult time'. They have sent a 'Deepest Sympathy' card with white roses on. Ruth's assistant, Kate, has signed with kisses. Robert Woolford, Pharmakon UK's managing director, has also signed, no doubt on Kate's insistence. His signature is the squiggle of someone who writes too many cheques. Nor is Ruth forgotten in New York. Gloria Beckenhauer has e-mailed: 'One never gets over the loss of a mother. My mother died seventeen years ago and I still think of her every day.' Gloria's message finishes with a postscript: 'Sending this via computer suddenly seems rather impersonal. A flimsy apology for a proper letter. But I just wanted you to know, as soon as possible, that we are all thinking of you.'

Ruth is thinking of the proper letter on the kitchen table. It is typical of Laura not to have used a self-seal office envelope, but chosen (as she did for 'The Testament') the heavier glue of an old-fashioned lick-flap envelope. Through the open study door Ruth listens. But it is far too early for Grace. She

189

won't be up for another hour at least. Alan is out too. He's in the studio and is unlikely to return to the house before lunch. Time for coffee, thinks Ruth.

In the kitchen she sets the kettle on the stove. This is the one advantage of having a kettle that doesn't switch itself off. An automatic kettle always cuts out just when the head of steam is sufficient to do the job. As she waits for the water to boil Ruth looks out of the window. Anyone coming from the studio has to cross the gravel drive. It is really quite impossible to get to the house without making a noise. When the kettle whistles she flicks open the turquoise plastic snout and the whistling stops. The steam does not stop. It hisses and billows from the hot aluminium belly. Ruth takes the coffee from the cupboard and the envelope from the table. If Grace would talk to her, there would be no need for this subterfuge. But Grace refuses to talk. Ruth spoons a heaped teaspoon of coffee granules into her mug. But she doesn't pour in the water. There may not be enough.

The envelope is fat. There must be at least three sheets of paper in there, even allowing for the air. For Laura has not folded the paper completely flat, as Ruth would have done, neatening the creases with her thumb-nail. No, Laura's jammed the letter in any-old-how the quicker to lick the envelope shut and get it in the post. Laura is urgent. As urgent to share secrets with Grace as Grace is to share with her. The two of them talking, laughing. Whispering together. With the door shut.

This is how clever her sister and her daughter are. Their cruelty is exact. To exclude Ruth, who has always had a terror of exclusion; to imprison her, where she has always imprisoned herself, inside her own skull.

In the kitchen, vapour clouds the air, breathing wet on the

window-panes. In the hazy swirl, sunlight darkens. Ruth takes the envelope and a knife, the one with a rounded blade, so as not to pierce the paper. She thumbs open the gap at the top of the envelope, making a tiny pocket, a way in. Then she lifts the letter to the steam. At once the glue loosens. It doesn't resist at all. She barely has to use the knife, the flap is lifting of its own accord. She can see the first of the pages inside and, even upside down, she can read the black word 'darling'.

She moves too fast then, pokes with the knife, fumbles, her hands in the steam, her fingers wet. The ink smudges.

'No!' Ruth pulls the envelope from the steam. 'No!' She bangs it down on the table, her fist on the flap. What is she doing?

What is she doing!

The flap won't lie flat. There are ridges, creases. She scrabbles with her fingertips, presses, rubs. The moistened paper tears. It tears! Now she's banging with both fists. She's banging the table. The knuckles of her little fingers are red. Her bones are banging on wood.

Bridie said that the head was mightier than the heart. Bridie said that, if Ruth used her brain, calmly, rationally, she could sort things out. Bridie said it would all be all right. Ruth will telephone Bridie. She will do it immediately. She needs her mother's advice. She needs her mother.

The phone trills into life.

Ruth jumps, grabs at it.

'Yes?' she says, she shouts, 'Yes!'

'Hi. Is that you, Ruth? It's Roger.'

'Oh.' Holding on to the receiver has stopped the banging. The banging has stopped. 'Yes. It's me.'

'You wanted to know if there was any movement on the Simon Trevor issue.'

'I did? Oh. Yes. Yes, I did.'

'Confidentially, he's leaving the company. Usual notice period suspended.'

'Oh.' The kettle is still boiling, the steam in Ruth's eyes.

'We're paying him a quarter of a million.'

'What?' Ruth flicks down the kettle snout. She turns off the gas.

'Pharmakon are shelling out a quarter of a million.' There is a rise of excitement in Roger's voice. 'Well, that's just hearsay, of course. But you know me and Finance. I have my sources.'

Ruth is silent.

'I thought you'd like to know.'

'Thank you,' Ruth says. 'Thank you very much.'

Roger rings off.

On the star-sign note block in front of her, Ruth has drawn a pair of hands. But the hands are too small. They should be huge and liver-spotted. Big enough to squeeze breasts, big enough to grab a quarter of a million pounds for the pleasure, the privilege. Bridie says be calm. Bridie says be rational. Under the hands Ruth writes a quarter of a million pounds in figures. Then she writes it out in full, *a quarter of a million pounds*. She stabs a full stop. The pencil lead snaps.

'For God's sake!' she cries.

'Are you all right?' says Alan.

She didn't hear him on the gravel, she didn't hear him in the hall, yet here he is, beside her. Her husband. He has clay on his hands and a terracotta smear on his cheekbone. He must have wiped his face with his fingers, pushing away his fall of hair so he could see to work. Or maybe he was simply moving among his pots, brushing against the earth of his everyday life. There is a basin in the studio where he is supposed to wash before he comes into the house, so he doesn't leave stains, marks. This is how she's kept him out, kept him at bay. But now he's come in. Just as he is. And her heart leaps at him.

For Alan is something solid, something true. No amount of vapour can blur his certain edges. The world turns mad but Alan endures. He is honest, honourable. He does not knife open letters not addressed to him. He does not stretch his big clay hands towards the white breasts of young women. He is a good man. Good on the outside and good on the inside. Not a masquerade. Not a mask. A rock of morality in an ocean of iniquity – loyal, trusting, trustworthy. Precious.

'It would be impossible,' she says to her husband, 'to tell you how much I love you.'

Alan blinks. He stares. He says, 'Oh,' with his hand almost over his mouth. He leaves clay at his lips.

Ruth wipes her eyes. 'I don't think I've said it.'

'Said it?' he repeats.

'Said it properly. Said it enough. 'I love you. I love you. I love you.'

She comes towards him, puts her arms around his neck, her face against his. She tastes clay, sucks on it.

'I,' says Alan, 'you . . .' And then he stiffens. They are being watched. There is someone at the door. He turns, but does not break the marble embrace. Grace is standing, hand on hip, observing the sculpture that is her parents. Her unmoving eyes are on Alan's right hand, which is clamped to Ruth's buttock.

'Hi,' says Alan, and he pulls away from his wife, hearing a crack that might be stone or might be his heart. 'Hi.'

Ruth shakes herself, smooths her jumper. 'You're up early,' she says.

'Going to London,' says Grace.

'London?'

'That's what I said.' She opens the fridge and pours herself a glass of grapefruit juice. 'Could you lend me some cash? Dad?' She's rocking from foot to foot, legs slightly apart.

'Of course,' says Alan, reaching into his back pocket. 'How much do you need'?'

'Forty pounds.'

'Hang on,' says Ruth, automatically. 'Hang on – she has an allowance.' Money is something about which she and Alan have always been united. 'And, in any case, it doesn't cost forty pounds to get to London.'

Grace shrugs.

'Where are you really going?'

'London. I'm going to London.'

'Why?'

'Just to see someone.'

'Who?'

'What is this – an inquisition?'

'If you want extra money . . .'

'Forget it. I'll hitch.'

'I'll drive you,' says Alan.

'I said forget it.' She looks at her father. 'Dad.'

Alan gets out two ten-pound notes.

'Alan! We hve an agreement. At least make her say where she's going!'

Grace drains her grapefruit juice. She licks her lips. 'Alan doesn't care where I'm going, do you? Just so long as I go. Keep out the way of you two love-birds.'

'That's not fair!'

'Oh, isn't it?'

'Grace . . .' begins Alan.

'None of what's happened is to do with your father!'

'Oh, sure. Right. Silly me. Dad's the nice guy, isn't he? The gentle, caring one. The one that wouldn't say boo to . . .' It's then that Grace sees the letter. She picks it up. It is wet. It's creased. The ink of her name is smudged.

'You're unreal,' she says. She thrusts the envelope in Ruth's face. 'I mean, if you want to read my post, why don't you just do it? Rip it open?'

'Grace . . .' says Alan.

'Go on, rip it open! Read it! Why don't you?'

Grace tears the envelope open. 'Look, here we go. Dear Grace, well, darling Grace actually . . .'

'No, don't. I don't want to hear.'

'Oh, sure you don't. Like you don't want to listen to my phone-calls or monitor my movements or legislate on who I can see and who I can't. You're unreal – you know that? You're sick.'

'Don't speak to your mother like that,' says Alan.

'I'm not,' says Grace. 'My mother doesn't live here.'

# 24

Ruth is sitting at her dressing-table. She is looking at herself in the oval mirror that belonged to Eva, her grandmother. In her hand she holds a silver-framed picture of Bridie, her mother. A death exposes you, she thinks. A death shaves off a generation and puts you next in line. How will it be when I am just a photo in a frame, just a legacy gift of antique glass and maple veneer? How will it be? One asks too few questions of the living, she thinks. Or perhaps, stroking the velvet back of the photo frame, it is only after a death that one understands what needs to be asked.

Why did you do it, Mama?

She has her mother's small nose, her small bird-like face. They share the arch of their eyebrows, the intensity of their gaze. Though Ruth's eyes are blue, of course. Mungo's gift.

And why did you never complain?

For Bridie lost a daughter too. Laura. Bridie lost a daughter and four of her grandchildren. Yet she never said. And somehow Ruth never noticed.

Bridie must have been about sixty when this photo was taken, grey and beginning to be hunched about the shoulders despite her emphasis on posture, the straightness of one's back. She's smiling, slightly, and has a dimple. Just one, on the right-hand side of her mouth. Ruth has this dimple also, though she has not noticed it before. They both have three frown lines, light crows' feet and deeper lines that run from the base of their noses to the edge of their lips. Laughter lines, Ruth supposes. Her mother maps her. Her mother shows her the way ahead. For she will be as her mother is. As her mother was.

Was.

A woman who loved not wisely but too well. For surely this must be it: Bridie loved Ruth too much. Couldn't bear to see her hurt, hurting. Wished her infertile daughter to be fertile. Demanded it for her. Sacrificed and died for it.

No. Now Ruth is being melodramatic. But what else is there?

'I owed a life,' Bridie said once, shortly. 'That's all.'

But that couldn't be all. For how could Bridie have paid such a huge price for Alice Watling? One only pays such a price for one one loves.

Holding her mother in her hand, both hands, cupping her face, fingers on the velvet, so soft it might be hair, Ruth tries to go backwards, to remember the Bridie who loved Mungo and lost him too. So that all she had was her daughters. The two of them. Before Ruth made it one. Made her choose.

'You can't have pictures of Laura in the house,' she'd said to her mother. 'Grace is old enough to ask questions now.'

The pause was barely perceptible. 'Yes,' Bridie said. 'I see that.' And she would have packed away those photographs, if Ruth hadn't come first with her knife and her scissors, arriving on an afternoon when she knew Bridie would be out, because she'd just left her at the hospital, at the bedside of her four-year-old granddaughter. Ruth had let herself into her mother's house with the spare key, the one that Bridie hung behind the trug in the garden shed 'against eventualities'.

There were two photos in the living-room and one in the bedroom. Ruth had removed the frames, laid the leather and silver aside, taking care over the glass, laying it flat so it wouldn't break. Then she'd stabbed and slashed at Laura, ribboning her sister, slicing her into smaller and smaller pieces. Next she'd gone to the bureau, to the bottom drawer where Bridie kept the albums. She had removed a picture of Laura pregnant, Laura smiling, her white summer frock loose about her swollen belly. The point of the knife had gone into the fattest part of that belly. A clean cut and then a twist, Ruth carving a jagged-edged hole, the knife catching, tearing. And then, because Laura still smiled, she'd put the Sabatier through Laura's throat. Nor did Ruth spare the children,

jabbing scissor points into Miranda's eyes, chopping away at
Sadie's face, dividing the boys' heads from their bodies,
amputating Toby's arms, Michael's legs. Finally, when
Laura's family was no more than gaudy, dismembered
confetti, she had sat down to wait.

Bridie had walked into the shining carnage, scissors
protruding from Sadie's head, a knife in Laura's neck. She'd
looked at the spiky rage on the floor and the explosive
stillness of her daughter on the sofa and she'd said only this,
'Why did you let Grace out alone in the snow?'

And Ruth had relinquished then, as her mother must have
known she would, and she'd said, she'd yelled, 'Because I was
inside with Alan. Because we were fucking. Because even
though we can't have children we can still fuck.'

Bridie had not replied, though the slight incline of her head
might have been a nod. A moment later she was in the
kitchen, getting the dustpan and brush. Ruth never moved,
just sat and watched as her mother went down on her knees
and swept up the sharp strips, tipping the garish debris into a
Sainsbury's bag and tying the handles together.

'There,' Bridie had said, rising at last. 'All done.' The key
she picked up from the carpet and took outside to rehang in
its place, behind the trug.

Ruth is crying. She is holding her mother in her hands as
her mother used to hold her, stiffly, matter-of-factly. She is
weeping for her mother who never wept. For the woman who
came to her the night the surgeons said she would never
conceive and held her straight-backed until her blouse was
transparent with tears. Ruth's tears. For the woman who
tried to sort something that couldn't be sorted and whose
daughter never even said, 'Thank you.'

If Bridie was alive she would walk in now and put her dry

arm about Ruth's neck. Then even the silence would be comforting. But Bridie is not alive. Bridie is dead.

Her mother is dead.

Ruth takes a handkerchief from the silk pouch (Eva's pouch) in her chest of drawers and she blows her nose. She is Bridie's daughter and she knows what she must do. In the secret drawer of her jewel box there is money. Just a little money, kept 'against eventualities'. She presses the padded leather panel and the shallow drawer springs open. Fifty pounds in ten-pound notes. She takes them all. Grace will use the money to visit Mungo, to stay with Laura. Ruth would like to write a note: 'Darling Grace, love, Mum.' But Grace's mother doesn't live in this house. So Ruth just puts an elastic band around the notes, to keep them together.

Then she walks down the corridor and posts the little parcel under Grace's bedroom door. She doesn't think she could hurt more if Grace had sprung from her own loins.

But then part of the hurt is not knowing.

# 25

The front legs of a hyena are longer than its hind legs, so their backs slope. This is what gives the hyena that alert, powerful-shouldered look.

I touched every bowl as I came downstairs, scraping at them with my nails, picking the clay pocks as if they were scabs. I promised I would not look back to see if she was watching from an upstairs window. But I did look back and there she was, Ruth with her hunched shoulders and her panting mouth. The skin of a hyena's jaw covers the incisors, despite their size, but I saw them anyway, the flesh grinning, pulled back. She wanted me to wave, to signal, to acknowledge the five debts with the elastic band around. Stood there, panting.

So I was glad to arrive at Lewes railway station and get on a train full of strangers. A whole carriage of people who want nothing from me. Nothing at all. And I, who am so antelope shy, want to hug them all for not wanting to hug me. I want to adore and embrace them, tremendous with gratitude.

'I love you all,' I want to say to these strangers.

Perhaps that was my mistake, to say this to Laura, at the door of my grandmother's death. A mistake to let my need and my shock nestle between her breasts. Impossible to say to her afterwards, it might have been the same with any stranger, a neighbour, an ambulance-man. Just someone standing there at the right moment. But this is not quite honest. For there was intimacy, of course, as she took me back to my own home, and we talked and talked at the kitchen table. Or she talked and I listened.

*My darling Grace.*

I'd forgotten that hyenas like to hunt in packs. Yes, they hunt as well as scavenge. If they're hungry. And these two are very hungry, these two are starved. A hyena will carry off a sleeping child or attack an antelope. But they don't face their prey, they approach from the rear, effecting the kill by tearing open the abdomen.

*My darling Grace.*

I don't know how long it takes for an animal to die this way.

My darling Grace, A fortnight until I see you again! So near.

So far! I've already gone mad with a duster in your room and wandered around the garden wondering which flowers will be good enough, which in bloom. Stupid, I know. Sadie laughs at me. But I'd no idea I could be so happy. Or so scared. As if you might be just an illusion after all. That's how much confidence I have in my own ears and eyes! I was mad for so long – maybe I still am a bit. Anyway – I can't wait to see you again, hear you. I could listen to your stories for ever, there are still so many gaps, so much I need to know. Not just about the big things in your life but the little ones too, the details. Like how old you were when you first walked, what your first word was, your first memory (mine was picking an apple at Bridie's house, finding myself at last tall enough to reach a branch), who your best friend was, your favourite colour, what made you most happy, most sad, whether you ever had night-mares . . .

Hyenas don't just strip a carcass clean of flesh. They eat the skin. They crush the bones. The molars of a hyena are huge and its jaw action is more powerful than any other mammal its size. They are called 'nature's undertakers'. Their job is to clean up the dead.

I put away the letter. I'm alive enough for this at least. I just fold the paper up (quickly and not very carefully, crushing it a little) and jam it back into the envelope. Of course the pages stick out, a leering panting tongue. But I can put the envelope away too, bury it in my bag, popper it into darkness. Then I only have the howling – or laughing, as they call it – to disturb me.

Perhaps I am ungrateful. This is what Ruth says. But what am I supposed to be grateful for? I didn't ask to be born any more than Ruth did, Laura did. So while I can be grateful for life, surely I don't have to be grateful for birth? Do I? Do *I*? Am I really any less natural than a child conceived in the bed of its loving parents? And if I am a freak, is it to be held against me? I am a freak.

I'm a freak.

I'm not as you are, sitting on the train reading your newspaper. It's cut in blood on my forehead. Freak. Calculation. Aberrant. Monstrous. Inhuman. And if you were to peel away the flesh, layer by layer, you would find it etched in the bones. Other. Other. Not same. Outcast. Cast out. Only this is the trick. I have no bones. They have been crushed and eaten by hyenas. So the flesh you see is just a bloodless case, a little balloon of skin with a space inside. Just one more incisor, one more bite could pop it all for ever.

Here's a thought. Do I make up stories because they made up stories? Or because I need to assemble my own pieces in my own way? Because some of my jigsaw bits are upside down and I still can't find all the edges? Or maybe it's just my attempt at their game. The control game. If I am the story-teller then I can control the story. Can't I? Because, one day, I believe I can write my own ending?

'Do you have the time?'

'I'm sorry?'

'Do you have the time?'

It is the man with the newspaper asking. He looks at me and he thinks I look normal. He thinks I inhabit the same universe as he does. One where the rules are known, quantified and quantifiable. I look at my watch.

'A quarter to four,' I say.

'Huh?'

'A quarter to four,' I repeat.

He retreats behind his newspaper. The freak label on my

head is ablaze with lights. But this is what my watch says.

About ten minutes later we arrive at Victoria. According to the station clock it is eleven fifty-two.

I make my way across the busy concourse and out into the open air where the bus ranks are. The tube doesn't go where I'm going, apparently. I get out my talisman, the scrap of paper torn from a diary with the address written in wobbly old man's letters: First Floor Flat, 4 Lytham Road, Camberwell. I half expect that the building will not exist, that there will be maybe a number two or a number six Lytham Road, but that number four will be missing. That this is just one more fiction, a story told by me to fill a gap.

The bus comes quickly and the bus driver, not understanding how shaky my destination is, takes my money.

'Where is it?' I ask.

'Two stops before the hospital,' he replies. 'I'll give you a shout.'

London is hot and the tarmac shimmers. A light breeze flicks sandwich papers around the feet of people too busy to notice. Purposeful people who know exactly where they're going and why. It is the same on the bus, almost everyone but me has a season ticket, a pass, a passport. I cross and uncross my legs, fiddle with the strap of my handbag, buffing the fake brass clip with my thumb.

Soon we are crossing the river, Old Father Thames, wide, flat, shining. Despite the blue of the sky the water is brown, the colour of mudflats and stirred silt. If secrets had colour, this would be it, I think, this blind, dredgy brown.

South of the river the landscape and people become more chaotic, more diverse. Tall buildings scatter around railed green spaces. Density changes. There is something more casual and colourful about the movement of the city. People smile and shout and joke. There are more children, more black faces, there is more litter.

'Lytham Road,' shouts the bus driver.

There is a wheesh of air brakes and the glass doors shudder open.

'Across the road, first on your right.'

'Thank you,' I say, as I step out into the noisome air. A drunk slumped in a boarded-up doorway drains a silver can of Special Brew.

'Top of the mornin' to you,' he says.

I cross the road and here it is, as solid as its black and white corporation sign. Lytham Road. I trace the raised black L with my finger. What am I expecting?

'Expect nothing,' my grandmother Bridie used to say. 'Then you won't be disappointed.' And I wonder, as I walk down my grandfather's road, if this is something he taught her.

Of course there is a number four. A two-storey Victorian terrace house with grey flat-conversion buzzers. Most of the houses in this road seem to be flats now, and there is a dingy, transient air to the street. Though Mungo, so he told me, has lived here for more than fifteen years, ever since he retired in fact.

I press the top bell. There is no name on the yellowing card behind the Perspex, just the typewritten words 'First Floor'. After a short pause the intercom buzzes: 'Hello?'

The voice, clear through the electronic crackle, is a woman's.

'Hello?' she says again, as I stand, silenced, on the doorstep. 'Who is it, please?'

Who indeed?

'Mungo's granddaughter.'

'Granddaughter?'

'He's expecting me.'

'He is?'

'I'm invited.'

'But he's not here!'

Number four Lytham Road exists but my grandfather does not. This is definitely one of my stories.

'I'll wait,' I say resolutely.

'Well . . . Well, I suppose you'd better come up.' She presses the door switch and I find myself inside. The walls are whitewashed. To the right is the door to the ground-floor flat, Yale-locked, and ahead are stairs with dredgy brown carpet. I ascend.

The flat white door of my grandfather's life opens a crack. The woman has it on a chain. She peers through. A tan and crinkled woman, wispy grey combed from her face. She regards me, squinting a little through her glasses.

'I didn't know he had a granddaughter.'

'Actually, he has three.'

'Three!'

'Miranda, Sadie and me.'

'Three,' she repeats, this time rather sadly. 'He never said.'

'No,' I say. 'I don't suppose he did.'

'And he didn't say you were coming. Didn't ask me to listen out for you. In fact, I rather fancy he said he'd be out all day.'

I turn then, my back to the door, my foot on the top step once more. Expect nothing. Nothing at all. A little scrap of paper floats to the floor, writing side up.

'What's that?' she says. 'Pass it here.'

I pass her the wobbly address. She pushes her glasses

further up her nose and studies the writing, then me again. Then she unchains the door.

'Sorry to be so suspicious,' she says, 'but you can't be too careful round here.'

I don't move.

'Come in,' she says. 'Please come in.'

'Who are you?' I ask then.

She laughs. 'Oh, I'm just the cleaner. Petal Amb – Well, you don't need to know that. Mrs P., that's what everyone calls me. Mrs P.'

Not my step-grandmother, then. Thank God. I go in.

'What time did you arrange to meet?'

'Twelve thirty.'

Mrs P. looks at her watch. 'Well, it's only a little past. If he said – well, I'm sure he'll be back.'

She leads me to the drawing-room. The flat is linear, just a corridor with rooms off to the left. The plasterwork is plain, off-white at the skirting, yellowing to nicotine stain at the ceiling. The only decoraton is a pair of tribal spears wired like a steel kiss to the wall.

The drawing-room is at the front of the house, overlooking the road. It is a strange, aged, masculine place. And it should be dark; heavy as the elephant-footed table, dismal as the fifties sideboard and the grey-tiled fireplace, black as the grimacing pair of masks hung above the mantel, thick as the fug of cigarettes. But Mrs P. has pulled back the floor-length brocade curtains. She has taken down the nets and flung wide the windows. In the assault of sunlight only the ash dances, motes caught in the glare. The rest of the room lies stunned, an eye from which the lid has been cut off.

'Make yourself at home,' says Mrs P.

I sit down on the brown leather sofa, which creaks under

my weight. Slung over the wide arm next to me is a brass ring ashtray on a fringed leather strap, its metal base grey from stubbings. I can't stop myself scraping a gap.

'Not my place,' says Mrs P., 'but he should know better, him a doctor and that.'

As the room comes into better focus, I see a large wall-hanging. A dazzlingly embroidered monster with the faces of women woven into its long tongue and red tail. Under his arm the monster carries a dismembered head. Mrs P. sees me looking.

'That's a burial cloth apparently. Peruvian, I think. Cheery, isn't it?'

And I realise then that Mrs P. probably knows a good deal about my grandfather. And that all I have to do to lay him as bare as his room is to ask.

But I don't.

I sit quite still and watch Mrs P. go about her business. She is standing in the centre of the room in her neat pink floral shift presiding over an ocean of freshly washed and starched net curtain. Thirty foot of net falls from her ironing-board in graceful undulations. Her hot iron hisses with satisfaction.

'Big job,' she says. 'Only get to it once a year. Has to be done, though. They come down filthy. Of course, a lot of it's to do with the dirt outside. The city these days, you wouldn't believe.'

I make a noise like sympathy.

She nods and hums, gets on with her work.

And I ask nothing. Nothing at all about the life that has ended up in this room. For the life, I see, has been lived already. It is a fabric of places and people and colours and thoughts all its own. It's discrete, even close to completion. It is not amenable to young girls sitting on its sofa. It creaks.

'Have you come far?' Mrs P. asks.

'A little way,' I say. At least I see the irony now. Realise that what I responded to in Mungo was his disinterest, a relation who didn't expect anything from me. Didn't need anything. Hadn't suffered for me. Someone to whom I wasn't obliged, didn't owe a debt. And yet here I am, waltzing into his life, as though, in a moment, I could inhabit it, draw it round me like a mantle, be intimate with it. Poor man. No wonder he's absconded.

Mrs P. up-ends the iron. 'Oh, gracious me, I should have offered you tea. Would you like tea?'

'No thanks.'

'Something cold, maybe?'

'No, really, I'm fine.'

The pressing is at an end. Mrs P. picks up the long sprung wire on which the net curtains are to hang and begins the slow process of threading. The wire's plastic coating has stretched and split so that every few inches there's a rusty glimpse of metal. The curtain is made of just one length of cloth so it is an unwieldy job to lift and guide the material without crushing it.

'Can I help?' I ask.

'Oh, thank you so much.'

So I stand and help to veil my grandfather's room once more. Mrs P. and I work in time with each other, passing the material between finger and thumb, hand to hand, mindful always of the hem at our feet, trying to hold it away from the floor to prevent creasing. We make a glorious billowing thing, crisp but soft too, sweet-smelling and – from the outside – impenetrable.

'You just hold on, I'll do the ladder.'

Mrs P. ascends the aluminium steps with the angel wing

flowing behind her, one upward stretch and she has the eye of the wire over the nail.

'Keep it high,' she commands, as she repositions the ladder in the corner of the bay window.

'There now.' She eases and plumps the gathers before hooking the wire behind the second nail.

And still, in my hands, is a foaming sea of white. I unfurl it, unravel it to her, so grateful for the task. Mrs P. works with grace and an effortless dexterity, but she has to pull now. The wire fits exactly, there's no slack, and if she doesn't get the tension right it won't fit, won't reach to the final nail. I'm willing her to get it right, to lift the last few feet of cloth from my arms and hook them up in one perfect movement. She tests the line from the third nail, moves the ladder for the last time. Then she goes aloft once more.

'OK,' she says, beckoning.

And I reach tall, I give it to her, this thin membrane. This flimsy thing that divides my grandfather from the outside world. Protects him.

'There we go.' Her strong cleaner's arm presses the spring.

Returning to earth she spends a few minutes realigning the folds, checking for evenness, brushing away invisible specks. At last she is satisfied.

'Thank you so much,' she says. 'I don't think I could have done it without you.'

'No,' I say, collecting my handbag, 'thank you.'

'Are you going?' she asks.

'Yes.'

'But it's not even one. I'm sure he'll come.'

'I don't think so. You see, we are a family who hide, who run away from things. It's in the genes.'

'I'm sorry?'

'I'll let myself out.'

She follows me down the corridor.

'I tell him you came. He'll be so sorry to have missed you.'

I have reached the door-handle.

'What's your name?' she asks. 'You never said.'

'You said names weren't important. You said, "You don't need to know." I liked that.'

She looks crestfallen.

'Hope.' I smile.

'Oh, that's nice. Not many people are called that, these days.' She bustles around me. 'Can I pass on any message?'

'No,' I say. And then I change my mind. 'Just tell him not to worry. Tell him . . . the hyena is not coming for him. Not this one anyway.'

'Oh. Gosh. Well, all right.'

As I go down the stairs, I turn and wave.

'God bless,' she says suddenly.

On the street, I take a breath as deep as my lungs. I've been running for far too long.

And now I'm going to stop. Now I'm going to turn round and face some things.


# 26


When I was a child I had a teddy-bear called Noozi. I still have him, in fact, keep him on my bed, by my pillow. I don't remember what colour he was to begin with but now he's a muted blue-grey, his face almost flat, his stuffing so limp that if you hold a finger under his back he flops in two. When I was about five, Ruth, my mother, hit me with Noozi Bear. I cannot remember what my crime was, and I'm sure it was nothing more on Ruth's part than a sudden, never-to-be-repeated temper. But I still feel the rage, the violation, the simple impossibility of that blow. Noozi Bear hit me? It couldn't be. It defied and defiled everything Noozi Bear was – that impenetrably private and secure place of perfect love. This is what I am thinking as I walk down the path to Adele's front door. I put my key in the lock and turn, at least I turn but the lock does not turn. I try again. And again. I thought being grown-up meant accepting that your Noozi Bears will hit you. Now I see that I have to accept something else, something more. That they can keep on hitting you. It's five minutes before I find the courage to ring the bell.

Julie sticks her head out of an upstairs window.

'Oh, it's you. She's moved out. Gone to Elaine's. Didn't she say?'

The relief is like laughter. Not Adele changing the locks on me, but Julie locking us both out, making us partners in exclusion. Hope flying out of Pandora's box after all. I give Julie a cartoon wave, my grin larger than a planet. Julie bangs the window shut. I hear it but I don't see it because I've already turned, I'm on my way again. It's four thirty now and I have been travelling all day, but as I return to the station I feel only anticipation, I'm getting closer, there has to be an ending. I'm on the right track.

Elaine lives in Eastern Terrace, a stuccoed strip of houses right on the seafront. It's only a thirty-minute walk from the station but my need to arrive is now imperative so I take a bus. Elaine lives at number four and her bell is the top one.

'Yeah?' And there it is, my destination. Adele's voice. The lilt of it. Flip, casual, bored. Adele home and, despite everything, my heart leaping.

'Hi. It's me. Grace.'

'Jees.'

A pause. My body pressed against the door.

'What kept you?' Adele lets me in.

After the glare outside it seems dark in the hallway, and it takes a moment for my eyes to focus the black and white flagstones, the curving banisters of polished wood and, directly opposite, the lift. It's one of those rickety, grilled lifts, which are panelled inside and smell of dust and cold carpet. I get in and clang the doors shut behind me, press for the top. Time retreats as I whir and grind three floors.

Adele is waiting on the landing.

'Babe!'

And all of a sudden I don't trust myself, can't quite bring myself to look at her, don't know whether I'm going to shout or cry. So I fiddle with the lift doors, taking excess care to ensure they are both closed properly, inner and outer, rickety and solid.

'D'you know?' Adele says, watching. 'I think I've missed you.'

'You have?'

I turn to see her beckoning smile, her ironic open arms. Habit, need, intimacy, all of it, propels me forward. It is so easy, after all, to walk towards her, to let her take me in. Beneath her thin white camisole, I feel her nipples hard as nuts. Around her neck is the sweet trail of Impulse. Adele changes her perfumes as often as she shoplifts, but Impulse remains a favourite. I inhale all the evenings we have spent together, the nights I have watched her dance. My mouth is so close to her neck I can taste her skin. The perfume bitter, the flesh salty-sweet.

'Come on.' The embrace is over, swift and, for Adele perhaps, perfunctory. She ushers me in and leads me up the final flight of stairs to the landing of Elaine's rooftop flat.

'Make yourself at home,' she says.

Elaine works in the Abbey National by day and the Tip Top club by night. The Tip Top is a karaoke place and Elaine waitresses and sings. Her flat is an extension of her divided personality, 'Acetate blouse meets fishnet stocking', as Adele once put it. The living-room is neatly tended pot-plants and abandoned takeaway cartons, suburban green carpet, a sofa from a skip and two blow-them-up-yourself zebra-striped plastic balloon chairs. Of course, some of today's takeaway containers (Chinese) will be Adele's. Just as the clothes, which I have to move in order to sit down, are Adele's. She's obviously having one of her try-on sessions, big boots and purple satin or silver shimmer and blue chain-mail? Decisions for tonight. That means she will be going soon, leaving. I let the gauzes run through my fingers, scent Adele again through their silken pores, familiar as sweat.

'So you moved out,' I say. Under my weight the zebra chair sighs, a long contented breath, like someone putting their feet up after a hard day's work.

'Moved on. Gotta grow up sometime, girl.' She smiles.

'How's Carl?'

'Carl?' Adele goes to the table where the budgie cage is. She pushes her fingers through the bars and pulls out the budgies' mirror. She turns her face to left and right, purses her lips, observes her profile in the shining disc. 'Carl who?' She lets the mirror go. It's on elastic and pings back on to metal,

juddering the cage and startling the birds. 'Now, if you were
to ask about Stewart . . .'

'How's Stewart?'

'Whoohoo . . . Stewart is . . . dream-topping with knobs
on. And when I say knobs, I mean knobs! Has a body to die
for. Gym instructor. Muscles in places other men don't even
have places. And he gleams – just gleams, like you rubbed
him in baby oil. Which I just might have done . . .' As she
talks, laughs, Adele begins to move, she can't help herself,
illustrating her points with her hands, the undulation of
them, the rub of her tongue against her lip, her teeth. 'Even
you would have trouble keeping your mitts off him,' she says,
and then breaks off suddenly, jabbing a blue nail at me. 'Hey –
what sort of friend do you call yourself?'

'Huh?'

'Your gran. I read it in the newspaper. Snuffed it, didn't she,
and I read it in the paper.'

'Yes, she died.' An edge, a warning sharpness to my voice.

Adele shrugs. 'I always wanted grandparents.'

'You never had any?'

'Well, not any that admitted as much.' Again that laugh.

And me ashamed, of course. 'I should have told you, only a
lot of things have happened.'

'Yeah?' Adele flings herself down on the second zebra-
striped chair. 'Such as?' And when I don't answer immediately she says, pulling to an upright, scrabbling against the
plastic in her excitement, 'You don't say, you didn't, you
haven't finally done it? You have, have you?'

'No,' I say, 'no. No.'

'Oh.' Her little nose wrinkling. 'What, then?'

'I found something out.'

'You did?'

I pause, leave a gap for her to jump into, but she doesn't jump, just sits and waits, her face unclouded. Somewhere deep inside me gladness blossoms.

'I've got two mothers.'

'Two mothers?' She whistles. 'Jees. One's bad enough.'

She listens to my story in complete silence, her legs curled tight beneath her. When I come to a stop she says, 'That's revolting. That's the most disgusting thing I ever heard.'

'Hang on . . .' I say.

'Oh, no disrespect, babe, but, well, if you can't do it like God intended, then . . .'

'Then what?'

'Well, jerking off in a cup for your sister-in-law . . . It's not right, is it?'

'Not right?'

'Not natural.' Absently, she pulls at the air teat of the chair, flicks it with her nails. ' "I fuck therefore I am." I read that in a lavatory. "They did it in a plastic cup with a turkey baster." Hasn't got the same ring to it, has it?'

'Adele, please – it matters to me where I came from, how I came.'

'Why?' Adele's face is a moon of surprise. 'You're here, aren't you?'

'But that "revolting " stuff, as you see it, is part of me. My freaky past. My history. Me.'

'Hey – what happened, happened. History, to use your word. Past. Gone. Done with. Finished.' She picks a Baltidome menu from the floor, reconcertinas it. 'Besides,' she says, suddenly tearing off the back page, 'who's going to know?'

'Well, you know.'

'Well, I'll forget.'

'It'll come out. Things come out.'

She looks at me. 'No, they don't. At least, they don't have to.' She stands up, screws up the Baltidome menu into a ball and puts it in the bin. 'What the eye doesn't see the heart doesn't grieve over.'

I'm silent.

'Look, Grace, if God wanted you to have a miserable life, why'd He give you a cunt?' She laughs. 'Mind you, with you it was a bit of a long shot, I agree.' She raises a hand aloft. 'Poor God, didn't have a clue what He was up against.'

And that's it. The world set to rights.

'Can we go on the deck, Adele?'

Adele looks at her watch. 'OK.'

Attached to Elaine's flat is a very small balcony. For some architectural reason I have never understood, it juts out from the living-room window at sill level. This means that not only do you have to climb out of the window to get on to it, but also, when you're in the room, the height of the balcony wall obscures the road and the promenade below. So being in Elaine's living room is like being on the prow of a ship. All you can see ahead is sea and sky.

Adele pushes up the sash window and we both climb out. The concrete wall is whitewashed, the balcony both secure and sheltered. At once Adele strips off her camisole and her sharp breasts bob as she turns to plump up an orange cushion, relic of some previous homage to the sun. She lies back and closes her eyes. I sit at her feet. The sun is still brilliant on the sea and the wind has scalloped a million gold coins on the surface. Somewhere in that sea is my father's penknife, dropped sharp through the pier slats by me, but blunt now from rubbing on rock. I take Adele's feet and unstrap her sandals. Her feet are bony and the skin hard from ill-fitting

216

shoes. Her impeccably filed and shaped toe-nails are, today, aquamarine. I begin by rubbing my own hands, to get them warm. For even in summer I have cold fingers. Then I begin to massage, starting at the balls of the feet, keeping the pressure firm to avoid tickling. But Adele squirms none the less.

'Tell you what,' she says, 'even Stewart can't do this.'

I move up and over her feet, around her arches, into the hollow behind her anklebones, and then back, in small sweeping strokes, to her toes. I use both hands simultaneously, to grip and to keep the flow, my thumbs working in circles, pressing and easing, feeling the familiar ridges and roughnesses of her heel, the pair of pinprick callouses on her fourth toe. I also honour the thinner, more supple skin, the little webs between her toes, the delicate blue veins that fan over bone. I take time at the joining places of hard and soft, passing from one to the other with my stroking fingers, making no distinction between the two. Before I move from her left to her right foot, I pause a moment, my hands a complete circle about the foot I'm about to leave, holding it hard and still and warm. Just as always.

'Does it really upset you?' she asks.

'No,' I say. And in that moment, sitting cross-legged on the balcony, with the glittering skin of the sea and the hard bone of Adele, it doesn't. And it seems to me then that only Adele has ever been able to rouse me from myself, and that's why – though I don't forgive her – I can never stop loving her.

# 27

'Never underestimate the dead.'

I can't remember when I first heard Bridie say that but now it runs through my head like a refrain. She's left her house and her money – of which there is not very much – to be divided equally between her daughters. But all her possessions, her personal effects, she has left to her grandchildren: to Michael, Toby, Miranda, Sadie and me. We are to gather, so instructs her will, at her house on a day agreed between us all. No other person is to be present. If any child fails to show, their portion is forfeit.

Michael's job precludes a weekday meeting and there is only one weekend between Manda's return from Bulgaria and Toby's departure for Namibia. Sadie has some engagement on the Sunday, so: 'Saturday suit you, Grace?' It is Michael who asks, formal, solicitous, taking charge. Michael to whom the executing solicitor gave the keys.

'I'll order a skip,' says Michael. 'There's bound to be stuff we need to junk. And a removal van for late afternoon, get it to do a round robin.'

So I have prepared myself to see, in Bridie's driveway this morning, the giant yellow bin which is to gorge on my grandmother's life, but Michael's maroon Mondeo is a shock. I had wanted – needed – to arrive first.

'Are you sure you'll be all right?' Ruth asks, dropping me at the gate.

'Yes,' I say.

And I am all right as I walk up the drive in the shadow of the leylandii. But then there is the door. Open. On the latch. Just as it was that day. As I cross the threshold Bridie falls again. Her body arching, thrown back in a curve, snapping like the neck of a bird.

I pause by the umbrella stand. The door to the drawing-room is shut, so at least I am able to cross the hall. They are in the kitchen. I hear them. Not just Michael but Sadie also. Of course it makes sense for him to have driven her down, for them to have come together. Brother and sister.

'Hi, Grace,' says Michael, rising from Bridie's chair at the head of the table. 'Come in. Take a seat.'

Sadie smiles, her mouth a line. In my grandmother's place Michael's body looks too large. It sprawls.

'Help yourself,' says Michael.

They have brought croissants and put them on the blue platter. The one my father made for Bridie, the one she only ever used for cheese.

'No thanks.' And then, because I sound abrupt, 'I'll just have coffee.'

'Tea's in that gold and black tin, but we couldn't find any coffee.'

I go to the walk-in larder. It's chill and untouched. Bridie's neat stacks of tinned tuna, the fleur-de-lis biscuit barrel for her wafer-thin Cheddars, a slab of unsalted butter still on its white china plate. As though she'd just stepped out. As though it will be but a moment before she's back. I take the tiny jar of Nescafé from behind the tangerine segments. 'She didn't really drink coffee,' I say, coming back into the warm, shutting the door behind me. 'Only kept it for guests.'

'Hallelujah,' says Sadie. 'I was about to expire from caffeine withdrawal.'

I switch on the kettle, take cups from the dresser, open the coffee. There isn't much left and what there is has fused together to form a shiny brown crust. This means, as I was one of her few guests to demand coffee, that I must have neglected her in the months before she died. I take a knife, hack at solidified granules.

'Terrific,' says Sadie, as I chip a dry triangle into her cup.

'She'd probably have got fresh,' I say, 'if she'd known you were coming.'

'Come on,' says Michael.

In the driveway there is the sound of a car.

Sadie goes to the window. 'It's them.'

Them. Two again. Toby and Manda. The four of them. Coming in pairs.

Michael and Sadie both go into the hall. I go as far as the doorway.

'Hey, Manda, how was it? How the hell was it?' Sadie launches herself at her sister. They kiss, holding each other tight.

'Hi. Hi, gang.' Manda is taller than me and thin, her mouse-brown hair held from her face in clips. Her face is rugged and exhausted but her eyes are a throw of diamonds.

'Hi, Michael!'

His bear-hug big, easy, fond. He pulls her round to face me: 'This is Grace.'

Manda stands and looks a moment, simultaneously shaking her head and smiling. A rainbow of herself. A bridge. Sunshine and showers. 'I've imagined this so many times . . . wanted it so much . . . and now, I really don't know what to say . . . except welcome. Oh, welcome, Grace.' And she puts her arms about me.

She's wearing a thick khaki shirt, which smells of detergent and dried sweat. Her loose olive green trousers are held on her thin waist by a large black leather belt. She pulls me so close the buckle digs into my stomach. I think of her taking children from cots in Bulgaria and hugging them too. Maybe my absence of response is not so odd to her.

She releases me.

'Hi,' says Toby, clearing his throat. 'Nice to see you again.'

'Hi,' I say.

'God bless Grandma for this,' says Manda. 'God bless her for this, at least.'

Sadie tap-taps at the door of the grandfather clock. Tap tap.

Then Michael says, 'Croissant, anyone?' and directs everyone past me into the kitchen.

I remain in the door-frame, stiff as the door-post.

'Go on, then,' says Sadie to my sister. 'Tell us, what was it like?'

The four of them open drawers, get plates, knives, cups. They clatter, laugh, talk over each other. Manda pulls on Michael's sleeve: 'Do you know? It smells just the same. Don't you think? Like we could just open the door to the dining-room and there it would all be, the lunch Mum made us leave on the table.'

'Roast lamb,' says Michael. 'With rosemary she picked from the garden. And those crispy roast potatoes. I was starving.'

'Anyone's name on that *pain au chocolat*?' says Toby.

'Yours,' says Sadie. 'Of course. The almond is for Manda.'

'God. Food,' says Manda. 'It seems a little obscene. I'm not

221

sure I could. Croissant, Grace?' she calls at me.

'I can smell cabbage,' says Toby.

'You can't,' say Michael.

'Remember how she always made you eat something green? Couldn't just have carrots. "Carrots *and* broccoli, young man,"' Toby mimics.

'It was great, Sadie, but totally knackering.'

'I don't s'pose there's any butter?'

'Grace, aren't you having any? Coffee?'

'Boy.' Toby swings a string of vegetables which hang against the wall, carrots and onions made of coloured straw. 'I used to love these, God help me.'

'You should see the other rooms,' says Michael. 'Twelve years and almost nothing has changed at all. Remember the toasting fork?'

'The toasting fork,' shrieks Manda. 'Oh, my God, the telescopic toasting fork!'

'Bags I the toasting fork,' says Toby.

Laughter rolls between them like a wave.

I force myself, push myself in – get as far as the draining-board. The brass toasting fork, which Bridie kept with the fire irons. The prongs shaped like Neptune's trident, the brass ring which you could pull to elongate the handle, four tubes of metal slotting exactly inside each other. Cutting a slab of bread ('Really, Grace, that's a bit of a doorstep') and spearing it on, waiting for the flames to dull to a red glow. Holding the bread over the heat, not resting the fork on the grate, but holding, turning, watching the bread darken, the golden scent of the baking lifting into the room, a warmth to take the chill from winter.

'Was toasting bread part of your childhood, Grace?' asks Manda.

'Part of my life,' I say.

They are quiet then.

'Look,' says Michael. 'This isn't going to be easy.'

'It's OK,' I say.

'Why don't we just give Grace first choice in everything?' says Manda, simply. 'I'm sure it's what Bridie would have wanted.'

'Dead right,' says Sadie, flashing me a look. 'Grace Thomas. Grandchild of choice.'

'Sadie . . .' begins Michael.

'Bringing the five of us together,' I say, quickly. 'That's all Gran wanted.'

'And what do you want?' Michael asks of me.

'I don't know.'

There is an awkward pause.

'Did you really never know about us?' asks Manda.

'No.'

'I saw you born,' says Manda. 'I was five. When Ruth took you away she gave me a doll. Took my baby sister and gave me a doll.'

Four pairs of eyes stare at me. 'I'm sure she meant it kindly,' I say, door-post solid.

'Look,' says Michael again. 'We've got less than a day and it's a big job. We ought to get on. Any suggestions on how to proceed?'

'Why don't we do it room by room?' says Toby. 'I mean, we probably won't all want the same stuff anyway. If someone wants something and no one else does, fine, it's theirs. If there's more than one claim – well, we negotiate.'

'Sounds good to me. Manda? Grace? Sadie?'

There's general nodding.

'Right, well, why don't we give ourselves half an hour to

look round and then meet back down here?'

Michael leads us to the drawing-room. I follow gratefully close, knowing that if I don't go in with them I won't go in at all. Someone, Laura presumably, has tidied up the parcels from the chest. The clothes, the Red Riding Hood cape, the fairy frock, the baby smocks are carefully folded beside the shoes. The books are stacked again. The shells and rocks gathered together in neat handfuls. When she fell Bridie scattered everything, falling with mussel shells and starfish, clipping her head on the corner of the bureau, flumping down, air from a sack, blood on the fairy gauze. Blood which must have leaked, seeped. There's a small brown stain on the carpet.

'Jesus Christ,' says Toby, 'my Pluto toothbrush!' He crouches down and extracts the splayed specimen from a pile that includes a Noddy egg-cup, a harmonica and a cross-stitched mat. 'Boy, were you lucky to get this!'

'Only I didn't get it,' I say.

Manda picks up the red velvet cape, rubs it against her cheek. She fingers the silver gauze. 'Oh, Mum,' she says.

'Obviously,' says Michael, indicating the piles, 'all that's yours. Supposing you want it.'

'No one in their right mind could turn down this tooth-brush.'

'Shut up, Toby,' says Manda.

Toby moves to the fire, picks up the toasting fork and pulls it full-length.

'*En garde*, pussycat!'

Sadie, at whom he points it, laughs.

Michael runs a hand over the bureau. 'Remember how she used to hide the fifty ps?'

'Yeah,' says Toby. ' "Going-home money." I remember that.'

'Bet I only got ten p,' says Sadie.

'You didn't get anything. You were only a baby.'

Michael pulls out the oak runners and lifts down the bureau lid. 'This was my favourite place.' He removes the central drawer and pushes his large hand into the cavity behind. 'Secret spaces. Gran's forte. Oh-oh, what's this? His fingers have found sharp edges. He extracts photos.

Manda comes to look. 'Boy,' she says to her brother, 'your haircut.'

Boy. A verbal tic. Like their physical tics, the way they blink when they're excited, the way they use their hands, the same flick of the wrist, an open-palmed exclamation. ('That's cute that,' says Adele to me. 'Like a little wave. Why d'you do that?')

'Speak for yourself,' Michael says, thrusting Manda the tinselled Angel Gabriel under her nose.

'Can I see?'

Michael passes the photos to me, Manda in a nativity play, Toby on a bicycle, a family group, the four of them together under a tree.

'You never saw these, obviously?' says Michael.

'No.'

'So you didn't get going-home money, then?' Toby laughs.

'No.'

'She didn't really have to go home,' says Sadie.

'I wonder if Bridie knew the pictures were here?' says Manda.

'Of course she knew,' I say.

Manda looks at me. 'I'm going to choose to believe that,'

she says. She takes the photos from me and puts them in her pocket. 'If no one minds,' she says.

On the mantelpiece is a small, oval, pierced-ivory picture frame. My six-year-old face shines out of it. I go to the fireplace and fold it flat.

'It's not your fault,' says Michael.

At the window-seat I sit and put my back against glass. The others move about the room touching my grandmother's – their grandmother's – things. Sadie knocks against the orange tree and a bitter globe of fruit falls to the hearth.

There is only a small bookcase here, the larger ones are upstairs. I take books from the bottom shelf: *Renaissance*, *Byzantium*, *Rise of Russia*, *Age of Faith*. TimeLife books Bridie bought on subscription.

'They hurt me, those,' she said. 'Ten shillings a month for a year. Never take more than you can pay for, Grace.'

I flick through *Variations on a Tradition of Humble Toil*, *A World Held Secure by Discipline and Obedience*, *Con-quest by Crusade*. The pages are thick and creamy and smell of mould. I put them back and move on to *Pevsner's Sussex*, *The South Downs Way*, some Ordnance Survey maps of the area, a pamphlet on Newick church with its watercolour by Charles Winston of an early fourteeth-century Agnus Dei in the south chancel window. Dusty parts of Bridie's life, though occasionally, very occasionally, there would be a bright spine here, a red *Grimms' Fairy Tales*. So I still looked when I came, as a matter of habit. Though most of the magic was to be found upstairs.

On the landing is the mahogany bookcase, its polished shelves deep and wide. I can't help the rise of anticipation as I approach it, even now. There are biographies here and more works of general reference, but most of the books are medical. *Black's Medical Dictionary* with its dense type and line-drawings of the spine, branched like a tree: the arachnoid, spinal ganglion, ventral nerve root, *ligamentum denticulatum, dura mater.* Black's definitions, litanies of words I would repeat to myself like a mantra, not having any idea at all what they meant: cryosurgery, cryptococcus, cryptorchidism, culdoscopy, curare, curette, Cushing's syndrome. Next to the dictionary are the works on anaesthesia, Wylie Churchill-Davidson and J. Alfred Lee. Books I left on the shelf because, if I drew them out, she swallowed. Bridie's swallow just like Ruth's, inarticulate pain. So I just touched the books in passing, marking the closed pages with my nervousness. I tip Wylie Churchill-Davidson backwards, the prints of my nails are still indented. A random scattering of small brown grins. I wonder now why Bridie didn't hide these books away; but perhaps to see them, to collide with them occasionally was another way in which she punished herself. I push the book away.

*Gray's Anatomy* is next. By contrast, *Gray's* was encouraged, delighted in by both of us. I lift it out with something akin to joy, this huge volume with its thousand see-through thin pages, this Bible of my childish imagination. Impossible to number the times I sat here cross-legged looking at the fantastical shapes of the body, fascinated by the heart-shaped android pelvis or tracing the muscles of the hand, the red elastic bands tight around the finger.

'Annular and cruciate pulleys of the flexor tendon sheath,' Bridie might say in passing, putting a dry interested finger on the page. Or perhaps: 'Don't miss skin. People always bypass skin. But it's the biggest organ. The interface between you and the outside world.'

I'm not sure that 'interface' was a word I knew any more

than 'cryptococcus', but it was part of the strange and vivid landscape of Bridie's house, Bridie's world. Which is why I never thought it odd to find the fairy-tales tucked in here. Different pictures, same magic. The nervous system illustrated like skeletal seaweeds, neurons adorning the rocks where mermaids played. So, of course, I looked for the seal story here. Not just between the books, but in the books, flipping page after page, scouring contents, footnotes, captions, in case it was hidden in the pictures, written in the margins. But the only thing inked here was Bridie's youth, the businesslike annotations of the medical student. If A then B.

'Are you looking for something particular?' Michael asks, stepping over me.

'No,' I say. Gently I put away my book of bones and spells, return it to Bridie's shelf, Bridie's order. No. I'm not searching any more. Just trying to find a way of saying goodbye. Oh, Grandma, goodbye.

'Twenty minutes and counting,' says Toby, emerging from the spare bedroom.

I realise then that I have no need to go into her rooms. I have inhabited them all, could describe the fall of light from her bedroom window on to the maple-framed tapestry of Moses in the basket. Could pick from the carpets, as if I was a needle, the threads of Afghanistan scarlet or Chinese blue. Could tell among a million scents the dry earth of her orange tree and the smoke of her Lapsang Souchong, the sharp hanky cleanliness of her eau-de-Cologne and the wood darkness of her linen press and her chest-on-chest. These gifts she has given and I have taken already. These and other things we never spoke of. Dredgy secrets made gold between. Grandmother mine, who both chose and denied me.

'I don't remember any of these jewels,' says Manda to Sadie. 'Did she wear these, Grace?'

I go into Bridie's bedroom. They have the wooden jewel-box open, have turned the dark metal key in the lock. Laid out on the lace mat of Bridie's dressing-table is her cameo of the Three Graces, her cracked ebony and ivory ball necklace, her five-pearl ring, her black and green enamel chain, hung with the tiny funeral urn with the hinged gold lid. Sadie is holding a crystal locket with a blond curl of hair inside.

'I think that was Mungo's,' I say. 'Mungo's hair.'

'She kept that!'

'Yes.'

'Did she wear it?'

'No.' I reach into the box and take out Bridie's amber brooch. 'She did wear this.' A large misshapen pear-drop of translucent gold, bubbled with honey and cracked with light. I stroke its smooth, warm resin surface. Inside is a fly. Black and trapped, its wings outstretched. My grandmother pinned this brooch to her olive-suited breast, where it rose and fell with her breathing. Manda and Sadie watch my thumb, excluded from this knowledge, this intimacy with my grandmother. Who is their grandmother.

'Are we all ready?' says Michael.

I lay down the insect and follow him, as we all do, to the drawing-room where we stand silent, called to account.

'Well, it doesn't really matter who starts,' says Michael, 'as everyone's going to get their say, but for argument's sake, why don't you begin, Grace?'

'No.'

'Oh, go on,' says Sadie.

'No. I mean, I don't want anything.'

There is a clamour. Surprise, disappointment, persuasion,

embarrassment, even anger: come on, Grace; think of Bridie, what she would have wanted; and Ruth, what will she feel; take something for Ruth at least; what not even the toasting fork? It's yours if you want it.

Manda says, 'Do you mean you don't want anything from this room particularly, or you don't want anything at all?'

'I don't want anything at all. I'm sorry. I don't mean to be rude. And I don't want to make it difficult for all of you. But I just can't.'

'Does that include my toothbrush?'

'For God's sake, Toby!'

'You may change your mind,' says Michael gently. 'Why not take some things now, just in case? If you find you don't want them later – well, then, your choice.'

'No,' I say. 'If I take them now I'll never be able to get rid of them. That's the whole point.'

'They'll become yours,' says Manda. 'That's what happened with Grandpa Alder's things. Dad's dad. He left us a few bits. At first they were his. Painful to look at. His little silver retirement box on my dressing-table. Sacrilege. But it's somehow become mine now. I don't bump into it any more. It's just there – part of some silent but shared history.'

Manda. My stolen sister.

'There must be something,' says Michael, 'just one thing you want. Just say it, whatever it is, it's yours. Isn't that right, everyone?'

Everyone – which is everyone but me – nods.

'No,' I say. 'No.'

There's a short pause and then Manda says, 'What about the amber?'

'No. No!' And I know I have to go then. 'Look, don't mind me. You get on. I'll go, leave you to it.'

They make to follow me, Michael, Manda, but I wave them away. My hand palm-open. 'Please,' I say, retreating. 'Please.' I sit on the lawn, in the shade of the leylandii. Of course I feel shabby, as though I have let them all down. As though I have let Bridie down. But there is also a relief, sweeter than the pine, as if I have finally shed something. As if I have made a stand about beginning again, relinquishing a past. I pick a daisy, pull the petals off one by one: She loves me, she loves me not. She loves me. She loves me. Oh, Grandma. The Alder children had my mother but I had their grandmother. And now all I can return to my siblings – who aren't my siblings – is a few of her things. The little bits Bridie gathered about herself. Not much. Not enough, and certainly not something I can explain to the four of them. But perhaps what Bridie wanted. Her last gift. Her legacy. That I should understand what she – and they – lost too.

I sit a long time. Until my brothers and sisters have all gone upstairs and their voices come from bedroom windows, then I go back into the house. I carry Laura's things to the bottom of the drive in armfuls, dresses and shawls and shoes and books. I take her shells, eggs, pressed flowers, a Christening candle. I even take Toby's toothbrush. I throw them one by one into the skip. But before I throw them I hold and honour each in turn. I admire the skill of smocking stitches and the delicacy of embroidered flowers, I trace the whorl of sea-snails and marvel at the pearly interior of mussel shells. I touch the picture of Rumpelstiltskin, who stamped himself into the ground because he was cheated of the child he had been promised.

When I am stroking Red Riding Hood's velvet cape into the bin, a man comes past on a bicycle. He stops to watch as I add a pristine book, and two starfish, the ones that Bridie wore in her hair as she fell. When I put in the white dress of fairy gauze he gets off his bike and comes to join me at the skip's edge. He stares at my face and then at the silver frock with the almost indiscernible brown stain.

'My girl would die for that,' he says, his hand over the metal lip.

'A girl did die for that,' I say.

'Oh,' he says. 'Oh, I see.' His hand comes back as if on a spring, then he jumps on his bike and pedals furiously away.

That's why I don't notice Sadie until she is almost on me. Out in the sunshine her body looks smaller, clenched and so terribly young I feel old beside her. When she looks into the skip she trembles. 'Couldn't you just take something?' she says suddenly, and with such ferocity she might be continuing an argument we've been having all our lives. 'I mean, would it kill you just to keep a shell? A stone?'

'I think the time for these things has passed,' I say, as quietly as I can.

'Oh – for you maybe,' she retorts.

'And for your mother.'

'*Your* mother!'

'Sadie,' I say, 'Sadie, what is it you want from me?'

'Want? From you? What could I possibly want from you?'

I am holding bluebells, pressed dry. It seems provocative to throw them into the skip, so I keep holding them. 'I'm not coming to Laura's,' I say, feeling the flowers becoming dust between my fingers and thumb, 'if that's what concerns you. I've written to her. Told her I can't come.' I offer this as a gift, expecting – needing, perhaps – to see something give in her. But she only gets smaller, all of her retreating behind her eyes.

'Can't come?' She repeats, a tiny pinprick of panic. 'Can't come?'

'She wants something I can't give, Sadie.'

'But you have to come!' Now her arms go wide and wild. Her cheeks are flames of red. 'You should see what she's doing. What she's done for you. She's made new curtains!'

'Exactly.'

'Please,' she says, then. 'Please, you have to come. If you don't come . . . You've no idea how it will be if you don't come.'

Nothing in her demeanour asks for pity, yet compassion wells in me as it did all those years ago for the girl in the mirror. 'Sadie, I can't love Laura. I can't have the relationship she wants of me. The relationship all this,' I gesture at the skip, 'represents. I'm not some lost child any more. I'm, I'm just . . .'

'Just the person my mother loves more than anything – anyone – in the whole world.'

'Your mother doesn't even – '

'Not mine,' interrupts Sadie. 'Yours. Your mother!'

'No,' I refuse. 'My mother is Ruth.' I say it to ward her off, but I hear it as a truth, the years reeling suddenly past me, the days, hours, minutes of Ruth's care. Ruth, my mother. The softness of her neck where the starched white collars gave way to flesh, the lingering smell of her in the house even when she was away, her hands between the stalks of flowers and the folds of my clothes, the lean of her body on the edge of my bed, intent, listening, telling me it would be all right. It would all be all right. All through the shouting and the screaming. Being there. And, when there was nothing left to say, pushing banknotes in a bundle under my door. Loving me when I was – when I am – unlovable. 'I don't think it's possible to have two mothers.'

'Two mothers.' She mimics. ' "I don't think it's possible to have two mothers."' Then she goes still as stone. 'Well, I think you're wrong about that. Because you've always had two mothers. Yours.' She pauses. 'And mine.'

And I want to say it's not my fault. But it is my fault and I want to say that too. But the words in my mouth are all wrong. For her eyes explain that I was loved too much and she too little and nothing can make that fact less harsh. And of course I want to return to her the fifteen years of her childhood. But it's not in my gift.

'Forgive me.'

She laughs.

Then all of a sudden I see how it must have been for Laura, standing fertile before her infertile sister all those years ago. How she must have ached to make it better, to reach up and crush away the pain. And despite everything I can't stop my arms lifting to Sadie. My sister pushes me from her. She turns away.

And perhaps that is right as well.


# 28


Alan has made a decision. It has come to him over many weeks, a piece of clay drying gradually in his mind, slowly becoming hard. It is not truth that he is after, or even some kind of absolution, it's just that he's fifty-four years old and he's been too long adrift. He has not said, 'No.' He has never said, 'No.' He has gone with the flow, with the passions of others. Two women brought him a plastic cup and said, 'Perform,' and he performed. Another – a girl – brought him her naked body and he acquiesced at once. He neither blames the women nor excuses himself, he has just become aware that it has to stop.

He doesn't think there was a defining moment, but if there was one, it was when Ruth, in the kitchen, standing in a cloud of steam said, 'It would be impossible to tell you how much I love you.' Adding, a moment later, 'I love you, I love you, I love you.' And although these were the words he had worked for so doggedly, words he knew he wanted more than he wanted his own life, he'd just stood there, baked dry, his own words just incomprehensible hieroglyphs scratched on the inside of his mouth.

It was as if, in offering him paradise to gaze upon, she had inadvertently shown him his own nakedness. And, after that, when he looked at the curve of her thumbs, or studied the shape of her nails or the rise of her moons he no longer fooled himself. He was loving his wife in such detail to try to fill the gap where his daughter had been. Of course, it had been easy for him to deflect his own attention. Grace had made it easy. She had avoided him, derided him, frightened him. She had gone to her room and shut the door. And she had called him Alan.

That is why he is sitting in his car at the end of Bridie's road. Why he has not waited passively for his daughter's call, 'We're through now, could you come and collect me?' (chancing, of course, that her mother might pick up the phone) but driven out early, to wait however long it is he has to wait. Because even if he cannot reclaim his daughter's love (the expression of this thought – just the expression of it – grinds glass in his heart) then he must at least try for her respect. This is what the decision is about.

He has parked some way from Bridie's drive, close enough to see but not necessarily to be seen. It is hot in the road. Hot in the car, though Alan has opened the windows. He would stand in the open air but that might attract Grace's attention and he doesn't want that. Besides, Grace is completing something of her own. He watches her take armfuls of things to the skip. Tender armfuls, he thinks, as the things (he's not close enough to see more than cloth and colour – red and silver) fall so very slowly from her hands. Watching the float of things makes him think that they have never, none of them, been any good at letting go. One of the Alder girls joins Grace now. The youngest one. Sadie. She stands between Grace and her father, partially obscuring his view. Her feet are apart, her stance angry. Alan leans forward, his hand hard on the steering-wheel, if she touches his girl, if she lifts a hand . . . But no, these are the thoughts he is no longer allowed. These are the rights he has abrogated, the rights of a father. This is what his daughter means when she calls him Alan.

Alan.

Alan puts his head on the steering-wheel.

When he can bring himself to look again, the scene has changed. Grace's tender arms are lifting towards the Alder girl's neck. Arms that used to lift towards his own neck, hang there. He could not have believed how the lack of something could have such a solid presence. His body is bruised with it.

The Alder girl pulls back, turns briskly on her heels. And Grace is left looking startled and bereft, as if she's just walked round a parked car that drove off in the meanwhile, leaving her to finish her curve around an empty space. Or perhaps he just wants this to be the case. Wants his daughter young and vulnerable again. As she was before she grew up. Before she saw her father fuck.

236

Alan gets out of the car. He cannot help himself. The not-knowing is suddenly more than he can bear. Grace sees him immediately. There's a moment when she might simply turn away, but she doesn't. She starts to walk towards him. She is coming. His daughter is coming.

She walks with the quick steps of a girl, but her head is down, hung. She is wearing a sleeveless yellow T-shirt and a short yellow skirt. Her arms and legs are summer bare and she is thin, unbearably thin. How can he not have noticed how thin she has become? All of him longs to move towards her, to scoop her up like he did when she was just a child. But she is a woman now, though thin. And he is a serpent who has swallowed her whole. So he stands leaning on the car.

'Dad,' she says, arriving.

Whatever he had expected it was not this. He tries to breathe the measured breaths of an ordinary father in an ordinary encounter with his daughter.

'Oh, Dad,' she says, and she lays her head against his chest.

She has not been so close since she shook her strawberry nipples in his face. He has no right to put his arms about her. No right at all. But he does.

'I'm so glad you're here,' she says against him.

She mustn't speak again. If she speaks again the thousand million impurities that make up the brick clay of him will fuse together, they will burst. He will burst asunder.

'Can we go?' she asks.

But if they move it may not be true. Or if it's true, it may not be true ever again. 'Of course,' he says, 'of course we'll go. If you want.'

He guides her round to the passenger door, his hand on her shoulder. Her flesh is warm. He does not linger in opening the door, in tucking her in, for he knows it has to end. He knows he has to walk the lifetime to his own door and get into the separate driving seat. It's only when he's in that seat that he realises he hasn't asked her if she's OK.

'Are you OK? he asks.

'Yes,' she says.

Michael Alder said it would probably take the five of them till dark to clear the house and it is not even midday, but Alan doesn't query this. No more, he notices, than she enquires why it is he has come for her so early. He just puts the key in the ignition and drives. The two of them drive away together, Alan and Grace. Father and daughter.

Alan concentrates on the road, though he has driven to and from Bridie's house so many times he might make the journey with his eyes closed. Grace stares out of the window as though the familiar landscape is quite new to her. She observes, or seems to observe, the splashes of red poppies on the hillside, the sudden escarpment of chalk, the lower land with the yellow harvested fields, the corn tied up in huge rolls like giant curls of butter. She sees the small towns, the country churches, the Cobbler's Inn on the corner where they sometimes stopped, Alan and Ruth and Grace, for a drink on the way home from Bridie's, where they sat outside in the summer and talked about nothing in particular as the sun went down.

'Do you want to stop?' he asks.

'No,' she says.

From here it is only four miles home and he hasn't even begun. But maybe he doesn't need to begin, maybe this is what Grace is telling him with her silence. He has never, he thinks, shared such quiet, such unspoken companionship with any other human being, not even his wife. A mile

238

passes. A mile that he spends remembering the time Grace and he went to the river and sat on a slab of shale. Rock laid down on thin, sparking layers. Layers he lifted with his penknife. He puts his hand in his pocket to feel for the familiar knife. But it is gone. His knife, which is never gone. That's when he blurts it out.

'I'm going to tell her,' he blurts.

'What?'

'I'm going to tell Ruth, about . . .' he says, 'about . . .'

'About what?'

'About . . .'

'About Adele?'

'Yes.'

'No,' his daughter says. 'Don't. You mustn't . You can't do that.'

She has stopped being the dreamy comfortable presence beside him. She's gone white, hard around the edges.

'I thought,' he says, 'I thought you'd understand. I thought you'd be pleased.'

'Pleased!'

He has made a mistake. 'But you know about it,' he continues stubbornly. 'About lying. About being lied to.'

'But I didn't know,' she says, 'until you told me.'

He doesn't quite understand this, needs time to think about what she is saying, but he hears his pause like a drumbeat. If he doesn't say something, if he doesn't continue the momentum . . .

But it's Grace who speaks again: 'What possible reason could you have for telling her?'

'But that's it,' he says, forging on now, for this is the thing he has rolled obsessively in his mind. 'We said you didn't need to know. That it would hurt you, so you shouldn't know. Your happiness was more important than the truth, I suppose. And it wasn't,' he finishes. 'Was it?'

'No. No. But this really isn't the same.'

'It isn't?'

'No.' She turns to look at him then and, even though he keeps his eyes on the road, he feels the burn of her as if he'd opened a kiln in mid-firing. 'Because you love her. Don't you? You love Ruth beyond anything. That's the real truth.'

And then he wants to tell his daughter that he loves her too. Loves her beyond anything. But his tongue is too big for his mouth. He can't even swallow.

'Oh, Grace,' he manages at last, 'Grace . . . I just don't know how to say sorry.'

'Then don't say it.' She pauses. 'There's no need.'

'No need?'

'I forgive you.'

'What?'

'I said, "I forgive you." Supposing I'm allowed to forgive. Supposing I have the right.'

'I'm sorry,' he says, 'I'm so very sorry.'

'Don't. There's no need,' she repeats. 'In fact, in a way, I'm grateful for it. About it.'

'Grateful!'

'Yes.' She stares at him. 'You see, you finally exploded it for me. Flesh and blood. If your own flesh and blood can do that, well, what hope did Ruth have?'

This isn't said in anger, just stated baldly.

'When did you grow up?' he asks. 'How did you do it and me not notice?'

'Promise me you won't tell her,' Grace says, suddenly stretching up to tap the rear-view mirror with her finger-nail. Tap tap. 'Promise?'

240

'What if Adele tells her?'

'She won't. Adele forgot it all the moment it happened.'

'Oh.' The humiliation spiking him, deflating him. Despite everything.

'And you?'

'I'll never tell,' says Grace.

'No?'

'I wanted to. Would have done at first. Wanted to kill you. Kill you both.' She shrugs then, as if it were all such a very long time ago. 'But people – people suffer enough.' Her beautiful brown eyes, with their strange hazel flecks, go vague for a moment, faraway. Then she shakes her head and those same eyes pinpoint. 'Besides, if I keep this secret from Ruth then I can't blame her for keeping her secret from me. Can I?'

They have arrived.

Ruth is looking out of the window. Before Alan has even parked up she's out of the door.

'I have been a pig,' says Grace, looking at her. 'Haven't I?'

'No, you haven't,' says Alan. 'You really haven't.'

'Is everything all right?' Ruth cries through he car window. 'Are you all right, Grace?'

'Yes,' Grace says, 'yes, I am.' And then she says, 'Mum.'

# SUNRISE

# 29

Laura is making drop-scones. She pours exact spoon-fuls of viscous batter on to the piping hot, cast-iron griddle. The griddle was her grandmother's, a huge upturned disc of black, with a finely wrought handle, the metal beaten into a loop. Laura likes to see the batter fall into creamy circles, the heat making it hold its shape. She likes to wait, watching the thick liquid begin to bubble from the underside. She enjoys knowing the precise moment when the scones need to be flipped, to cook on the second side. It's quite an art, keeping four or five of them going at the same time, each browning at a slightly different rate depending on its precise size and position on the griddle, its distance from the central heat source beneath. Thus, though Laura has done this job many times and her hands are nimble, she still needs to concentrate. Which is why she has chosen drop-scones to make at five o'clock in the morning.

It's September and warm still, an Indian summer. Outside the darkness is ever lightening, though its quiet and still in the house, which makes it seem darker somehow. Thomas and Sadie are asleep upstairs, Thomas breathing through his mouth and Sadie lying, as she has since childhood, still as a stone. Manda would throw off all her covers but Sadie was always to be found at seven o'clock in the morning in exactly the same position she'd been left the previous night. As though, Laura thought once, many moons ago, she was afraid to move.

Laura slides her spatula under another two golden scones and wraps them in a cloth napkin with the others, to go in the warming oven. She eats nothing herself, even though drop-scones are best straight from the stove. Drop-scones become limp and rubbery if they are left too long, as these will be.

She has read the letter twice. Four times maybe. She has read the lines and in between the lines. But it all says the same thing. Grace isn't coming.

'We expected too much,' Thomas said. 'We went too fast. It's only natural. That she'd want to pull back.'

Laura had been making drop-scones that first ever time, when Ruth rang, almost eighteen years ago to the day. When Ruth asked, 'Will you carry a baby for me?' Carry like it was in a papoose.

'I think we just need to give Grace time,' says Thomas.

Men, thinks Laura, pouring batter, have a different understanding of time from women. Women lived in fused time, the past and present indivisible, the future just one more overlay, soon to be the present, to be incorporated, to be interpreted as part of the whole. Men live in separate time, able to close off, close down. Which is why men could send their fellows to the gas chambers and then eat a hearty dinner. Why Thomas could give her the piece of paper that signed away the life of her child and say, 'Leave be.'

Three more scones go in the napkin. Already the ones at the bottom are feeling cold. They lose their heat so fast, she thinks. They just give it out through the bubbles, the pores, giving out until there's nothing left.

And now her own children – her girls – are separating

things, closing off, closing down. Forgetting. What Sadie brought from Bridie's fitted on the back seat of Michael's car. A box of books and a jewel case. Inside the jewel case only one jewel – an amber with a fly inside.

'Didn't you want anything else?'

'Why would I? None of it means anything to me.'

And Grace? She hardly dared to ask what Grace had taken. But she did ask because she had to know.

'Grace took nothing. Grace threw everything she could in the skip. Especially your stuff. That fairy thing. The Red Riding Hood cape. The smocking frocks. Whooopt!' Sadie whistled through her teeth. 'Just chucked it all away.'

'And Bridie's things, her grandmother's things . . .'

'Nothing. Zilch. Didn't even want to stay in the house as long as lunch. Pushed off and never even said goodbye. Manda was quite offended.'

Another neat spoonful of batter. And another. Perfect control with the spoon.

'At least,' Thomas has said, 'you know Grace is well. You know what she looks like now. You can stop searching.'

She knows what he means. And she has stopped – almost. Stopped scouring the face of every seventeen-year-old she sees in the street, in Sainsbury's, on a bus, a train. Though it is difficult to stop, so long has she had the habit. Scanning the six-year-olds in the park when Grace was six, the sevens in the swimming-pool, the eights on holiday, the nines . . . Yes. He's right. It is something to know what Grace looks like. Now, when she lies awake in bed, she is able to conjure every living inch of Grace's body. She can look in her daughter's eyes and count the million golden brown hairs on her head. She can open Grace's hands and see her white palms, trace the whorls of her thumbs . . .

'What the hell are you doing?' Sadie, in jeans and T-shirt, is standing in the doorway.

Laura is caught in mid-flip. 'Do you want one?'

'What?' Sadie stares. 'I don't like drop-scones. I've never liked drop-scones. You know that. And I don't eat breakfast. What would I want one for?'

'Where are you going?'

'Out.'

'It's not even five fifteen.'

'Well, if it's a good time to make drop-scones, it's a good time to go out.' Sadie takes her jacket from the back of a chair. 'Besides, I often go out at this time.'

'What?'

'I go out. Creep out. Been doing it for years.'

Laura has splashed the batter. There's a drop, two drops running down the griddle.

'Where do you go?'

'Just the pits.'

'The chalk-pits?' The batter is so thin, it's solidifying already.

'Yeah.'

'Why?' says Laura.

'Dunno. It's just where I've always been.'

'Since when?' Laura begins to scrape. Scrape, scrape at the blackening batter.

'Since for ever.'

'Since when?' repeats Laura. The chalk-pits are dangerous. All the local children know not to go to the chalk-pits. The sides are sheer, the water deep. If you fall . . .

'Since I was five, six. I can't remember.'

'No,' refutes Laura. 'No. You couldn't even have reached the bolt then.'

'I could if I stood on the stool. Which I did.'

'Oh, Sadie.' Under the black batter tears, the knife.

Sadie takes her keys from the dresser. 'See you, then.'

'Sadie,' her daughter is almost out of the door, 'can I come with you?'

Her daughter stares at her. 'Bit late for that, don't you think?'

'Please?'

'No. No, I don't think so. I really don't think so.' And then she says, 'Mum.'

A moment later Sadie is gone, closing the front door behind her, softer than a breath.

Laura wipes her hands on her apron, she sits down on the stool by the cooker. She never wanted to be Bridie. That was to be her gift, the thing she'd learned. *Never to shut the door on the children, never to retreat down long corridors. Not to be Bridie.*

Bridie who always loved Ruth more than she loved Laura. Bridie who recognised herself in Ruth, who understood her, adored her, so that even when Laura offered her own flesh as sacrifice, it wasn't enough, because nothing could be enough for a mother who loved one daughter above another.

The last remaining scones are turning black. Two creamy white scones on the griddle going black. Grace may come. Grace may not come. Grace may or may not forgive. But Sadie, Laura knows, will never come. And she will never forgive. Just as she, Laura, never came and never forgave.

The scones are burned. They are just ash on a griddle, thin flakes curling, peeling away to float for a moment in the air, before falling, falling. From the cupboard under the sink,

Laura gets a wire brush. She begins to scrub. She scrubs and scrubs, drawing the shrieking brush across iron.

# 30

Mungo is asleep, his blue-striped arm about his pillow, the flies of his pyjamas undone. Unlike other men of his age – seventy-seven – who tell him over a pint how difficult they find it now to fall asleep, Mungo simply lays his head down and falls into a distant, soggy slumber. And if he dreams, if phantasms come and go, they do not trouble him.

This morning it is different. It's a warm early time, perhaps five a.m., and there are three women licking round his body. The women are like Russian dolls, stacked inside each other. The largest doll, the outer one, is Paquita, Horst's wife. Her skin is the colour of molasses in sunshine, pale sparks of honey in the thick, treacly brown. She would oil herself, Paquita, as her grandmother had before her, the old woman like a slick black walnut. But Paquita . . . oh, Paquita.

The second doll is Lucrece with her French blue colonial eyes and her amber skin, which would have been white if it hadn't been for the fierce African sun. Lucrece who rested in a coil only to rise, to order, like a serpent from a fakir's pot.

The central doll, the one that doesn't come apart, is Bridie. A tiny, dark, darting bird. She of the quick, quick fingers and sharp, probing tongue. Bridie who explored with arching limbs and sharp teeth.

The women, above him, slide in and out of each other as he used to slide in and out of them. Their eyes flicking brown, blue, brown and their triangles brushing against him, black, blonde, brown. Six arms embrace him and three tongues come for him. They move easily, the women, they laugh for their bodies are young and their sex brazen.

Somewhere between the rasp of a tongue and the silk of a honey hair, Mungo comes to a hinterland, an edge of consciousness. It is a sweet place, a sugar place and he is unwilling to move from it, to let the dream – for he knows he's dreaming – go from him. Just as he's unwilling to let the hands and the mouths go. So he tries to know nothing, think nothing, but just let the tongues and the lips and the hands touch where they will, kiss where they will, for his old body has lain a long time alone.

But he finds himself greedy. His loins will not lie still, they will not wait. He has been stirred and his prick requires attention. He cannot help his own hand pushing down between his legs, grasping for his hot cock. Searching for it, fingers rootling. Finding it – at last – small and flaccid, lain on his thigh. But he still takes it, thumbstrokes some comfort, keeping his eyes closed. For the women may reach out again, as they did, as they used to. And besides it's good to hold himself. He can sleep again like this, drift off, without the women, for they have slipped away now and in their place is Mrs P.

Mrs P. waving an iron at him and saying, 'She came. But you weren't here. Why weren't you here?' That's how he knows he must be asleep, must be dreaming now, because that's what Bridie said, all those years ago. 'She came and you weren't here.' Or perhaps it was less than this. Perhaps it was just 'You weren't here.' As if he had deliberately gone abroad, when going abroad was what his job required, was what he was paid to do. As ridiculous as what Bridie had said about his other women. Because he hadn't had any other women then. Hadn't even thought about it until she mentioned it, made it a possibility.

A sudden deep cough racks at Mungo's chest. He is forced upright, forced awake. He hoicks phlegm into a cotton handkerchief. Normally he doesn't cough until the winter and it is only September and warm, very warm, though he lies down and pulls the blankets close about him. One should never go back. He probably should not have returned to England. He pulls at the eiderdown, which seems to be slipping off the bed. But when Paquita died, it was so very empty in Caracas. The teeming city just footprints in the dust. The vibrant colour of the market – her market – bleached out. But in the *barrios* on the steep mountainside, the slums where Horst's brother lived – well, it had seemed sensible. Yet he still might not have returned, might have stayed and faced them all if it hadn't been for the stall-holder calling, '*Hallacas, hallacas!*' Because when he looked at the Christmas pastry, its stew of meats in an envelope of maize-flour pastry wrapped round with a plantain leaf, he knew he was in the wrong place. Needed roast turkey and sage and onion stuffing now, even if he had to eat it alone.

And he had eaten it alone. Had learned to be alone. It hadn't been easy. But he'd persevered. Which is why it had been madness to go to Bridie's funeral. Wouldn't have considered it except that they'd happened upon Paquita's day, the anniversary of her death. Just a stupid coincidence, of course, but he'd acted on less. He'd acted on *hallacas*. So he went. For the women. The ones who had died on him.

Lucrece had just run away. He never quite discovered what happened to Lucrece.

Still. It was no excuse. He should not have gone to Bridie's and he should not have said what he said. It had not been at all sensible to look upon his daughters again. Ruth particularly. Ruth coming at him with that fierce, twitchy neediness, so like her mother's. So like Bridie. That's why he'd invited Grace to tea. Pure spite. Inviting the grandchild but not the daughter. Just to be annoying. Though it was quite spontaneous. Not a premeditated crime, albeit he was sorry later. On the appointed day he'd hidden in the library, read the newspapers until he could have recited them, stayed until they rang the bell and threw him out. But he needn't have bothered because the child (what was the child's name?) had only waited the half-hour. That's what Mrs P. said. So she can't have wanted to see her grandfather that much, can't have minded. Had the impatience, he supposed, of youth. The devil-may-care.

Mungo sighs. He is awake and he doesn't want to be awake. He's never awake. He's a man who sleeps well. God forbid that's going to change. He lifts his pillow, which seems remarkably heavy, and turns it over so as to be able to put his head on the cool underside. But the pillow-case is polyester. Not what he's used to, and not cool. He'd bought polyester on his return from Caracas, not concentrating, not knowing, as he now knows, that he had spent all his life sleeping on pure cotton. Of course, one only had cotton in Africa, in Latin America. In Bridie's house.

It was not quite what he'd intended. Somehow none of it is quite as he intended. But it is what he has. Mungo puts one hand through the open flap of his flies and tucks the other around his pillow. It's less than a minute before he falls into the stolid sleep from which he is never to wake.

It's Mrs P. who finds the body, stiff and cold, two days later. The orifices have all evacuated, black trials of slime from nose and mouth and ears and anus. But it is not this that upsets Mrs P. What upsets Mrs P. is that Mungo Henderson's right hand is clasped around his lower member and, no matter how hard she pulls in the cause of decency, she cannot get it free. Eventually, before she calls the police (there being, she reckons, no point in the ambulance, for her employer is profoundly dead) she resorts to pinching his pyjamas together as best she can, and pulling up the eiderdown from its place on the floor. If anybody complains that she has exceeded her responsibilities, she will simply tell them straight. It is not what she's used to.

After this she sits down to wait, making herself at home with a pot of tea, pouring the good quality Assam into Mr Henderson's favourite mug, the Spanish one with the jagged pattern which he, for some reason, called his 'conquistador' cup. As she stirs in two sugar cubes she thinks three things almost simultaneously: firstly, why it is that Mungo Henderson has been allowed to go so peacefully in his sleep when her own husband, darling Percy, had the lung cancer when he (Percy) never smoked a single cigarette in all of his life; secondly, what is she going to do for money now that her most lucrative employer lies beneath the sheets with his hand . . . well, with; and thirdly, what is she to tell the police as regards Mr Henderson's family? For though she knows now that he has family, she is blessed if she really knows either what their names are or where they live. She can't even remember the name of the child.

Hope.

Oh, yes. Hope. Before she forgets again, Mrs P. writes it down on Mungo Henderson's African elephant memo pad.

# 31

Gav lies on his back, half in and half out of the lift. He is a big man is Gav. Not as big as Carl, or Stewart, but big none the less. Adele gives him a kick with the toe of one of her flame orange shoes. The satin scuffs against his black sole.

'Jees-us.' She's a good mind to leave him right here. In the hallway, bedded down on the black and white flagstones. Serve the bugger right. Only getting him out of the lift, now he's half-way in, seems as much trouble as forcing him the final couple of feet. She squats and pushes at him. He groans but he does not move. She stands up and peels off her skimpy big-fur jacket. She's hot from alcohol, dancing and dragging Gav. He'd bettter be worth the bother when he finally wakes up. If he wakes up. She kicks him again, his flesh this time. In the harsh light of the hall he looks pale and flabby. Not at all the man he seemed to be in the strobe lights of the club. The sexy one making such a play for her and Stewart looking on. Carl looking on.

'Move, damn you.' She steps over the bulk of him and then turns to lock her hands under his shoulders. She pulls from the head end, nails in his armpits. He shifts an inch, grating over the metal runners of the lift. If she can get his arse in, she ought to be able to fold his legs. That's what she did once with Pete. In a hotel. Why they can't hold their drink she'll never know. And her, half their body-weight, keeping pace, cocktail for cocktail. She grits her teeth and heaves again. His arse bumps in. Bump, bump over the metal ridges. With any luck he'll have bruises. She'll make sure to check. Then she leans out of the lift and gathers his legs, pulling his ankles towards his knees, bending him up. And still his foot drags, the buckle of his ludicrous shoes stuck on the runner of the inner door. She twists at the obstruction and the buckle, which is cheap, breaks on the metal. She takes the shoe off then and flings it into the hallway. He'll be glad enough to find it tomorrow. The bloody Cinderella. The socked foot is easier to maneouvre. At last he is in. She pulls the outer door to, bangs shut the grille door and presses for Elaine's. How she's going to get him up Elaine's stairs, God only knows.

She puts her right foot under his cheek and rocks it. Dangerous, because he could vomit, of course. Most of them vomit. But she's past caring now. She just wants him to wake up, just a bit. Enough to support some of his own weight going up the stairs.

'Wake up, you crap artist,' she says.

He snores. She rocks more savagely. Then she squats down and pinches the fleshy part of his nose, digging with her nails.

'Oi,' he says.

'Nearly home, lover boy.'

'Uh.'

The lift comes to a stop. But Gav has slumped during the ascent, his feet, and therefore his weight, are braced against the iron grille. She cannot open the door.

'For crying out loud.' She rearranges him once more, but

it's difficult, trying to open the door with one hand and keep his legs from wedging it shut again with the other.

'Oi,' Gav says again.

'Stand up,' she orders.

But he doesn't. So she rams as much of him as she can into the small gap she's managed to create in the doorway and then steps over him once more to begin operations again from the leg end. Eventually he clunks out and lies, full stretch on the beige landing carpet.

'Leave me alone,' he slurs, turning himself on to his arm.

This is good. This resembles consciousness. And she is going to need his help for she has to be quiet. The Abbey National makes Elaine work on a Saturday morning. Adele consults her watch. Five thirty a.m. Elaine will be up in a couple of hours. She will not want to be up now. This much has been made plain to Adele. In fact, it was almost the cause of a row – of mention being made of overstaying one's welcome. Adele slides both lift doors shut. Elaine had to walk the ninety-six steps of the building once because Adele, apparently, omitted to shut the gates properly. Though how Elaine could be sure the culprit was Adele, Adele doesn't know.

'Because the sodding lift was on this floor,' said Elaine.

Gav draws himself in around his stomach. He burps. Adele waits. Not here. Please, not here. On the other hand, maybe better here than in Elaine's flat. Gav vomits. The speed and splash is as violent as it is sudden. Great gobs, slicks of red pour from his mouth. Adele has to jump, for fear of her skirt, her stockings. An orange blob of undigested something lands on her shoes. Perfect match, Adele thinks, wiping the satin on the carpet. Gav coughs and splutters.

'God,' he says.

But it's over now and at least he's missed himself. The sick is mainly on the floor. Both things good news for her bed. What's more he's not completely prone, but in a kind of crouch. Maybe he can walk.

'Better?' she asks.

'Uh,' he says.

'Here.' She reaches down and takes his arm.

'Hang on.'

She waits and then he heaves himself upwards, rubbing his forearm across the spit at his mouth.

'Mind your feet,' she says, steering him. She doesn't want vomit footprints on Elaine's carpet.

'Uh.' His breath is acid.

Despite her slight frame, she manages to get the weight of him as far as Elaine's front door. She fumbles for her keys, hand under her skirt (thank God for the micro mini) and into her stocking tops for the Velcro purse. Got it. Don't move now, you creep. Somehow she extracts the key and gets it to the lock, possibly only because she's managed to lean him against the door-post. There's a chance he'll fall quite flat when the door opens, but that's a chance she's going to have to take. The door-hinges squeak. Well, that's not her fault. Elaine should get some oil.

'Come on now.' She supports him through, shutting the door behind her with a steel-tipped heel. 'Gav, you gotta walk, boy.' She points him at the stairs. Fifteen steps, though at least it's her bedroom not Elaine's that's at the top of the stairs. Elaine's bedroom is at the front of the flat, next to the living room, a corridor's length from the stairs. Gav moves, though most of his weight is still on Adele. It's like trying to carry a mattress, big and unwieldy and bent in all the wrong places.

'Come on, Gav.'

'The name's Paul,' Gav says.

'Jesus,' says Adele. 'Jesus Christ.'

'Paul,' Gav repeats. But the mattress is moving, she and the mattress are making it up the stairs. He bangs his foot into the skirting. Bang. Whack. Enough to wake the dead. She holds her breath but there isn't a shout, so she keeps on going. They are nearly at the top. They are at the top. It's only five steps to her room.

'Good boy,' she whispers.

She was wrong about the sick. There's some on him somewhere, he's smeared it on her silver body, the stench of it rising from her breasts. The body is metallic, it repels most things, but if he's got it on her jacket, which she has tucked under her arm, she'll kill him.

Her door is open, she lunges at it, the final propulsion that exhaustion allows her now that the end is in sight. Paul trips on something, a shoe, perhaps, an underwired bra. He falls. There is very little space between the chest of drawers and the bed, but he contrives to find the gap, only glancing his head on the bottom drawer. The noise is cushioned by the duvet, which was half on the floor anyway. He lies quite still. She reaches for his hand, lifts his heavy arm and lets go. It drops like a lead weight. Well, that's it. He's out.

She hangs her jacket over the door knob and then strips off her top and sniffs at her chest. Acrid. But not with sick, with perfume and sweat. Lucky, considering. The flat's water system seems to come to a head of pipes in the wall of Elaine's bedroom. Wshing is not an option. But Adele doesn't want to wash much anyway now. Adele wants to sleep. She takes off the rest of her clothes and lets them lie where they fall. The shoes are ruined anyhow. Naked, she stands above

Paul and tugs at the duvet. Of course it won't move. How come the bastards always get the duvet? She pulls again, but only half-heartedly. She doesn't want to wake him now, doesn't want him in the bed. It's only a single after all. His flies are half undone. She unzips them completely and puts a hand inside. Boxer shorts. Tartan. Not a good sign, not for a Friday night. She parts them to pull out the penis beneath. He doesn't stir and nor does it, the soft, pale sausage. She gives it a little squeeze, all of its limpness contained in the palm of her hand. Men are revolting she thinks, letting it go, watching it flop obscenely on his trouser leg, where she leaves it for him to find in the morning.

She lies full stretch on the bed wondering without enthusiasm where her cleanser is, her hairbrush. She's cold, although it's only a moment since she was sweating. There's something chill about lying naked on this single bed when the bastard has the duvet. She pulls at it again, releases a small corner. Now, if she lies right at the edge of the bed, she can have a triangle of cover. Just about big enough for her groin. Great. She gets up to see if there is anything in her wardrobe resembling a maxi coat. But there isn't. Then she remembers the rug in the living-room.

Stepping over Paul (who is snoring now, which at least proves he's alive), Adele goes to the prow of the ship. The living-room window is a painting. A huge navy sky giving way to morning, a ridge of pink-yellow light on the horizon, the promise of the sun. While, hung high in the upper darkness, there is still a moon. A perfectly round silver moon, like a coin tossed up in the sky.

Adele opens the casement, even though it may wake Elaine, and, wrapping the rug about her, she climbs out into the dawn. On the road beneath the balcony there are already one or two car engines running, lights ablaze. But she can still hear the sea, the slap of it on the shingle beach. She watches the dark water, its rhythmic swell, listens to the wash, wash of it, its constant breath, in, out, on the stony shore. And all of sudden Adele thinks of Grace, wants her. Remembers each of the times she's climbed the hill in the dark to Grace's house, slipped into her friend's bed. Lain with her head against Grace's shoulder and listened to the rise and fall of her friend's chest. The soft, steady breathing rocking her into sleep. A sleep she has never experienced elsewhere, not in her mother's house, not in the beds of the men. Not alone with herself. The carefree, tucked-up sleep of a tiny child.

Adele pushes the thought away. Comes in and shuts the casement window.

In the doorway of the living-room is a lurching Neanderthal, its dick hanging out of its trousers. It grunts, it moans, it says, 'Do you wanna fuck or not, then?' and then it falls like a post to the floor.

A light goes on in Elaine's room.

# 32

The curtains of Ruth and Alan's bedroom are open. Alan has always liked the curtains open in summer, and the room overlooks the garden so there is no one to pry.

'We live too much in artificial light,' Alan says. Artificial light has no rhythm,' he says. 'It kills the body.'

And yet, for seventeen years, Ruth has been closing the curtains – winter and summer alike.

'I can't sleep,' she said, 'with the light.'

But she does not recall seeing this light before, the diaphanous dawn, which is now birthing things around her as she lies unmoving but not unmoved in her bed. The light is stroking things out of the dark, painting pale new edges on objects Ruth had thought familiar, a ghostly corner on her dressing-table, a milky curve to the blue ginger jar, a white rim on the beam above her head. The last silver of night warming as she watches, becoming flaxen, day breaking in her room, touching things yellow now, revealing more than edges, brushing in the surfaces, making things whole, the face of her mirror a pool of pale gold. Her mirror and not her mirror. The stiff antique rippling, the bevel of glass soft as water, the maple frame dappled, splashed with light, sunshine through autumn leaves on a windy September morning. As though she'd never looked before. As though she'd never known. Her mirror new-born. Or else her eyes. For it may not be the rise of the sun, but the rise of her heart, for she saw him too. Alan. A man made light. A rippling effulgent creature that first night when he came to her naked in the moonlight. When he stepped across the room with the open curtains and she rose to meet him.

'You are so beautiful,' he said. Which is why she dared to take off (though he helped her) her protective cotton night-dress with the high Victorian neck. Why she was able to stand in the moonlight, open to the world and to him. Though, only a moment before, she had been hard, wrinkled as a nut. It was his eyes. He made her young by looking. Just as he made her gauche hands expert when he kissed her, when he murmured a second time in her ear, 'you are so beautiful.' Because her body remembered then, responded to the desire dormant inside her and the strong, slow touch of her husband who, so long ago, had been her lover. He began with her fingers, tracing nail and knuckle and bone. Stroking her into being – elbows, shins, ribs – as if she were indeed beautiful. As if every part of her was as tender to him as cheek and breast and lip. Inside his embrace, inside his mouth she ceased to be arid. She flowed once more. As though he found in her what she had lost, fashioned a woman from a barren rock. And she let him hold her, mould her, always remembering he made only what was to be made, the shape that he knew and understood of her. Her own shape. So long lost. And she loved him for his truth and his patience. But she said nothing for there was nothing to say that his hands didn't already know.

And now she lies in the dawn with the sweetness of him once more upon her. For that was the first, but not the only, time. He is not in the bed beside her now, but she knows where he's gone and will join him soon. But not yet. For there is luxury lying here, waiting, knowing what's to come. Luxury, too, in the happiness, the tiny wrapped parcels of happiness she opens with care, one at a time, in privacy. In case they should overwhelm her.

'I'm not going to Laura's.'

This is what Grace has said. Grace looking Ruth in the eye and saying it so simply, so honestly and so definitely that Ruth had cried, 'Oh, but you must!'

And, of course, in time, Grace will go to Laura's. In time. Ruth knows this. Indeed, she wants her daughter to visit her sister. For there has never been a moment in Ruth's life when she has not loved her sister, though the love has been carved with knives. And Grace needs to know this sister, who has borne so much. This gracious, giving woman. This mother. Grace's mother.

Grace's mother.

Ruth can say it now. At last. Without the swallow. Ruth opens a second parcel, tight string around two small words: 'Tell me.'

And Ruth told her: told Grace of fear and panic and powerlessness, but also of passion and love. And Grace listened.

It is, Ruth thinks in the breaking dawn, as if she has spent all of her life in tight bud. Afraid to open herself to the elements, to the wind and rain but also to the sun. And now she is unfurling. Painful, crinkled petals uncurling to find that they have sap and shape after all. That they can be beautiful. That they are beautiful. A blossom to be picked and cherished. To be chosen as Alan chooses her still. As Grace chooses her for now. For a blessed now. And though she knows that she cannot be a rose in full bloom for ever, that she must dry and brown at the edges, wither and die, be discarded, be thrown away, it is all right. For she cannot return to what she was. She cannot be tight any more, crushed inside herself. The fear has gone. She can let go because she has something to let go of. A daughter. A child who knows everything and still returns. The young woman who calls her Mum.

That's why Ruth is going to ring Laura today, try and make a time when the families may meet. She is going to tell her sister how warmly Grace spoke of Manda, of Sadie. Just a beginning, she knows. Of course, they must all guard against going too fast, expecting too much. But the children are sisters, half-sisters, and . . . and . . .

Laura.

Oh, Laura, how am I ever to make it up to you?

Ruth gets up then. Puts a thin, lawn cotton shift over her nakedness. A dress of floating yellow. She brushes her hair from her face, sees its glossiness in the moon-gold mirror. Then she pads downstairs in bare feet, feeling the tufts of the stair carpet, the warm smooth wood of the hall floor, its parquet cracks. A moment later she is opening the front door on the coming day.

The grass underfoot is wet, among the green a silver dew-drop spider's web. She pauses, because she's never taken enough time for pausing. Always too busy, always locked up inside her own head. She crouches down and looks, sees the individual water drops, the delicate tension of them as they cling to the gossamer web, each one a misty pearl in the sun. Sees the spider, balanced on a blade of grass, waiting at the edge of his intricate handiwork for whatever the day will bring. Even if it is only to begin again, spin again. For some oblivious foot may destroy in a moment all that he has laboured to create. Ruth stands up. It will not be her foot. She steps to the side of the spider.

The windows of the studio are spattered with clay. The pale sun glancing off obscurely. But she still sees him, head bowed over his work. Just the shape of him and his moving hands, on the workbench, above the rim of the sofa. Big, slow, kneading hands. Beginning again with the brick clay.

Nothing, she thinks, as she opens the studio door, can ever again divide me from this man.

# 33

Alan has sacked Jerry. Told him, very politely, that his services are no longer required. Though he nearly changed his mind when he saw the look of astonishment, the stunned incomprehension on Jerry's small, nut-brown face. But Alan didn't change his mind and now he has Aaron. Aaron is big and his hands look like dog paws, huge and clumsy. But his big fingers are, in fact, quick and accurate. He can throw seven longtoms an hour, sometimes eight. He's recently out of college and he smiles. He's also keen to help out, he says, on the administrative side. If there's anything to do. Which there is. And he's done it. Quite a lot of it, which is why Alan has been making pots again. Real pots.

The pots are also to do with Ruth. About her saying, as she lay close to him on their bed, 'Why don't you make pots any more?'

'I do.'

'No, I mean real pots. Like the jug women. The amphorae.'

'Well, then, I will.'

And he had. It had been surprisingly easy. Just like making love that first time after so long. He'd thought that celibacy might have become a habit, that the shadow of Adele would be long. He wasn't at all sure that he would be able to touch his wife the way he had, the way he wanted to. But when she'd moved across the room in the moonlight, looking at him, her eyes on his, the light dancing on her, out of her, he'd just reached up and taken her as if she'd been part of his own body, the natural and always extension of him, the piece of life's jigsaw he would always lack if it wasn't there, in its rightful place beside him. The piece he might have searched all the universe for and not come upon such a perfect match. Even now. Even after everything. Or perhaps because of everything, because they have shaped each other after all, the attrition of twenty years. And so his hands and lips touched her lightly, with love but without claim, for how can one claim something already one's own? And she had responded from the part of her that knew him, knew him for what he was, and always had been. Brick clay. No more. But no less.

So he has a sense now, sitting at the workshop bench at five thirty in the morning, that everything is going to be all right. That, though he has stood on a precipice, the sea has now receded, the ground extended under him, or perhaps just that the drop is nowhere near as high as he had imagined.

'Why don't we work towards an exhibition?' Ruth said. 'About time Pharmakon did some more enlightened sponsorship.'

'I don't know,' he said.

'You can do it,' she'd said. 'I know you can.'

And so he had. Just a few words and he'd become bold, gone straight to the studio desk where drawings for the lightshedders were. But when he'd pulled out the pictures he'd no longer felt any association at all with these strange insular forms, their ugly exteriors concealing dark and unknown spaces. Even the pencil marks seemed rough to him now, ragged and untrue. So he'd taken the sheaf of designs, the paper curled and brittle, and thrown them into the bin. (A bin that Aaron emptied almost immediately, so they were gone for ever.) And the feathers and beads and eggs, he'd tossed them away too. Well, not the feathers, because they might be useful again. But the eggs and beads.

'What were you attempting here?' Aaron asked, interested, thumbstroking the curves of the white egg.

And Alan looked at him then, his big golden face upturned. Not dark like his name suggested. But big and golden and handsome. He had not thought of this.

'Voodoo,' said Alan. 'Throw it away.'

'Seems a shame,' said Aaron. But he threw it as instructed. Alan checked, rifling through the bin.

Once the eggs were gone, the bowls began to appear. Not the large fruit bowls of so many years ago, the shallow, giving dishes in the bold colours of sky and earth and sun. But smaller bowls with muter colours. Delicate mushroom bowls, with short brown stems and smoothed gills of washed pink. He worked on the wheel at first, making perfect thrown shapes, stripping the edges with the bamboo rib. But then it seemed to him that the sides were too straight, too stiff, too perfect and he wanted something else, something more fluid. So he took to the autumn woodlands to think and to look. And there he found, nestling in the damp soil, the palest orange cups of *Otidea onotica*, Hare's Ear. The lopsided irregular growths bedded down with clover. Exquisite forms that demanded a finger, which asked to be touched, though Alan did not touch the fragile, bewitching, hollows. And only when he could carry in his mind the precise shade of their ochraceous interiors, the pinkish blush of their tiny backs, and the frail flow of their rims, did he move deeper into the wood to sit, on a log, for the pure pleasure of remembering, re-creating.

There'd been a fire, the log was charred. At his feet, grown from the ash, was a cluster of *Peziza echinospora*. Incurved cups of reddish-brown, no bigger than the palm of a baby's hand. He might so easily not have seen, have stepped on them, crushed them underfoot. But he had not, and they seemed to him a gift, a confirmation of the rightness of his path, a recognition of happiness. For he was happy. He knew that there in the wood. Not a short bubble of happiness, which might burst at any moment and be gone, but a slow, dark happiness that had spored deep in the ground and which produced these sudden, strange shapes of unlooked-for joy.

And when he returned to his studio, he did without the wheel, worked with hand and clay and joy, kneading a whole. Of course he made mistakes, was inadequate. Coiled the clay too thin so it cracked in the firing. Mixed colours too bright, or too artificial, or simply wrong. Yet he never felt set back, attacked the work each day with renewed vigour. Laboured to bring from his earth the shade and flow and form that nature had blessed in the dark wood. He began with single bowls, working to get just one to look as God might have dreamed it in an idle moment. But then he became entranced by the idea of clusters, making three or four bowls together, each quite different, separate, but obviously belonging together, grown of the same spore dispersal, the same breath of wind.

The first sets were crude, the clay too thick, but Grace still took them one at a time in her hands, turning them, touching their terracotta-dark mouths and their flushed brown-white backs.

'I really like these,' she said. 'These are really good.'

'Not good enough,' he'd said.

'Can I have them, then, if you don't want them?'

And he'd said, 'Yes.' Meaning, until there was something

better. She'd taken three bowls to her room and put them on the window-sill where he could see them from the garden. Just as she used to take the beads they made together when she was a child, string them round her neck for a few days, and then leave them on a window-ledge.

'They look different in the sun,' she said. 'They shine.'

So Alan feels touched, not just by his wife and his daughter but by the universe itself, as if there was a conspiracy to make him happy. As if every plant and tree and blade of grass had been put on this earth for him alone, his pleasure to notice and describe, care for, re-create and love. That's why he is up again at five thirty. For he needs to rise with nature's beginning and sleep with the night's repose. This is the rhythm his body understands.

And now, his hands deep in the clay, he sees her coming. She's wearing a light dress of fragile yellow. He cannot imagine where she has kept this frock all these years, his wife, his Ruth, who chooses stiff navy and starched white. This dress moves with her, floats as she floats barefoot across the grass towards him.

He does not move from the workbench. For there is no hurry, she will come to him in her own time. Look, she pauses, she kneels in the grass. Some small thing has caught her attention, her body curled in concentration round it. A shell, perhaps. A stone. A beetle. The girl in her looking. But now she lifts her skirts and comes again, she turns the handle of the studio door, she is in, she has come in.

He has been working some time, has clay to his elbows. She smiles and throws herself down on the sofa. Says nothing, just waits. And he gets up to wash, but she says, 'No, no.' And comes to him immediately, quickly, pressing her body against his. And when he stands, dripping red clay from his arms, she takes his hands and puts them on her, on the yellow dress where they leave prints of earth. She laughs. 'Remember?' she says. 'Remember?'

And, of course, he does. The time when they first moved here, when Ruth escaped at last, felt free at last. How she came to him of an evening, when the sofa was new, or newish, and smiled on him. Grace tucked up in bed in the house.

He lifts the dress from her and she is naked beneath. She takes his hand again, smears clay on her breasts, bringing the spread of his fingers down to her abdomen. And, of course, he cannot help but remember also when these same (clean) fingers traced the sharp shape of Adele, when her body and his sank to the sofa as he and Ruth sink now. And, of course, despite what Grace says, he has to tell his wife. For there is no secret that will not out in its time. Grow its filthy head above the violets. This much at least he has learned.

But Ruth has her mouth over his mouth. She is kissing him, she is tracing the ridge of his teeth with her tongue. So he cannot speak. Not now. Not just yet awhile.

# 34

I have to accept that I made it up. The seal story. That I never sat and read it at Bridie's, my back pressed into the glass. Glass as cool and hard as the shale rock in the river though 'made-it-up' makes it sound like a lie, so maybe I should say 'created'. Or perhaps simply 'knew'. Because I did know, of course, long before Laura sang to me in the hospital, keening above the thin white sheets.

Ruth has told me how the story of the glass tummy came to her. How the tale of my birth appeared, suspended in front of her, an unseen spider's web made suddenly visible by dew-drops. Something that already existed, which she merely had to describe. Perhaps, she said, the seal story came to me like this. But I don't think so. I think I gathered it like bones over the years, painstakingly fashioning a skeleton. And, of course, being only a child, I put some of the bones in the wrong places. Which is why I have to return to the rock.

I tapped none of the bowls on my way downstairs. Though I did touch the ruby insides of the mushroom cluster before I left my room. Three frail fungi clinging together on a window-ledge. Not frail enough, my father says, though a breath would shatter them. The house was quiet. Empty even, and I knew they were both up, before I saw my mother's footprints in the dew. She was wearing the muslin yellow dress she used to wear when we first came to this house when I was five. A dress she gardened in, planted in, her hands in the soil. And I realised, looking, that it was a long time since I had seen her dance, as she was dancing, on the lawn. Not formal steps, of course, not someone else's dance. But her own lightness, the dress billowing.

I waited while she danced, paused, danced again, to arrive – as I knew she would – at my father's door. The door planted behind the mock-orange. She went in. Through the clay-spattered window of the studio, I saw them come together. I watched as they put their arms about each other, making a circle of themselves. A fragile cluster. Two of the three. Yet not so fragile. For a circle has no beginning; and therefore no end. A moment later they disappeared beneath the rim of the sofa.

'Why does your dad have a sofa in the workshop?' Aaron asked me.

'Because he sleeps here sometimes. When he's working very hard.'

But Alan's working harder than he has ever worked and he is not sleeping in the studio. He's sleeping in my mother's bed. The house heavy with them, the air charged. And me alone in my room. Thinking of Aaron.

Aaron looks at me and he smiles, his eyes as big as mirrors. I see myself in him, the reflection of me. I look in the mirrors and I don't see a child. I see a young woman.

He hasn't touched me. Or, if he has, only with the hairs of his forearm, brushing against me as he moves about the studio, carrying pots. His arms are beautiful and his hands are like my father's.

I watch him at the wheel, pulling a pot from a lump of clay. He wets his fingers as he forms the cone, the clay's strongest shape, then he presses down for a weighted, centred base before lifting up again. And again. He works slowly, rhythmically, altering the angle of his hold, using his knuckles at first and then his fingers to make the vase wall thinner, checking the height with a needle and then going for the final shaping pull. He hums as he sponges water from the base, cuts off the tail and erases his fingermarks with the bamboo rib.

'I'll teach you,' he says. 'If you like.'

'Grace was five,' says my father, 'when I first showed her how to throw a pot.'

'Ah,' says Aaron.

Then he asks Alan about the old days, how it was for Alan

when he first started out. And Alan tells him how he used to lay clay in beds to winter. How he would let the air come to it and the frost break it down. How he and I laid damp sacks on it, to stop it drying out in spring. He describes the blunger and the slip the consistency of double cream. He mentions my hands, how I turned the clay in the pit with my baby hands while he used the spade.

'It takes a long time,' Alan tells Aaron, 'to become a potter.'

'I'd like to make clay the old way,' says Aaron. 'Watch and work it for a whole year. Is there a part of this garden where we might bed clay?'

'No,' says Alan sharply. 'It's not economic.' But he knows what Aaron means and I know what they both mean.

I carry this with me to the stone. I am as barefooted as my mother, feeling the meadow wet beneath my feet as she must have felt the lawn beneath hers. Ahead of me is the river, the light on the water so pale the river is just a glimmer of itself. As if the world has only just begun and the river is the first note in a symphony, which will only later become oceans. I begin to run or maybe I dance, running and dancing through the dawn mist on the valley floor. The song already taking breath in my lungs.

I'm soon at the slab. A grey rock with the sun rising round it like steam. Normally I jump to the stone but today I step into the swirl of the river. The chill of the water is shocking, so I'm glad to take a second step, up, on to the shale. The rock is, by comparison, warm. I lie full-stretch in the shimmer, spine on the stone, eyes on the sky. When I first came here the rock was huge, surrounding me wholly. But I have become tall and I barely fit now. For the first time I see that I have almost outgrown this rock.

I begin it then, or it begins me. Hymn of the shore mother and the moon milk seal. It's not a melody, but a low, parched tone, as if someone had struck a tuning fork on bone. This is how it comes to me, the past, the hum of my mothers' tears. Both my mothers. And I embrace the sound, let it reverberate within me, claiming it as one claims grief, knowing that loss is only and ever the under side of love. And from this bleak beginning comes the eddy and hiccup of some kind of gratitude.

The notes deepen then, swelling into something new, the first faint stirrings of a tune. It comes from the hollow of me, the dark place under my ribs. The anthem of what was never to be. A lament for the minnow catcher, a gentle, rippling sound, the lilt of wind on water, the ruffling of grass where a hare has run. And I let it rise in me as they, the ghosts of all the people I might have been, rise. I breathe around the sound, exhaling it into the morning air, rising up on to my elbows, wanting to let go the regret, to accept that I am that I am. But the song won't wait, it's ahead of me, sudden in my throat, staccato stabs. Sister. Sister. Oh, my sisters. I sing then of siblings. I name them in song: Michael, Toby, Manda and Sadie. But it is the psalm of my sisters that crescendos, the fierce, elusive melody that is Manda, and the low, pained pulse of Sadie. And my heart would chant with their hearts but we beat in a different time. The music thins – pure and cold and difficult now. A thread of notes that flays me as I sing and yet still I hope and so must sing: oh, my sisters.

I don't know how long I sing, but when I look again the dew has dried on the stone. There is a pause, a silence – which is music too. I rise to my feet and undress, slowly, feeling the sun warm on each new piece of my nakedness. Then I wait. And as I wait, I see the Earth changes, the valley turns gold. Then at last it is here, the new tune, rising from me like a heron from a river, wild and resonant. And I strain for the descant, the flight of the song that I don't yet know. And even as I seek it, it comes to find me. Singing that I am no longer the child of my mothers, shore and sea, but the child of my future, my own possibilities. I owe my mothers but am not in their debt. They gave me life but I am not their creation.

On the stone, in the river, I beget myself. The cry of my becoming is urgent. The mad and maddened shriek of new lungs, sweet and savage and quite alone. And I sing with it and it with me until we are both exhausted and the sun high in the sky.

Then I quietly clothe my nakedness, leave the rock and climb the hill without looking back.